Lessons in Gravity

MEGAN WESTFIELD

Entangled Publishing, LLC
2614 South Timberline Road
Suite 109
Fort Collins, CO 80525
Visit our website at www.entangledpublishing.com.

Embrace is an imprint of Entangled Publishing, LLC.

Edited by Karen Grove
Cover design by Letitia Hasser
Cover art from Shutterstock

Manufactured in the United States of America

First Edition October 2016

embrace

For Eric

Chapter One

April had curled herself into a snail-tight ball deep within her sleeping bag, but still she shivered. Her air mattress had gone flat in the middle of the night, and the chill that wafted up from the ground was distinctly similar to the flow from a refrigerator door left ajar.

But the cold wasn't the only reason she couldn't sleep. At first, it had been the nighttime forest noises: the creaking branches, wild animal calls, and wind scraping across the top of the tent—it was like living inside a 1950s horror film. Then her mind switched over to the horror that been real. Her father. The air show. His falling plane. The screams. The flames. And once the adrenaline from the memories kicked in, there was no way she could relax enough to fall asleep.

Making things worse, the same tight ball that helped with the cold and the mental images was also causing unbearable pain. When she drank a beer with her crewmates, Madigan and Theo, last night after the drive from the airport, she hadn't realized how far away the bathroom was and just how much she would not want to leave her tent once she was zipped safely inside. If bladders could burst, hers was about to.

It took great effort to uncurl and inch to the top of the sleeping bag. The much colder air outside stung the tip of her nose and the whites of her eyes. She stared at the ceiling of the tent for a moment, planning her next move. Wait, she could see the ceiling. That meant dawn had arrived. The hellish night was finally over.

With clunky fingers and arms stiff like chicken wings, she pulled her jacket on over her pajama top and struggled into jeans and shoes. She scooted to the tent door, hesitating as she reached for the zipper. It had been dark when they'd arrived from the airport, and she had no idea what—or who—was outside. The last thing she needed was to encounter her crewmates for the first time in the daylight before she'd had a chance to clean up.

She unzipped the tent as quietly as she could and peeked outside. Madigan was already up. Thankfully, he was over at a picnic table with his back to her. If she could just get out of the tent before he turned around, she could escape to the bathroom without being seen.

Unwilling to risk any more zipper noise, she dropped to her hands and knees to push through the partially open flap. Sharp, frigid gravel pressed into her palms. As she lifted her second leg over the threshold, her foot caught and she tumbled forward.

Madigan turned around. *Shit.*

She fought to free her legs as he came over to see what was going on. He stood above her and offered a hand. *Oh, god.* She wanted to turn to dust and blow away.

"Good morning," he said, attempting to suppress a grin but failing miserably.

April choked down her humiliation and unhooked her toe from the door. *Way to start your internship, champ.*

Madigan pulled her to her feet and then went back to

the picnic table. Even from behind, she could tell he was still grinning. *At least somebody thinks it's funny.* She brushed herself off and joined him at the table, where he was screwing a collapsible burner onto a can of propane.

"We have a pretty relaxed schedule today," he said. "Once Theo gets up, we'll go over to the cafeteria and grab something to eat." He lit the stove and balanced a pot of water on the burner. "After that, we can do some location scouting."

"You think Theo will be a while?"

Madigan laughed. "Theo would sleep all day if we let him."

The walk over to the bathroom building warmed her up enough to stave off the shivers—just in time for the icy toilet seat and the sink's frigid water. The aluminum mirror above the sink was hardly reflective, but she could make out enough to confirm she looked as haggard as she felt. Her dependably well-behaved, straight blond hair had a brassy cast, and it was inexplicably matted against the side of her head.

She finger brushed her hair and tucked in the tails of her pajama shirt that were hanging out of the bottom of her jacket. Not wanting to go back to the campsite just yet, she sat outside on the cement bathroom stairs. This campground didn't look anything like the pictures of Yosemite she'd seen online, and it definitely didn't live up to Theo's use of the word "sublime" last night when describing the main valley. Sure, there were a lot of big pine trees here, but other than that, it was just a flat expanse of dirt with half-buried cement tubes dividing it into campsites. There weren't many other people up yet, just a few campers boiling water on spindly stoves like Madigan's and a guy climbing around on a house-size boulder a few campsites away.

She rubbed at her dry eyes, which made them hurt more. Between the cold, the hard ground, and not sleeping, it was like having the world's worst hangover combined with a severe case of strep throat. She'd barely made it through one night. How would she be able to make it through three *months*?

She'd held it together so well last term—the whole school year, really. And the flight last night from L.A. to Fresno hadn't tripped her up like she had feared it would. Flying commercial as a passenger was very different than flying your own plane. Or sitting in the audience of an air show. Instead, she'd completely failed what should have been the easiest thing: sleeping. And as she'd learned the hard way, sleep deprivation was the quickest way to a really bad place, mentally.

Her chest tightened. Not only would she not be able to function coherently, she wouldn't be able to function at all. She'd be fired from the internship, and what would happen then?

This internship was the opportunity of a lifetime. Walkabout's documentaries were stunning. Big. Bold. Different. Its founder, Danny Rappaport, was easily her favorite documentary director, and he'd picked her for this position out of more than a hundred applicants. Further, she'd be part of the filming crew instead of the typical intern role of being a footage-logging slave. Although she'd be doing plenty of that, too. This internship was the key to getting a full-time job in the documentary industry, and a ten-year head start to making her own films someday.

If you don't get a handle on sleep, you'll lose it all. Your dream will be over before it even starts.

Be brave, April girl, her dad would say if he were alive. It had been his advice for every situation, whether it was her first airplane landing at fourteen or asking her chemistry partner to prom two years later. But being brave had been easy for her dad. He was never afraid.

If she could just be more physically comfortable, then

maybe she'd be able to keep the upper hand on her mind long enough to fall asleep tonight. Yes, that was the solution. She would start by not drinking any liquids after dinner so she wouldn't have to pee in the middle of the night. She'd wear her jacket to bed and listen to music on her phone to block out the forest noises. Maybe there was a camping store here where she could buy an air mattress that wouldn't go flat overnight.

Having a plan created a nice warming effect on her body and loosened some of the tightness in her chest. If she could just get through these three months on location, the remaining six months of the internship—postproduction back at Walkabout's headquarters in Seattle—would be a piece of cake.

She turned her attention to the guy in the gray hoodie on the enormous boulder. *This* was what she needed to focus on. The climber guy's movements were smooth and controlled, like a choreographed dance, as he moved back and forth across the boulder's longest side. She realized that the entire time she'd been sitting there, he hadn't touched the ground or paused for a break. His deep focus was inherently dramatic, and she could see that this, thousands of feet in the air and set against some of the amazing vistas that supposedly existed in Yosemite, would make for some stunning cinematography.

Climbing might be a bizarre sport, but she had to admit, it was also a little sexy. The height. The fearlessness. The confidence. The apparent impossibility of it all.

It was the daredevil's siren call.

The guy stretched diagonally, locking onto a section that was slightly overhanging. His hood fell back, revealing light brown, tousled hair. Now hanging by his arms, he tucked and lifted his legs effortlessly though the air, placing the tips of his shoes back on the rock with precision. Even though she couldn't see his face, her heartbeats quickened with interest.

God, April, no!

She would have to be very careful here, surrounded by a bunch of sexy guys like this. Not only were crew-talent flings expressly in violation of the employee conduct contract she'd signed, she would never allow one to happen. Daredevils die young, and after what happened to her father, she would never—*not ever*—fall for a guy who risked his life for a living.

The guy climbed up and over the far corner of the boulder. She waited for a few minutes, and when he didn't reappear, she walked over to take a closer look. Running her hand across the rock, she tried to find something to hold on to, but there was nothing. She pushed her fingertips into the rock, and it became sharper and a little bit tacky, like sandpaper. But, still, it wasn't enough friction to hold someone's body weight.

Not wanting to stay away for too long, she headed back to the Walkabout site, where Madigan lounged in a camp chair with his sleeping bag wrapped around him like a shawl. She was still embarrassed about falling out of her tent, but it would be worse if she let it show, so she sat confidently at the picnic table, facing him.

"How'd you sleep?"

"Great," she lied. "How about you?"

"I froze, but it's just because I was too lazy to go get my warmer sleeping bag from the van."

There was a day's worth of stubble on his jaw and a few tufts of dark brown hair sticking out from the bottom of his wool hat. He was younger than she'd guessed in the dark last night, probably in his late twenties.

A savage roar made April leap off the bench. She wheeled around, half expecting to find one of the scythe-wielding maniacs she'd visualized last night.

Madigan burst into laughter. "Theo's awake."

Theo's tent shook as he fumbled to unzip it. He stuck his

head out. "Whaz up, guys?"

His hair was shaggy like Madigan's, but it was red and an inch or two longer. He crawled out of the tent, staggered toward them, parked his butt on the picnic table, and pulled a ragged yellow beanie over his head.

"It's about time," Madigan grumbled. "Get off your ass and let's go eat."

The cafeteria was down a short trail and across the road from the campground. As they approached, April's mouth watered at the smell of sausage and bacon sizzling on the grill.

"Guess Josh arrived early," Madigan said as they sat down with their trays of food.

"Who?" she asked.

He gestured toward a cute guy about her age with light brown hair a few tables away—a guy who wore a threadbare gray hoodie and was reading a newspaper. The same guy she had watched climbing around on the boulder.

"That's Josh Knox," Madigan said. "He's our star. He's been out of the country all winter on a sweet climbing trip."

Madigan and Theo stood, and April dutifully followed them, her stomach rumbling in protest at having to leave her food. "How was Indonesia?" Madigan asked Josh.

Josh set his newspaper down and man-hugged the guys. "It was good, man. Real good." His smile faded as soon as he noticed April standing there with them.

"This is April," Madigan said. "She's our intern for the project."

Josh was thin, but he was tall and his posture was imposing. His eyes were an arresting combination of green and brown that she longed to study further, despite the marked lack of expression in them. Even as he shook her hand, he didn't seem any more interested in her than the napkin dispenser on the table his eyes shifted to next.

She drew back from the group, feeling small and

unimportant. She *was* unimportant: a lowly intern. It was time to toughen up, because she'd probably be experiencing this type of thing a lot.

"You're welcome to join us," Madigan said to Josh.

"Thanks, but I better stay here and catch up with what's been going on in the U.S.," he said.

Back at the table, April dug into her syrupy French toast and chugged down the coffee that would be her lifeblood for getting through the rest of the day.

"Josh is parked out behind the search-and-rescue camp while we're filming," Theo said. "He lives in his truck."

"Permanently?" she asked between bites.

"Whenever he's in the States," Theo said.

She looked over at Josh, who was reabsorbed in his newspaper. There was something vaguely familiar about him.

"How long before the rest of the talent arrives?" she asked.

Theo stopped chewing. "They're climbers, Hollywood, not *talent*."

"When are the other *climbers* getting here?" she asked.

Theo snorted. "That's something you'll be helping us puzzle out."

Madigan slugged Theo. "Stop being a jerk, you ass." He faced away from Theo. "A lot of it's weather dependent. We can't shoot up in Tuolumne until the snow's melted. And it's really going to be determined by Josh's climbs. His are the riskiest, and the rigging we have to do for them is the most complicated."

April looked over at Josh, who was now listening to messages on an old-fashioned flip phone. He was definitely cute, in a unique, somewhat exotic, unkempt sort of way. Perhaps "striking" was a better word.

From the number of messages he was going through, it had to be the first time he'd checked voicemail since getting back from his trip. Either that, or he was really, really popular.

As if he could feel her eyes on him, Josh looked toward their table. Just as quickly, he looked away, and she immediately placed where she recognized him from.

Back when Danny Rappaport was still working for the American Geographic Channel, he directed a series about the modern Southwest. One of the segments was about rock climbing, and Josh had been in it. She was remembering him not for his looks but for his terrible interviews. As in off-the-charts bad. One-word answers, ogling the camera, staring off into space. In fact, she had only watched a few of his interview spots before skipping past the rest. It was the only skipping she had done while watching all forty-five hours of Danny's filmography after she'd found out she got the internship.

Her specific role on this internship was to run the interviews. *Fantastic.* Her job just got infinitely harder.

"Anyone want more coffee?" Theo asked.

April and Madigan held out their empty cups. Theo took them and walked brazenly through the out turnstile into the food area.

She looked over at Josh. A lot of time had passed since the American Geographic special. He'd probably been in lots of films since then. Surely he had improved.

Josh snapped his phone closed. His face was somber. Girl troubles, perhaps? Strange, though. What kind of girl would date a guy who lived in a truck? Perhaps that was the problem.

Theo returned to the table, gripping the three paper coffee cups in an impressive counterpressure triangle.

"Here you go, Hollywood," he said with a wink.

April took her cup. "You know, I've never done any work in Hollywood."

"You went to film school in L.A. That counts."

"Like you didn't."

"Nice try. Colorado Film School for me. UNC for

Madigan."

Theo sat down and started talking about some newly climbed mountain in the Andes.

A few tables away, Josh folded his newspaper and stood up. He turned their way, and his eyes locked with April's, making her breath pause. The sadness from earlier was still hovering over him like a cloud. His expression went sharp, and she looked away with the distinct feeling she'd seen something she shouldn't have.

Her stomach churned uneasily. She didn't even know the guy, but the intensity of his sadness was speaking directly to the hard place in her heart she kept so carefully locked down.

Madigan and Theo waved good-bye to Josh. His frown relaxed as he nodded to them, but by the time he'd reached the exit and glanced at April once more, the sorrow was even more deeply rooted in his eyes and etched in the lines around his mouth. Goose bumps popped up on April's arms. This time, she couldn't look away.

Chapter Two

April and Madigan climbed into the avocado-green Walkabout van parked in the campground lot. The van, though rusty on the outside, was completely refurbished on the inside, designed to store equipment, charge batteries, and manage footage downloads and backup.

Madigan started the van and eased it through the parking lot's deep potholes and onto the main road. Within a minute, they broke through the shadows of the forest into a breathtaking meadow surrounded by cliffs as tall as skyscrapers. April was transfixed.

Rounding a corner, they came face-to-face with a cliff so massive that she gasped before she could stop herself. The monolith jutted into the meadow like the curved bow of a ghostly *Titanic* returned to this world even larger than it had been in real life.

"That's the captain," Madigan said. "*El Cap-e-tan.*"

She followed the edge of the buttress from the ground, up, up, up to where its angular profile met the cloudless sky.

Madigan watched her reaction. "Amazing, isn't it? That's

a lot of granite. Look behind."

Through the side mirror, there was a clear view of the head of the valley: a supernatural amphitheater of warm gray cliffs, with one particularly remarkable, sheer-sided dome perched high above it all. To complete the panorama, there was a shimmering waterfall dropping from the tops of the cliffs to the valley floor.

Now, *this* was sublime.

Ahead, the meadow was wider, with a creek running through the center and a deer and fawn grazing along the banks. The sun was still behind the rim of the valley, but its rays were beginning to separate and bend over the cliffs.

"Stop!" April cried.

As Madigan pulled onto the shoulder, she unzipped her camera bag and unbuckled her seat belt. She threw the door open and raced into the meadow, only vaguely aware of the muddy water flying up and soaking through her jeans in icy little pinpricks.

In the middle of the meadow, she halted and lifted her camera. Slowly, she turned in a circle, holding her breath to steady the shot. Sunbeams poured over the rim, fanning into a thousand rays of golden light that reached down into the meadow. Her mind was going to explode from the beauty of it.

She completed the pan as the top of the sun itself appeared, thrusting the valley into a gorgeous patchwork of shadows and brights that would be too much contrast for her camera.

"Sorry," she said when Madigan caught up to her. "I got a little excited."

"No—that was awesome! Did you get the shot?"

"I think so," she said. She replayed the footage for him. "It would have been better with a Red Dragon."

"Looks great to me," he said.

They sloshed back through the meadow, toward the van and the base of El Capitan.

"There are some climbers up on Pacific Ocean Wall." He stopped and pointed.

All April could see was rock, rock, and more rock.

"They're like pinpricks. Look for shadows. See there—right above the tree line?"

April stood behind Madigan's pointing arm, straining her eyes to pick out a miniature human. She couldn't see anything.

"Try your camera," he said.

Even zoomed in all the way, she couldn't see any people on the wall. Then, in a sunny patch, she spotted a hair-thin black bar that didn't look quite natural. There was a crumb-size lump on top of the bar and a black speck no bigger than a newborn spider hovering on the rock above it.

"The belayer's still on the portaledge," Madigan said. "It's probably their first pitch of the day."

"They spent the night up there?" She squinted. "On that little thing?"

"It's actually eight feet long. Yes, it's small, but when you've been standing on buttonheads all day, it feels pretty big."

"You've slept up there?"

Madigan laughed. "No, not on El Cap, but on other climbs. Theo's climbed it twice."

April watched the climbers through her camera. When she'd accepted the internship and found out the subject of Walkabout Media & Productions's next film was rock climbing, the company's secretary assured her that she would be doing interviews, not filming up on the rock. Faced with the dizzying height of the granite in front of her, she was thankful her feet would stay firmly planted on the ground during this internship.

For interviews, though, she still needed to know a lot

more about rock climbing. She had wanted to study up on it before she left L.A., but it was her last quarter at school and she was too busy wrapping everything up. One of her film school friends worked at an indoor climbing gym, and he had stockpiled a bunch of video clips and back issues of rock-climbing magazines—all of which were waiting back in her tent, unwatched and unread.

"El Cap is twice as high as the Empire State Building," Madigan said. "Took forty-five days the first time it was climbed. That was in the late fifties. Strong aid climbers do it easily in a day now."

"I'm assuming Josh Knox is one of them," she said, thinking of the power in his grip when they'd shook hands.

"Josh doesn't do much aid climbing. He doesn't need to. He can free-climb routes that even the best climbers need aiders on."

"So free-climbing doesn't use gear?"

"Well, free-climbing uses gear, but it's just for protection if they fall. Aid gear is used for climbing past the hardest parts. We use aid gear a lot with filming, actually."

"Sorry you have to explain all of this to me. I don't have any experience with rock climbing."

"Don't worry about it. It's actually a good thing."

She raised her eyebrow dubiously at him.

"This isn't a climbing flick," he said. "Vera—the woman financing the film—was very specific about that. This is a film *about* climbing and about Yosemite, for a general audience. And think about it—I climb, Theo climbs, and even Danny climbed when he was younger. Danny wanted a *filmmaker* on our full-time team here, not another climber. Believe me, we had plenty of those apply."

"So you're saying I'm an asset *because* I'm a climbing idiot?" She smiled.

He returned her smile. "Precisely. Danny picked you for

your people skills."

"For interviewing?"

"Yep. You're the lens we need for focusing on telling the story while Danny, Theo, and I are absorbed in getting what we need from up there," he said, gesturing to the lofty heights of El Capitan.

The sample movie she had sent in when she applied for the internship was just one of her student film assignments, but like most of her assignments, she was so excited about the project that she went way beyond what was asked. As in, all-night editing sessions, living and breathing the project for weeks on end. In this case, all that extra time and effort had paid off. And if Danny had chosen his intern based on interviews, then her movie—featuring seven tight-lipped homeless teens dependent on the dumpsters behind UCLA's dorms—had been the perfect submission choice.

When they got back to the van, Madigan spread a map of Yosemite Valley on the hood and pointed out the major features to April. The high, curved cliff at the head of the valley was Half Dome. The gorgeous waterfall was Bridalveil Fall. The sharp, twisting tower was Sorcerer Spire.

"That'll be Josh's big climb for the film," he said.

Like El Capitan, the Sorcerer rose from the valley floor to the sky in an uninterrupted swoop. But unlike El Capitan and the other formations, the rock of the Sorcerer was nearly black.

"It's so smooth that there's only one route that can be climbed without aid gear," he said.

The top of the spire was incredibly sharp. Something about the jagged profile of the shadowy hulk was distinctly sinister. She turned away from it.

"Josh was the first one to climb it free," Madigan said. "That was five years ago. Now, for the film, he's going to solo it."

"As in, without a partner?"

"Yeah. And without a rope."

She thought about Josh on the boulder earlier that morning. He hadn't been very high off the ground, but he didn't have a partner or rope then, either. "Is it normal to climb ropeless?" she asked.

Madigan laughed. "No. It's not normal. Only the crazies and the insanely good do it. When you climb without a rope, it's one wrong move and you're toast."

She knew more than anyone should about "one wrong move and you're toast."

"Technically, he'll be free BASEing. Climbing with a parachute in a backpack. It could save him if he falls from high enough, *if* he pulls the cord fast enough."

"That's a lot of *ifs*."

"Yeah. It's pretty much free soloing."

She wasn't liking the sound of this. "Does he ever climb *with* a safety rope?"

"Not 'safety rope.' Just 'rope.' And, yes, most of the time, I think. Definitely with his new projects. He's just doing the one free solo for the film."

She looked at the gnarled spire, imagining someone being on its great height without a rope. Suddenly, it was like she was a mouse in an open field with an owl circling overhead. She quickly got in the van and shut the door. The feeling was just the hypervigilance that had plagued her ever since the crash, but that knowledge didn't do anything to slow her pulse.

Although she knew rock climbing was dangerous, she didn't know there was a death-defying extreme to the sport — or that Walkabout would be involved in documenting one such feat.

• • •

It was nearly dusk by the time April and Madigan got back to the campground. The day had been exhilarating and the temperatures warm, but cold was filling in behind the fading light, renewing her dread of the coming night. The caffeine from the morning's coffee had worn thin, and her sleep deprivation hangover had returned.

Madigan pulled into a parking spot next to Theo, who was unloading the back of a beat-up station wagon that Danny Rappaport had driven down from Seattle.

"Danny's meeting with the public information officer right now," Theo said. "I'm going out to pick him up when we're done unloading."

The three of them grabbed boxes of food to carry back to the campground.

"Group dinners are a Walkabout tradition when we're on location," Madigan said as they walked. "We all take turns cooking and cleaning."

"The talent, too?" April asked.

Theo cleared his throat.

"No, we don't make the *talent* cook," Madigan said, as they returned to the station wagon for another load, "but they usually eat with us." He glared at Theo. April glared at Theo as well, and he shrank back with a pleased smile.

"So Josh will be coming tonight?" She thought of his tan skin that glowed with the sun despite the gloominess hovering around him this morning.

Theo gave her an odd look, like she'd shown too much interest in Josh. "I don't know a single climber who would turn down a free meal," he said. "But with him, you never know."

At the campsite, Madigan handed April a five-gallon collapsible container. "Mind getting the water for dinner while I start a fire?"

April took the container across the campground to the

bathrooms, where she recalled a small, scullery-like room with a deep sink. That's when her eye caught the big metal sign on the backside of the building.

On it was an enormous bear with Freddy Krueger claws prying the door off a car. The hairs on her neck rose.

ODORS ATTRACT BEARS TO PARKING LOTS, PICNIC AREAS, AND CAMPGROUNDS. NEVER STORE FOOD, GARBAGE, OR TOILETRIES IN A TENT.

Her toiletry bag—with winter mint toothpaste, pomegranate shampoo, and sunscreen that smelled like coconuts—had spent the night two feet from her head.

BEARS CAN BE ANYWHERE IN THE PARK AT ANY TIME. ALLOWING A BEAR TO OBTAIN HUMAN FOOD, EVEN ONCE, CAN RESULT IN AGGRESSIVE AND DANGEROUS BEHAVIOR.

Her face went numb. She'd spent all that time last night thinking about movie monsters and an accident that happened almost three years ago when there were actual bears roaming free out there. Now she really wouldn't be able to sleep.

She filled the water container in the utility sink and hauled it back to camp.

"There's a spigot right there." Madigan pointed to the neighboring campsite.

"Now you tell me," she said, massaging the crease where the handle of the heavy container had left an imprint in her palm.

He laughed. "Danny just texted. Should be here in a half hour. It'll be perfect timing with the food."

April unpacked the boxes of food into the metal storage cabinets, which she now understood from the Freddy Krueger sign were actually bear-proof lockers. She grabbed the toiletries bag from her tent and stored it inside a locker alongside Walkabout's cases of Mexican beer.

By the time she was done, Madigan's fire was already raging in the twilight. She approached cautiously, her pulse quickening as she got closer to the flames. She told herself to be rational. This fire smelled nice, like pine pitch. It was bright orange and homey, the kind of fire that belonged in a brick hearth with a happy family gathered around.

Madigan squatted to blow on the fire, making it flare. She flinched and stepped back, but relaxed as the fire settled into a comfortable burn.

He stood up next to her. "Cold?"

She didn't realize that she was trembling, let alone trembling hard enough to be noticed by someone else.

"You might want to put on a jacket before we start dinner," he said.

"I *am* wearing a jacket."

"That's not a jacket. That's a windbreaker. Temps will drop a lot by the time we're done with dinner. Did you bring anything warmer?"

"No. This is plenty of jacket for where I'm from."

"Los Angeles?"

"Yeah, and Arizona. That's where I grew up."

"Okay. I get the picture. Wait here a second." He disappeared into his tent and came out holding a puffy down jacket.

"Thanks," she said, slipping it on. Her body heat was reflected back like a mirror in the sun. A down jacket: it was the magic solution to keep her from freezing to death during her first job in the film industry. She liked that Madigan wasn't aloof like the assistant directors she'd worked with occasionally for school assignments. He didn't seem like a boss at all, actually.

"So, uh, if you thought that windbreaker was sufficient for Yosemite in March, maybe we should talk about the rest of your gear," he said. "What's your sleeping bag rated?"

She shrugged. She'd borrowed it from Sophie, who, like her, had only ever been RV camping.

"That's not good. You must have been cold last night."

"It was pretty chilly."

"Okay. You're going to want to get a better bag. And probably some other gear. What kind of air mattress do you have? What kind of layers did you bring? You'll want some good polypropylene long underwear for our early morning work. And, of course, a warmer jacket."

Poly-prop-a-what? From a financial perspective, it would be better to quit the internship, charge a plane ticket to Tucson, and beg for her high school job back at Kids Are Wee Videography.

Madigan caught the concern on her face. "Walkabout has some pro deals with a couple of companies, and between Theo and me, we have more than enough gear to get you through until everything is delivered."

She wanted to throw her arms around him. Tonight—and for the rest of their time in Yosemite—she would be comfortable, which meant there was hope of not descending into complete incompetency from sleep deprivation.

"We were really lucky the Park Service agreed to give us a camping permit for so long," he said as they watched the flames. "And being here before the tourist season makes it all the better. Come June, this place will be crazier than spring break in Mazatlán."

After a few more minutes next to the warmth of the fire, they went over to the picnic tables to start dinner. The sky was nearly black beyond the silhouettes of the pine trees. Madigan lit an old-fashioned lantern that made the whole cooking area glow brightly.

Despite the primitive kitchen, the spaghetti they were making was far from just tomato sauce and noodles. They sautéed ground beef, onions, and green pepper for the sauce, then wrapped a loaf of garlic-buttered French bread in foil and left it to warm by the fire. Even the dinner table was fancy, with a red-checked vinyl tablecloth, metal silverware, and blue enamel camp dishes.

Theo swept into the campsite like a tornado, going straight for the cache of beer.

"Beer, Hollywood?"

"Where?" She backed into the picnic table, scanning the darkness for beady animal eyes.

Theo howled. "Not a bear, a beer!"

Sticking to her resolution of no liquids in the evening, she said no.

A short, muscular black man carrying an enormous backpack stepped into the circle of lantern light. He had a neat beard, a shiny bald head, and wore thickly rimmed eyeglasses.

This was Danny Rappaport.

"April Stephens," he said, gripping her hand firmly. "It is a pleasure to finally meet you."

She was too starstruck to find the words for a polite response, but it didn't matter because he was already over at the tent the guys had pitched for him, putting his backpack inside. Which made sense, because Madigan and Theo had both described him as hyperactive.

The four of them filled their plates and sat down. "Where are the candles?" Danny asked.

Madigan hopped up and dug through one of the bags in the bear lockers.

"My wife sells Candlerama," Danny explained to April sheepishly. "She swears by candles for group cohesion."

As they ate, the candles flickered gloriously against the black night. She was thankful Theo was dominating the conversation with his wild tales so she could eat uninterrupted, because she was starving after only eating one small hot dog for lunch.

Without any warning, Josh Knox stepped out of the

darkness and into the glow of the candles to dish up a plate of food. April dropped her fork.

"Hey, guys," he said simply as he sat down in the only open spot, across from April.

He'd apparently startled Theo as well, because he stopped talking. In the silence, she was suddenly aware of the chirping of insects all around them and the whir of the lantern over on the cooking table.

"So, April," Danny said, "how do you like it here so far?"

"It's nice. It's really beautiful." She glanced at Josh. Something about him, or perhaps their silent exchange at the cafeteria, made her nervous. She wished she hadn't turned down Theo's beer earlier.

"The guys haven't been too hard on you, have they?" Danny asked.

"Are you kidding? We've been fantastic," Theo answered.

"I'm sure," Danny said, returning his attention to April. "Were you able to finish everything up at college?"

"I'm done, but I don't get my diploma until I finish the internship," she said.

"We'll do our best to help you out with that," Danny said.

She'd better finish! The aftermath of the crash had kept her out of school fall quarter of her junior year, and with most of UCLA's School of Theater, Film and Television courses needing to be taken in order and only offered once a year, she had been pushed two very expensive additional quarters into her fifth year.

Without looking, April knew Josh's eyes were on her. It was strange how someone who was being so quiet could have such a formidable presence.

"Loftycakes for dessert, anyone?" Madigan asked.

April hopped off the picnic bench to get them before Danny could hit her with another question. Concealed by the darkness, she observed Josh at the candlelit table. In person, he was just as aloof as he was on camera. Although he was currently laughing at something Theo said.

She carried the marshmallow sandwiches to the table. She didn't think Josh would be the type to eat such a juvenile dessert, but he took a lime-green one from her.

"Thanks," he said. Through the flickering candlelight, their eyes met. She pulled her eyes off him, but they rebelled, going right back and scanning across his torso, down to the large, strong hands that dwarfed the beer can he was holding.

She froze. *Oh, shit!* She had just checked out the talent. Did he notice? *Please don't let him have noticed.* But how could he not have? He was right across the table.

"What's with that jacket, Hollywood?" Theo asked. "I didn't know they made down dresses."

"It's Madigan's," she said. She fingered the hem of the jacket, which reached midway down her thigh.

"Ooh, ooh," Theo said to Madigan. "What a gentleman you are."

April blushed, even though most of the film majors at school were guys and they said stuff like that all the time. It was Josh being there that made it embarrassing.

The guys inhaled their Loftycakes, and she escaped to the bear boxes to get more. Squatting in front of one of the lockers with her hands on the cold metal top, she chastised herself for the bad start with Josh: staring at him across the cafeteria, and then blatantly checking him out just now. She was going to have to interview this guy, and she could not keep gawking and getting tongue-tied around him. Sure, he was good-looking and intimidating, but this was also true for pretty much any film star, even in documentaries.

There was something else going on in her body besides that. Something a little unsettling and irksome. What was it?

She looked over at Josh, thinking about how he would be climbing that bone-chilling spire without a rope. That was it.

She was still uneasy from her damned fight-or-flight reaction to the Sorcerer this morning.

She had to stop getting wigged out when other people put themselves in danger. Otherwise it would be like that party junior year, when that drunk guy stood up on the roof. She *knew* he was going to fall, and her body locked up even though she and Sophie were in the middle of a crosswalk on a busy street. Sophie had been clipped by a car while trying to pull her the rest of the way across. April's hands were sweaty just thinking about it. Sophie could have *died*.

The climbers in the film were *choosing* to take risks, and she couldn't let her body react to their danger. Besides, from all Madigan had said throughout the day, it didn't seem like climbing was nearly as risky as she had initially thought, with the all the ropes and safety equipment involved. Except Josh, of course, when he climbed the Sorcerer.

Josh.

What she needed to do in order to stop being all weird around him was go back to the picnic table and have a normal conversation. Like Madigan said, Danny had picked her for her people skills. The better she could get to know him beforehand, the smoother the interviews would be.

But when she stood up, Josh wasn't at the table. He was over by the dish tub, drying his dishes. He said a quick good-bye, then disappeared into the blackness of the forest.

Her heart sank. Back at the table, his absence was palpable.

"April," Danny said, "I asked Josh to pop over here for a quick interview tomorrow at ten."

Oh, no. Already? There was still so much to do. All those magazines to read so she could get up to speed about rock climbing and Josh's background…

"We'll go over the exact content we'll need for the film later on," he said. "This is just to test the location Madigan picked out, and for Josh to start getting comfortable with you."

"Oh, okay. Sure." There was no way she was going to admit to the great Danny Rappaport that she wasn't ready. She had the whole night ahead, during which it was doubtful she'd be sleeping anyway. By tomorrow, she'd *be* ready.

Chapter Three

After helping with the dishes and hanging out around the fire with the guys, April made her final trek to the bathroom building and then retired to her tent. Lying on Theo's thick bouldering pad and being toasty warm with her thin sleeping bag zipped inside Madigan's extra one made the tent almost cozy. It was kind of like being in a blanket fort at a sleepover, except instead of a teenybopper magazine in the beam of her flashlight, it was a rock-climbing magazine.

The issue she chose had Josh on the cover, climbing the underside of a rock arch in the middle of the Mediterranean Sea. She turned to the story, "Deep Water Redpoint Soloing With Josh Knox."

The opening photo was a steamy close-up of Josh that could have easily doubled as a page in a hunk-of-the month calendar.

Wow.

He was shirtless and dripping wet from a fall into the ocean. His eyes were fierce, his jaw determined, and his wet hair spiked in an array of defiant points. And his back! She couldn't stop looking at his back, which was an incredible patchwork of muscles, from the waistband of his low-slung shorts all the way to his powerful fingertips stretching for a hold.

Now, tomorrow was going to be even harder. Knowing what an amazing body Josh had would make her even more intimidated by him.

The next page, with a close-up of him facing forward, revealed that the front of his body matched his back, with his taut, defined stomach, and the intricate, naturally derived muscles of his arms that were so opposite of the puffy-buff, gym-going frat guys at school.

She skimmed the rest of the article for anything that would be useful in her interview, but there was nothing. Absolutely nothing. This was not the case for the other climbers in the magazine. They shared all sorts of candid details about themselves—stories about their dogs, favorite foods, mishaps, and climbing goals.

Despite flipping through several more magazines, she found nothing but hunky climbing photos of him and dry write-ups. It was almost deliberate how little he revealed of himself.

The beam of her flashlight was growing gradually dimmer. In a panic, she snapped it off. Hopefully, there would be just enough power left in case she needed to get out of the tent tonight because of, say, a bear attack.

She flipped onto her back, trying not to imagine the sound of Freddy Krueger bear claws ripping through the nylon of her tent, and how the tent poles would creak and snap as the massive creature forced its horrible, ursine head inside.

Despite the extra sleeping bag, her blood grew heavy and slow in her veins. She hated this feeling—it was exactly like the paralysis she had experienced immediately before she consciously realized the free fall was not part of her father's air show act.

She curled into her tight, protective ball. Why had she assumed her father's crash wouldn't follow her all the way out here in Yosemite? Would it follow her everywhere, for the rest of her life?

She needed to sleep. She *had* to sleep. In just a few hours, she would be interviewing Josh, and she had to do well so she'd make a good first impression on Danny. Not only would she not get her degree until she was finished with the internship, but her out-of-state college debt had crossed into six figures last term, and there was no way she could get a steady job in this ultracompetitive field without a recommendation from a director like Danny. Not to mention her secret hope that this internship might lead to a permanent job with Walkabout.

There was a refill left on her sleeping pills from last year, but she wouldn't be able to get it filled out here in the middle of nowhere. Besides, sleeping pills were just a temporary solution. This was a problem that had implications for her whole career. Documentary crews never had the budget for nice accommodations, especially in remote—and hopefully someday foreign—locations. She had to learn to sleep somewhere other than a familiar, comfortable bed.

She needed to be rational about the bears. All the food and toiletries that would attract them were locked away in the bear boxes. There was a reason none of the other campers were lying awake, petrified about bear attacks—although it happened, likely, it was rare. It was probably similar to the rattlesnake warning signs on the Hollywood Hills jogging trails. In four years of running there, she'd never seen a single snake.

Turning her mind to a relaxation technique she'd learned back when she was still seeing a therapist after the crash, she focused on the soft foam of the bouldering pad beneath her sleeping bag, and how the damp nylon of the tent smelled a little like the common room in her freshman dorm. She listened to the pine tree branches shifting in the breeze before remembering her plan to listen to music to cover up these noises.

There wasn't much battery left on her phone, but she'd happily drain it if it helped her fall asleep. She closed her eyes and recalled, one by one, the few details she'd learned about Josh from the magazines tonight.

Grew up in Las Vegas
Started climbing at five, at local rock-climbing gym
Six feet two inches
175 pounds
Isn't afraid when free soloing
Favorite place to climb: Yosemite
Favorite type of rock: granite
Hazel eyes
Very fit
Very, very fit

She visualized the close-up photo of him in the Redpoint article, the one where he was sitting on the rim of a rickety boat, looking up at a column of rock that rose from the water.

What was it about him that was so striking? She thought hard about his eyes, which were large and surprisingly communicative despite his bored expression. The tropical sunlight overpowered the flecks of green in his eyes, turning them instead into deep pools of chestnut. With his tan torso and sun-lightened hair, he was as much a part of the landscape as the palm trees around him.

Perhaps that was the X factor that had kept her looking at him today. He was the human equivalent of an indoor tropical plant. Wild and beautiful, but a little out of place.

• • •

The guys had just left to scout a rock formation called Flying Sheep Buttress, and she was alone in the campsite, savoring the sauna-like heat of Madigan's down jacket in the morning sun as she prepared for the interview.

She was treating herself to a second look at a Josh Knox hunk-of-the-month centerfold in an older magazine just as Josh himself walked into the campsite. What was he doing here so early?

Remembering what was in front of her, she slammed the magazine shut and thrust it under the picnic table. *Kill me now!*

"Hi, April."

She couldn't help being flattered that he remembered her name.

"Are you free?" he asked.

His eyes, in person, were even more magnificent than in the close-up in the Redpoint article. A little tingle ran up her spine.

"How about doing the interview right now?"

What? No! She needed this hour to prepare. "I still have some stuff to get together," she said. "Is it okay if we stick to the original time?"

"Sorry, but I need to get on a climb before it gets too late," he said, his eyes falling down her body to where she was still hiding the magazine under the table. She blushed.

"We could do it tomorrow if you want," she offered.

"I'd rather just get it out of the way today."

He was the talent, and he was clearly not willing to budge, meaning she no longer had a choice in the matter. "Okay, but can you give me a half hour?"

He looked at his watch. "I'm sure it won't take that long. I'll just wait."

"I've got to get all the equipment from the van and—"

"I'll just go with you. That way I'll be ready as soon as

you are."

He hadn't said anything mean, but she felt bullied. His demeanor was making her rush, and being rushed made her flustered.

She put her study materials away in her tent and walked out to the parking lot. His eyes burned a hole in her back as she struggled with the van's rusty door. When she came out of the van loaded down with the padded camera bag she had prepacked, tripod, collapsible interview stool, and all the sound equipment, Josh was seated with folded arms on the bumper of someone's car, like she'd taken so long he'd needed to rest his legs.

Had she done something wrong? Or was he just being a jerk? Theo was dead wrong about not calling climbers *talent*. Josh acted *exactly* like an A-lister.

She cut diagonally across the parking lot to the trailhead. Without a word, he fell in beside her. When the trail tapered, he took the lead, even though she didn't think he knew where they were going.

Her equipment was heavy and hard to balance, and she struggled to keep up with his long-legged strides. Chivalry from anyone but her dad made her uncomfortable, but damn it, would it kill him to take one of the bags?

The jacket that had been so comfortable just minutes ago was now a superheated torture device, but she refused to ask Josh to stop so she could take it off. With more determination than ever, she jogged to close the gap between them and then kept right at his heels.

As they rounded a sharp corner, she noticed his T-shirt. It was red, with a huge logo on the front from Esplanade Equipment, one of his sponsors. There was no way he could wear it for the interview.

Danny said he had talked to Josh about what to wear, but Josh had either forgotten or chosen to ignore him.

She took a big breath. "Josh?"

"Yes?" he asked without slowing down.

"Can you stop for a second?"

He stopped and turned. She rested the tip of the tripod carefully on the dusty trail. "Your shirt—it's not going to work."

Silently, he sized her up. How had they gone from the almost-friendly interaction at the picnic table to *this*? Clenching her jaw, she held her ground.

"We're all the way out here," he said. "What do you want me to do?"

She forced herself to keep looking at him. "I'm really sorry, but can you go back and change?"

He frowned. "I can just turn it around."

There was writing running diagonally across the back of his shirt in bright yellow typeface. She shook her head. "I'm sorry, but we're wasting both of our time if you wear that shirt."

"I live in a truck," he said. "There's not much room for clothes."

"You can keep your pants, but your shirt, it can't have any logos," she said. "It should be a muted color and there shouldn't be any loud patterns. It's going to be the same shirt you wear for all your interviews, so it has to be something you can keep clean and wrinkle-free."

She hardly dared to look at his face. "I'll go on ahead and start setting up. I should be ready to go by the time you get back."

After adjusting her grip on the tripod, she lifted it off the ground. He didn't move when she started to walk, and with the trail being so narrow, she had to brush against him to get by.

"No," he said, almost too quietly to hear.

She stopped. Dread filled her.

"Sorry, I have places I need to be," he said, keeping his eyes carefully off hers. "We'll have to try this another time."

• • •

April sat in the van, killing the time that should have been used for interviewing Josh. She would have normally been comforted by all the familiar equipment around her, but seeing as she didn't have any footage to download, it just made her feel worse.

The van door slid open. "Done already?" Madigan asked.

Theo pushed inside and started munching on some trail mix. "How'd it go, Hollywood?"

"Well—" It was too awful to admit aloud. "It didn't go well."

"I'm sure it wasn't as bad as you think," Madigan said.

"We didn't even do the interview. His shirt had a huge logo on it, and I asked him to change it and then he walked away."

Theo choked on his trail mix. "Classic."

"Don't be too hard on yourself," Madigan said. "I was there when Danny told him what to wear. It's not your fault. Flying Sheep Buttress is still damp from the rain last week, so you'll have plenty of time to try again before we start filming any of his climbs."

• • •

Danny returned from his morning jog as April, Madigan, and Theo were finishing bowls of oatmeal at the picnic tables.

"I bought two bikes from one of the rangers," Danny said. "They're not in the best shape, but they'll be good for errands around the valley."

April paused midbite. The second she got her hands on one of those bikes, she was going straight to the showers over at Housekeeping Camp.

Danny emptied two packets of oatmeal into a bowl, along with the last of the hot water from the stove. He joined them at the table, flipping through his planner as he ate.

"The gala's coming up soon," he said. "April, would you mind giving Vera's assistant, Gabby, a call to see what they need from us?"

"Is this something we're covering?" she asked.

"No, we're attending. It's a fund-raiser for HSSR."

High Sierra Search and Rescue. This was the small village of white platform tents next to the campground. The same place where Josh was parking his truck-house during filming.

"They've always been funded federally, but this year's budget cuts hit them hard," Danny said. "Vera's taken it on as a personal cause, because of her brother."

Theo's sharp eyes didn't miss the fact that April had no idea who that was. "Vic McWilliams. Yosemite climber from the sixties. Pretty much bagged the first ascent on every major formation in the valley." He slapped her back for good measure. "Good name to remember here, Hollywood."

"Vic was paralyzed in a climbing accident," Danny said. "Vera took care of him until he passed away last year."

She nodded and suddenly it clicked. Vera—the woman financing their film—was Vera McWilliams-Smithleigh, from the Smithleigh Company family. The face wash, aspirin, and shampoo April had brought to Yosemite were all Smithleigh products.

Danny scraped the last bite of his oatmeal out of his bowl. "Gabby said she'd reserve a block of rooms for us at the hotel, but can you double-check that when you call?"

"By the hotel," Theo said, "he means the Kingsbury."

The *Kingsbury*? As in the five-diamond hotel chain? It would have been nice to know about this before she left L.A. Her mom would have to mail her a gown from home.

Danny turned his planner to the current week. "I'm thinking Flying Sheep will be dry enough in about three days." He looked over at April. "How do you feel about filming the top out?"

Top out sounded a little frightening.

"We're only filming the bottom two-thirds of the route, but I want to show him coming over the edge when he finishes. All you have to do is hike around the back side, then wait for Josh at the top," he said. "It's very straightforward. If you're up for it, then I won't have to call in a contractor. Madigan will show you exactly what to do."

April fiddled with her paper napkin. "Sure."

"Madigan told me Josh was uncooperative yesterday, but let's try again with him tomorrow since we can't be up on the rock yet."

Tomorrow? She knew she'd have to face him again at some point, but she'd hoped it wouldn't be so soon.

"He's taking a rest day, so you should be able to find him over at his truck to schedule a time," Danny said.

Dread settled into the pit of her stomach. She wanted nothing more than to *not* go over to that camp of his and be alone with him again. Picturing Josh's stony face from the trail yesterday, she knew it was quite possible he'd refuse an interview altogether.

Talent or not, she couldn't let someone treat her like that, but if she stood up for herself, there was no doubt he'd report her to Danny. Either way, it would be humiliating.

Chapter Four

Josh eyed the camera as if he expected it to roar to life and suck the soul from his body. April frowned and paused the clip. In some parts of world, native peoples still believed this. But Josh had no excuse. He grew up in America, and as a professional rock climber who had been in at least a dozen films, being in front of a camera should be second nature to him by now.

It was the third Josh Knox interview she'd watched on her laptop as she, Theo, and Madigan drove back to Yosemite Valley after picking up the ranger's bikes in the miniscule town of El Portal. Although the clip was his most recent, it was also the worst, and that was saying a lot, because the first two had made her want to bury her head in her jacket.

It was a complete mystery to her why Danny had picked Josh to be the film's central character. She'd watched some segments of other professional climbers, and it seemed like there were plenty of others out there who were charismatic, energetic, and zany. In other words: likable. And cooperative.

Back at camp, Theo got to work tuning up the bikes, and

April watched another cringe-worthy clip of Josh. If only his climbs were at the end instead of the beginning of filming, she would have several dynamite interviews with the other climbers to prove her worth to Walkabout before having to tackle an interview with Josh.

How was she, an *intern*, expected to come up with something usable out of this guy? Further, it was very unusual to do one-person, small-channel, television reporting–style interviews on a documentary film, and Walkabout was normally no exception. Even for UCLA student films, everyone would take turns helping each other out with sound, because if you messed up the sound, the whole take would be useless.

She looked over at the search-and-rescue camp and sighed. Instead of going to find Josh, she sidled up to Theo, who was still working on the bikes.

"What do you think about helping with Josh's interview tomorrow?" she asked.

"No can do, Hollywood," he said. "Time to step it up."

She huffed.

"Danny thinks Josh will do better if it's just one person," he said. "You know, so he's not distracted with a bunch of extra people hovering around." Theo knelt down to put some oil on the bike's chain. "I saw the sample movie you sent. If you could get those guys to talk, a climber should be no problem. The other bike's done, by the way."

That meant she could shower. *Yes!* She needed to shower badly.

After gathering her things, she pedaled over to Housekeeping Camp. She took her time showering and getting dressed—the longer she stalled, the better her chances were that Josh would have other plans for tomorrow. She biked back to the campground slowly, with plans to volunteer for dinner duty so she would conveniently run out of time to go ask him.

Back at camp, Theo had already started dinner and Danny was at the stove helping him. "What did Josh say about tomorrow?" Danny asked.

"I haven't talked to him yet," she said. "I was just heading over there, actually."

She leaned her bike against a tree and started toward the search-and-rescue camp. Theo peered around Danny's back and smirked. She scowled.

Entering the woods between the campground and the search-and-rescue camp, she prayed to cross paths with a Yosemite superbear that would force her to turn back. It didn't happen. She continued around behind the white platform tents in search of Josh, halting as she came to the truck. Her skin bristled. It wasn't just the way he'd acted yesterday that made this hard. It was her having spent so much time watching videos of him today, and the fact she had fallen asleep last night picturing his serene but hunky Redpoint climbing photos. Entering his personal camp felt way too intimate.

The tailgate of his truck was down, and the camp chair next to the fire ring was empty. There was a hammock strung between two trees, which was where she found him, all bundled up in a hat, down jacket, and long pants. It was a stark contrast from the shirtless, ocean-backed Redpoint Josh.

He was reading a book and hadn't seen her yet. She could still escape.

Her father's voice came echoing from the past. *Nonsense, April. Just get in there and get it over with.*

She exhaled and clomped loudly into the clearing. Josh looked up immediately. He didn't say hello. Instead, he waited in silence for her to explain her presence in his campsite. *Great.* "Can you do an interview tomorrow?" she blurted.

He closed his book and looked toward the platform tents.

Someone over there was playing guitar. "Tomorrow?"

"It's okay if you can't," she said. "We can find another time."

His gaze returned to her. "Tomorrow's okay. After lunch. Does that work for Danny?"

"It's just going to be me again."

One of his eyebrows twitched. He frowned. What had she done to make him dislike her so much?

"Okay, then," she said. "I'll set up before you get there. Just keep following that trail we were on. One o'clock?"

"Sure," he said. He opened his book and started to read.

"And please make sure to wear a shirt that is—"

"I remember."

Her pride recoiled. This guy might act the part of a free-spirited, climbing-bum hippie, but really, he was nothing more than a spoiled athlete. *Jerk.* She turned back toward the campground.

"Hey, April?"

She stopped. As much as she wanted to ignore him and keep going, she was an intern and didn't have the privilege of returning his disrespect. She turned around.

He was still in the hammock, now looking up from his book. His face was distinctly softer. "What's for dinner?" he asked.

She closed her eyes for a fraction of a second to collect herself. "I don't know," she said. "Danny and Theo are cooking tonight."

Their eyes met, and she felt as if he were not looking at her but into her. Her heartbeat picked up, and she reminded herself that he was exotic looking, not hot. His eyes were too deeply set and his cowlick made his hair stick out weirdly. Even though his muscles were defined, he was skinny overall, not to mention the icy personality.

She sighed silently. Her mind's attempt to trick her body

wasn't working at all. She could nitpick his features all day, but in the end, he wasn't just hot, he was irresistible.

"Hmm," he said with such cool disinterest that she wondered if it had only been in her imagination that he'd asked about dinner. It was completely mortifying that she had such a fascination—okay, *attraction*—to this person who was so awful.

She walked quickly past his truck and back into the woods, the tight, intolerant line of his mouth burned into her head. How in the hell was she going to make it through this interview tomorrow?

Chapter Five

April set the camera up in the alcove formed by a band of low cliffs. It was a nice, private place for filming, with light that was bright but not blinding and a background that would be visually interesting but not distracting.

She pulled the penny out of her pocket to tighten the tripod screws before setting up the camera, and then sat on a log to review her video journalism class notes on challenging interview subjects. If she played her cards right, perhaps she could stay one step ahead of Josh and outmaneuver him into some decent sound bites.

That was, if he actually showed up for the interview. It was 12:55 with no sign of him. What if he stood her up? She started sweating. What would she say to—

Josh appeared around the corner. A wave of relief washed over her.

The new shirt he'd chosen fit exactly within the parameters she'd described, but it was downright hideous: a plaid, cotton, button-down shirt that was so faded and misshapen that it couldn't be anything other than a thrift store castoff.

Josh sat on the boulder between the camera and the cliff. He didn't bother to make small talk, and that was fine with her. At least he was here. She adjusted a few settings on the camera, and Josh came into clear focus. Through the camera, the shirt looked perfectly normal. She smiled at the tiny triumph.

What was unacceptable was the way he was sitting. His back was ramrod straight and his knees were pressed together, making her worry that the boulder she'd picked was sharp and pointy. She should have sat on it to test it first.

While pretending to adjust a knob on the camera, she frantically scanned the alcove for an alternate backdrop with good lighting and a softer place to sit. "I think over there might be better," she said, pointing to a fallen log.

Josh switched to the log right away, but even before she moved the camera, she knew the new position would never work. The barely perceptible breeze had turned the shiny-leaved bush behind him into a mirror ball, sending beams of light all around the alcove.

"I'm sorry, that isn't going to work, either," she said. "Let's try back by the rock, but this time, stand just behind it and a little to the left."

He silently obeyed. Once in place, he settled in with crossed arms.

"Would you mind uncrossing your arms, please?" she asked.

When he did, his hands dangled limply like scarf tassels. The view of him through the camera looked like a mug shot. She took note of the boulder in front of him. It was as flat and smooth as a bench. The problem had been *him* all along.

"Well, the first time was the charm," she said, trying to lighten the mood. "Let's go back to sitting on the rock."

Josh repositioned as she untangled the lavaliere microphone wires. She handed him the transmitter pack, which he clipped to the back of his pants before threading the mic through his shirt and fastening it onto the collar. Even though Walkabout seemed to be ignoring everything her professors taught her about sound technique, at least they had provided the most expensive, Hollywood-grade lav mic on the market.

"We're going to do a little something different with that mic." She pulled a piece of skin-colored blister tape from her pocket and peeled the back off. "Just put this across the base of the mic and then stick it right to your collarbone underneath where you have it right now."

She held the tape out to him, their fingers touching for a moment as he unstuck it from her finger. Turning on the sound monitor, she could tell, even without looking at the microphone itself, that Josh had placed it all wrong. The way things were going, he would probably whisper his answers; she had to get that mic in exactly the right position.

"Do you mind if I do a quick adjustment?" she asked, walking toward him.

He shook his head. Those killer brown-green eyes of his were wide and somber as she leaned over him to peel the tape off his warm skin. His breaths were deep and rhythmic against her hand as she hid the mic higher and a little farther under his collar, with a better angle toward his mouth. Her hair slid off her shoulder and onto his shirt.

She was close enough to smell his laundry soap, and the scent of his body beneath that, which she purposely tried to not focus on. Thank god she'd taken the time to go over to the bathroom to brush her teeth before this.

The fabric was scraping against the mic, so she fiddled with his collar to get it to rest lower, on the stem of the mic. Good thing she was wearing a crew-neck running top, otherwise he'd have a view straight down her shirt into her meager cleavage. She blushed just thinking about it.

Back at the mini soundboard, she focused on fine-tuning the mic while her cheeks cooled down. She could tell that Josh was watching her, but she didn't know if it was because he was mad she was taking so long or because of something else.

She clipped the soundboard to the camera and looked up. Finally, he was sitting normally on the rock! She smiled and gave him two thumbs up.

"Looking good. Are you ready?"

There was a hint of a smile at the corners of his mouth that made her feel light and carefree. Her own smile grew a little bigger.

But then, with his eyes still on hers, a shadow seemed to pass across his face. His jaw hardened, and his posture turned stiff.

"Go back to what you were doing before," she said, sitting on her collapsible stool to demonstrate. She dropped her hands into her lap and exaggerated her slouch. "You want to relax and look natural. Try shaking out your hands."

He gave a few halfhearted wiggles of his wrists, which did nothing for his stiff back. His face had not just lost its softness, he looked cold. Defiant, almost.

"Okay, how about—"

"Listen, if you're not ready…"

Not ready? Are you kidding? It was absurd that he'd even *think* of blaming *her* for his awkwardness in front of the camera!

She darted behind the tripod, pretending to check the focus as she let her anger simmer down. Returning to her stool next to the camera lens, she pressed the buttons to start recording sound and video.

"I'm going to start out with a few questions to make sure the sound is coming out okay." Her voice trailed. He was so stiff! Stiffer than he'd been the first time he sat on the rock. "You know, there are a few things you can do to make this smoother. I'd be happy to share a couple of—"

"This isn't the first time I've been interviewed," he said, his voice tinged with even more hostility than his face showed. "Could we just get started?"

She couldn't think. No one had ever been that directly rude to her. She opened her mouth to ask the first question, but nothing came out at first.

"Why do you like climbing?" she stammered.

"It's fun," he said.

"Why is it fun?"

"I don't know. It just is."

"Is it scary?"

"No."

"Can you expound on that?"

"What's there to expound on? It's never scared me."

He looked at her with a perfectly expressionless face as he waited for the next question. She tried to use the silence to her advantage, seeing if he would give a better answer if she waited him out, but the technique backfired. Suddenly, they were in a staring contest. Each second of silence stretched into eternity. She folded first.

"How old were you when you went climbing for the first time?" she asked.

"Five."

April caught a whiff of nervous sweat and, realizing it was hers, lost her train of thought. *If you lose control of your interview, pause and then take it right back*, her notes had said. She exhaled slowly. "What attracts you to the sport of rock climbing?"

"I wouldn't call it a sport."

"But there are competitions involved."

"Only for gym rats."

"I read that you used to compete in indoor contests."

"Used to."

"If it's not a sport, then what would you call it?"

"It's an activity. A pastime."

She was trying to keep her sound adjusted correctly, but his answers were too short to register reliable readings. "Tell me about the first time you went rock climbing," she said. "Where did you go? How did it feel?"

"I can't remember. I was five."

Damn it. "Tell me about the first climb you remember, then."

"I climbed the chimney on my house when I was in the fourth grade," he said. "It was made of river rock."

"How did you parents feel about that?"

"They didn't know."

"But if they had?"

Josh shrugged. "They would have been mad, I guess. It was three stories tall."

His eyes shifted immediately to April's left, which meant the camera lens. Had he been giving usable answers, the segment would have been ruined. Her breaths were fast and her brain was ready to short-circuit. How was she supposed to take control of the interview when she couldn't even get control of *herself*?

"Was that in Las Vegas? What was it like to grow up there? What was your family like?"

"I don't see what my family has to do with this film."

Josh must *hate* her. Her career would be over if Danny saw this footage. She had to come up with *something* she could show the guys. *Take a breath. Stay calm. This is* your *interview. You're in charge.*

"Describe what it was like the first time you saw the valley. And, please, repeat the first part of my question when you answer."

"What do you mean?"

"Like, say, 'The first time I came to Yosemite, I couldn't

believe how tall the rocks were—'And then continue on."

"Are you supposed to be telling me what to say?"

Tears of frustration stung her eyes. *Tears, April? Really? In the middle of an interview? He's just a rock climber. This is not a test. Nobody's watching. It's just a short little interview with a difficult subject.*

"No, it's just that I need complete answers for sound bites," she said. "The audience won't have a context for your answer if you don't repeat the question."

"Except they'll hear you asking the questions."

Ooh, this guy! She had words for him, all right! *That's because your answers were so terrible in every other film you've been in that they had to leave the interviewer's questions in.*

She forced herself to remain professional. "Can you answer the question, please?" she asked.

"What was the question?"

"Your impression of Yosemite, the first time you came here."

"I don't remember. I probably thought it was beautiful like everyone else."

How could a person be this awful to someone they didn't even know? Those damn tears were still mounting, threatening to escape her eyelids. She was so frustrated and embarrassed, and definitely at her limit of having to sit here and fake that this wasn't a completely messed-up situation. A traitorous tear slipped down her cheek. *God!* She hopped off the stool and ducked to safety behind the camera.

She no longer cared about the footage, she just had to get him out of there before she told him off or started to cry for real.

"Okay," she said. Infuriatingly, her voice was a little shaky. "I think we have enough for today. Thank you!"

She busied herself disassembling the equipment as he stood and undid the microphone wires. The second he was around the corner, she slumped against the boulder, which was still warm from his body. It was not possible for the interview to have gone any worse.

There was nothing on the SD card that could be used, and she'd rather quit than have the guys watch the raw footage of this. But she couldn't quit. Her degree. The loans. All the money she'd just spent on camping gear, and the fact that she had no job lined up after this.

She buried her face in her hands, now feeling defeated more than angry. It was all such a disaster. She had utterly and completely failed, and the film's central character hated her.

And she missed her dad so much.

Chapter Six

The night had been rough, with it taking her hours and hours to coax her mind out of its agitated state from the interview. Getting hung up on things like this was commonplace now, but it usually only happened for things that were life-threatening or related to the crash. But then, in a way, this *was* life-threatening. Livelihood threatening. Josh Knox could singlehandedly ruin everything she'd been working for.

Now, she was sitting at a cafeteria table with Madigan, making no progress on her task of posting some pictures on Walkabout's social media accounts. She kept replaying the interview in her head, trying to figure out where she had gone wrong or what she could have done differently. Over and over, she saw those stony looks of his. Those incredible brown-green eyes that had been wasted on a such a rude and abrasive personality.

She put her earphones on to watch yet another movie with Josh in it. Skipping past the climbing parts, she got straight to the interview section, where he was looking to the right of the camera even though the interviewer's voice was coming from the left. She sighed and paused the clip.

"What's up?" Madigan asked, peeking over at her laptop, where Josh sat in front of a bold panorama of snow-covered peaks. "Ah, Cerro Negro. That climb was groundbreaking."

"But his interviews!" She paused to rein herself in. "I mean, I get that Josh is a really good climber and everything, but…"

"But what?"

"I just don't understand why Danny picked *him* to be in the film."

Madigan thought for a minute. "Well, Josh Knox is not only an amazing climber, he's pretty much the centerpiece of the climbing world right now. To make a documentary like this without him—it would almost be sacrilegious. It would be like making a baseball movie without Derek Jeter."

"But what does it matter? Josh is unlikable on film. This is for a mainstream audience, not a bunch of rock climbers. He's going to ruin the entire project!"

So much for reining herself in. Madigan rested his elbows on the table. She'd gone too far. Madigan might be as friendly as a friend, but he was still her boss.

His face relaxed into amusement. "You're right. It's painful to watch. He's a superstar on the rock, but off it, he's a director's nightmare."

"Can we vote him off the film?"

"No." He laughed. "But even if we could, I wouldn't want to. The thing is, Josh embodies the spirit of climbing. He's living the life every climber in the world wishes they were. Completely free. He's pushed the limits of the sport beyond what anybody thought was possible, and then he kept going. He's Edmund Hillary. He's Muhammad Ali. He's—"

"Okay! Enough! I get it!" It might be possible that she hated Josh Knox just as much as he hated her.

"You just have to remember that for everything he lacks

in interviews, he makes up for in climbing. The things he can do shouldn't be possible. You've seen footage of him climbing, right? It's incredible to watch when he's on something hard. And you're right about the mainstream audience part—that's what makes the interviews you're doing so important. The audience has to be able to relate to him before they can appreciate what he can do."

She frowned. *Thanks, Madigan. Way to take the pressure off.*

"I'm guessing the interview didn't go well yesterday."

"Yeah. I just don't have good rapport with him, you know? He was short ending all my questions. I think he'd do better with someone who knows climbing."

"I wouldn't take it personally. He's not the type to pour his heart out to someone he just met. He'll warm up."

Doubtful. "I don't know…maybe it would be better if I shadowed one of you instead of doing the next one myself. Maybe I'll learn what I'm doing wrong."

"Unfortunately, that's not my call. But remember, Danny knows what he's doing. He wouldn't have given you this assignment if he didn't think you were capable."

She shouldn't have said anything. Now it would get back to Danny that she was freaking out about her task. She rubbed her temples.

Madigan continued to watch her, then he shifted closer. "Okay, so I'm not supposed to say anything about this, but just between us, Vera had a few stipulations in funding this film. Josh Knox being the central character was number one."

Her jaw dropped. He winked. "Yep. Danny didn't want to work with him, either, but Vera wouldn't budge."

With a smile, she shook her head and closed her movie player.

"Danny has a history with Josh that colors this situation with the interviews," he said. "He worked with him once before, in an episode he did for the American Geographic Channel, and he got so frustrated about how stubborn Josh was during the interview that it ended up affecting him when he was filming Josh's climb. Danny's a patient guy, but there is a limit. What we're doing here is significantly more dangerous, especially with Josh's Sorcerer climb, and Danny wants to keep his focus on the climb."

Madigan packed up his laptop. "I have to get over to the business center for a conference call in a few minutes." He looked at her as he stood. "You know, if you're really not feeling comfortable with interviewing Josh, don't be afraid to bring it up with Danny. Personally, I'm not convinced Theo or I—and especially not one of our contract videographers who Josh doesn't know at all—would be getting anything different than you are. But talk to Danny. You guys might be able to work something out."

In other words, *ask for help.*

It was just like the motivational poster she used to stare at in the campus psychiatry waiting room—a badly Photoshopped picture of a lake with a human hand sticking out: SOMETIMES ASKING FOR HELP IS THE BRAVEST MOVE YOU CAN MAKE.

This was not advice her father would have agreed with, but Madigan was right on. As much as she didn't want to, it was probably smarter to admit that she was having trouble rather than having Danny figure it out himself after she'd wasted another week.

She nodded good-bye to Madigan as he took off through the cafeteria. She finished her social media posts and filled her coffee cup one more time before heading down the road to the station where they usually went to recharge the van's power supply. Sure enough, the van was plugged in and Danny was inside, reviewing the B-roll she and Theo had taken of the valley's waterfalls.

"Good stuff here. It's been a dry spring, but we're getting nice runoff right now," he said. "Where's your footage from the interview?"

"Um, I wanted to talk to you about that," she said quietly. Apparently too quietly, because Danny hopped up and dug through one of the equipment bins for something, like she hadn't said anything at all.

He grabbed a beat-up light meter and brushed it off on his shirt as he sat back down. "Before I forget, I need to ask a favor. It's about the gala."

She should have seen this coming. She, the lowest person on the totem pole, was going to have to film the event instead of kicking back and enjoying it. Typical.

"Josh is giving a speech there, and he'll be sitting at Vera's table with a bunch of VIPs. If you don't mind terribly, I'd really appreciate it if you could be his date for the night."

She choked down a gale of laughter.

"I didn't mean to say date," he said quickly. "You'd be more like an escort. A coordinator, really. Vera wants someone to help with his tux. Screen his speech. Help him be social at the gala. That kind of thing."

Help Josh be social? Would this nightmare never end?

"Does Josh know about this?" she asked. "I don't think he'd be very happy about it."

"He's not. I talked to him this morning. But he agreed as soon as I told him it was either you or Theo."

Danny laughed, but April was far from amused. She couldn't picture grungy Josh in a tuxedo, but she *could* picture him parked in his seat at the gala, scowling at his bejeweled billionaire hostess.

If a thirty-minute interview had pushed her to the limit, imagine how terrible a whole evening with Mr. Awful would be! It was about the last thing in the world she wanted to do, but picking out a tux, editing a speech, organizing wardrobe details, and schmoozing—these were things she couldn't mess up if she tried, thanks to the countless air show functions she and her mom had attended with her dad. She so badly wanted—needed—to do well in Yosemite, to show Madigan and Theo and Danny that she was good at *something*. If she couldn't prove her worth to the documentary film industry through relevant skills, then she would have to do it this way.

"Sure," she said.

"Perfect, April, thank you." Danny turned back to the monitor.

This was her chance to bring up the interview again, but instead of speaking, she fiddled with one of the power cords hanging near her seat. Tough interviews were something she would have to face in the future, especially with the kinds of films that she wanted to make someday, films that covered highly controversial topics. There would undoubtedly be individuals who wouldn't want to talk, especially when it came to people who were accused of doing something wrong. These people would be way more hostile than Josh.

She thought about that hand sticking out of the water on the poster. *Sorry, hand.* At least for now, she was going to side with her dad.

April looped her laptop bag over her shoulder to leave. As much as she didn't want to, she would give it another try and face Josh again all on her own before she resorted to asking for help.

. . .

Madigan looked up as soon as April returned to the campsite after calling her mom and asking her to send a dress. He was at one of the picnic tables, using a thick black marker to sketch storyboards.

"Looks like Flying Sheep is a go for tomorrow," he said.

She sat at the table and scooted close to see his sketches. "All I'm doing is filming Josh coming over the top, right?"

"Yep. And a quick interview after."

Of course. There had to be an interview involved. "He's going to say, 'It went fine,' and that's it," she warned.

"Wear something cute and catch him off guard."

"Madigan!"

"I'm just saying! You're a woman. Use it to your advantage."

She suspected the iron-willed Josh would be immune to any such tricks, but perhaps this could be a strategy for the gala. She could call her mom back and ask her to send a different dress, one with as little fabric as possible. Then she'd really be acting the part of *escort*.

"I'll radio up to you once I finish shooting the off-width section," Madigan said. "You'll already have everything set up, but it will give you about a forty-minute warning. I'll call up again when he's about to go over the top."

He drew a map on a blank page in his notebook.

"Now, this is a climber's trail, so it's not marked. You really need to pay close attention to my map or you'll get lost. But if you do get lost, just go straight up."

"Straight up. Got it."

"The bottom part of the trail will be steep—very steep—so be careful, okay?"

He tore the map out of his notebook and handed it to her. His handwritten directions were neat and the drawing precise. The little notes with arrows, though, made her arm hairs tickle apprehensively.

Sheer cliff

Unstable edge, stay back

Look for the cairn, go left of the holly bush

"What's a cairn?" she asked.

"A pile of rocks that marks a trail."

"How do you know it's a marker and not just a pile of rocks?"

He reached under the picnic table and grabbed a few flat pebbles. He stacked them one on top of another until they were four high. "You'll know because rocks in nature don't look like this."

He added a fifth pebble to the pile and it toppled into a heap that looked like any other pile of rocks in nature. She hoped it wasn't an omen for tomorrow's shoot. Or her internship in general.

• • •

April and Madigan spent the afternoon rehearsing top-out shots in the boulder field behind the search-and-rescue camp. It was hot, and the work was uncomfortable and dirty, and the more she thought about it, the more irritated she was that Josh needed a babysitter at the gala. Although she'd be good at the assignment, it was definitely going to be an awkward and uncomfortable evening.

She headed back to the campsite with a headache, just in time for tuna mac dinner duty. Her partner was Theo, who wasn't much help, but at least he volunteered to go drain all the cans of stinky fish in the bathroom scullery room.

"Bear, Hollywood!" he yelled from the other side of the campsite when he returned.

She jumped. He cackled. "Want a beer?"

To hell with her bladder. Tonight, she needed the alcohol.

Josh was a no-show to dinner—big surprise. He hadn't joined them since the first night. The guys said he had been hiking to the top of El Cap in the evenings to practice his BASE jumping—illegal in all national parks—under the cover of darkness. Since he hadn't said he was not coming, she'd had to make a whole extra box of macaroni *just in case* he came, and now it would go to waste.

As the four of them ate, she stared at the line of flickering votives on the table. It was such an over-the-top romantic touch for this completely nonromantic setting.

April drank a second beer after dinner while hanging out around the campfire with the guys. She pretended to listen to their stories of film shoots past, but in her head, she was running through an imaginary alternate-reality interview with Josh.

"Can you please find a way to sit so that the audience doesn't think you have a crochet hook up your ass?"

"Let me remind you: you live in a truck. You don't have a job. We're giving you a stipend to be in this film and you better start earning your keep. Now, let's try that again. Tell me about the first time you went climbing."

She smiled in spite of herself. What would happen if she actually talked to Josh like that? Perhaps he would shape up and obey. But it could also go the other way, with him storming off and demanding a different cameraperson. She smiled again. Either way, it would be an improvement.

The guys went to bed, but she stayed up alone, planning to wait long enough so she could pee off the beer before getting in her tent. She poked at the embers with a heavy stick, then swirled the flaming tip through the black air in psychedelic patterns.

She thought about what Madigan had said about Josh not being the type to pour his heart out to someone he just met, but it seemed more than that. It was possible that he was exceptionally camera shy. One of her documentary-track classes at UCLA had a whole week of lectures about the psychology of camera shyness. Camera shyness could be overcome, just like a fear of public speaking.

She scooted her camp chair closer to the fire pit for warmth as the flames died down. What if she just leveled with him and tried to find out why he didn't like the camera? Maybe no one had ever taken the time to give him camera training before. She could show him some clips of what good interviews looked like and they could role-play. It would be a huge risk, but imagine if it worked! If she somehow managed to pull a good interview out of Josh, Danny would be so impressed that she'd be more than set for a recommendation. Maybe even a job offer.

After the fire went cold, she grabbed her toiletry bag and walked to the bathroom. For once—thanks to the beer—she wasn't paranoid about running into a bear.

While she was in the bathroom, a wave of joyous laughter floated past the windows. Ah, to be up late, surrounded by friends, laughing and having fun. It had been so long since she'd done that. After the crash, she'd stuck close to her roommates, and with all of them being film majors, hanging out usually meant watching movies.

She stepped outside the bathroom, keeping her headlamp off as she walked carefully through the darkness toward the laughter. Ahead, there was a campfire with flames twice as tall as Walkabout's fires, with so many people gathered around it that they fully encircled the campfire, with a full second row of people in front, sitting on camp chairs. Music from a guitar danced quietly beneath the rise and fall of the group's laughter and the crackle of the fire.

Even though she didn't know any of these people, it somehow stung that she had been left out. How had everyone known to rally for a campfire tonight? Had there been a posting at the registration kiosk? Or were they a private group, like a church youth group or something?

Trusting that the brightness of the flames would enable her to remain out of sight in the darkness, she crept closer to the fire. She slid behind a pine tree to observe, slowing her breathing so she could hear them better.

The group's profuse swearing ruled out a church group, and the addition of words like "quick draw," "whipper," "knobs," and "rappel" revealed they were climbers. That, and the smell of weed mixed in with the campfire smoke.

April rested her head on the tree trunk and closed her eyes. The night was cold, but the sounds of the campfire made her feel warm. In a way, it reminded her of winter nights at home in Arizona, when her parents would turn on the gas fireplace and play jazz on the old CD player.

There weren't many women in the group, but she recognized a girl with long dreadlocks she'd seen around camp. April studied her, wondering if she was a climber, and if so, how good she was. She leaned down to say something to the guy sitting in front of her. The guy turned toward her, and firelight shone on his profile. Josh.

The dreadlocked girl said something else. Josh's subsequent laugh was sincere and hearty, ringing out above all the other voices.

Josh, laughing? She squinted to make sure she wasn't mistaken. It was him. He was even wearing his gray hooded sweatshirt, with the hood up.

She studied him as he turned back to his original conversation. He doubled over at something a guy near him said, and then started telling a story of his own. From the distance, she could only hear snippets.

"…and then this kid…"

"…I didn't know what to do, so I…"

By the end of his story, Josh had entranced everyone on his side of the campfire ring and they were laughing along with him.

This was Josh Knox? Mr. Awful? The same guy who had completely humiliated her during the interview?

Aha! This was absolute proof that his stubborn, abrasive on-camera persona was not camera shyness at all but a complete act. Willful film sabotaging. Think of all the projects he had ruined—and Walkabout's would be next! Josh Knox was just a selfish athlete who wanted sponsorships but none of the spotlight or responsibility that came along with them.

April squeezed the tree trunk so hard that a chunk of bark broke loose. It disintegrated into flakes, sliding out of her fist like sand. She was furious, yet she couldn't take her eyes off him. She just kept seeing that look on his face from the cafeteria, and how it contrasted so much to his laughter now. Who was this guy?

Unable to see his face from this angle because of the shadows from his hood, she closed her eyes and listened for his voice. There it was, clear and joyful. He was relaxed. Natural. Likable. Relatable. Attractive. Interesting.

"Dude, you don't even understand. It was sick!"

"…gnarliest climb…absolutely never getting back on that thing."

She opened her eyes. As much as she was angry at him, she couldn't help wishing that someday he might laugh that way around her.

Chapter Seven

Was *this* what Madigan meant by "climber's trail"? The path cut up a slope so treacherous and steep it might as well have been vertical. If this was some sort of elaborate hazing scheme the guys had set up, someone was going to pay.

April pressed her fingers into her temples, trying to find relief from her throbbing hangover headache. She checked Madigan's map against the terrain in front of her. Yep, this was it. The guys would soon be on their way to the base of the climb, and she had to get moving.

She adjusted the gargantuan backpack that held her gear and started up. Three steps later, the trail spit her back to the bottom in an avalanche of pebbles and pine needles. She grabbed a sapling and yanked herself back on to the trail. The sapling snapped under her weight and sent her sliding.

She threw the tree to the side, gritted her teeth, and then sprinted the first hundred yards to the place where the slope was a little less steep. She was drenched in sweat in no time and used a few of her precious minutes to strip to her bottom layer: a dry-fit running top with a tight, low neckline and a barely there halter back. After seeing the dreadlocked girl with Josh at the campfire last night, she'd decided to take Madigan's advice about skimpy clothing.

The trail steepened again, and she found herself caught on a seventy-degree treadmill of loose gravel. Her feet jetted out, and she slid down the hill on her hip, straight into a brittle, thorny holly bush.

She cursed Madigan for knowing how bad this trail was and still letting her come on it. She cursed Theo for not giving her better warning: surely he must have known that a girl he'd nicknamed Hollywood would not do well on this trail. She cursed Danny for subjecting his staff to such miserable working conditions. She cursed herself for not doing an internship in nice, clean, urban, familiar L.A.

Most of all, she cursed Josh. They were doing all this for him, yet he was secretly sabotaging everything. It was worse than any A-list prima donna story she'd ever heard.

The more she thought about him, the angrier she got. That anger fueled her up the gravel treadmill and another half mile of equally heinous slope and onto a zigzag of faint trail that rose straight to the sky.

She crossed the last switchback, gasping for air and furious. Her hands were caked in pitch and gravel, and rivulets of sweat ran down her body, turning dust into mud.

The slope eased a little after the switchbacks, but the top was still impossibly far away. Through the gaps between the trees on the ridge, she could tell the morning's overcast sky had already cleared. It was probably going to get hot, and fast.

She gulped down some water and continued her ascent past three cairn-marked turns. The next section of trail didn't require as much effort to remain upright, so her attention turned to the discomfort of her running shoes and socks, which were filled with twigs and pebbles. She longed to empty them, but she didn't dare take a break that long. She absolutely could not miss Mr. Awful's top out.

She climbed across a wide field of boulders, then reached the crest, where the trail was a tidy rut of hard-packed dirt through short green grass. The path kept her close to an apron of white-gray rock that swept up to a high band of cliffs.

Rounding the corner of the apron, she was met by a jaw-dropping unobstructed bird's-eye view of Yosemite Valley. A gentle stairway of granite slabs took her to an expansive plateau that was the top of Flying Sheep Buttress. There, a tiny alpine lake was nestled among pine trees and a carpet of new green grass that looked as soft as silk. In the cliffs above, a waterfall streamed thick with snowmelt. She breathed deeply, the pristine air refreshing her lungs after kicking up all that dust on the trail.

She looked at her watch. Despite it all, she'd made good time. She slid her pack off and dug for her radio. "Madigan, this is April. I'm at the top."

She rubbed the backpack indents out of her bare shoulders as she waited.

Unlike the valley's crowded landmarks, there was not a soul in sight up here. It was no wonder, seeing as the climber's trail and the cliff face were the only ways up. She carried the pack over to a log and set her equipment up exactly like she and Madigan had rehearsed in the campground yesterday.

"Madigan, this is April, I'm all set up," she said into the radio. "I'll start rolling as soon as you give me the sign."

She didn't receive a response from him, Danny, or Theo. She flipped through the other channels to make sure the radio was working. A Park Service conversation about an aggressive chipmunk at the visitor center was her confirmation.

What if coming all the way up here really was some sort of Walkabout hazing?

She walked over to the place where Josh would be coming over the edge of the cliff. When she was as close as she dared, she lowered on her butt to scoot closer and then rolled onto her stomach to peer over the edge.

The valley floor fell away from her like a sweep in an IMAX film. Her stomach dropped, and she pulled back. Good thing she wasn't afraid of heights, otherwise she might have fallen over the edge just from the shock of the sight.

She peeked over again, this time gripping the sharp edge of the cliff. She couldn't see the guys, but, then, from her perspective so close to the plane of the face, she couldn't see much at all of the cliff itself.

She could tell how high she was by the size of the cars on the road below: bumblebees. Her father used to have her fly at this height when he was teaching her low-level aileron rolls. In the Decathlon, it always felt too low, and she would chicken out until he let her do it a thousand feet higher. Sweat beaded on her forehead from the memory. Without the metal sides of the airplane around her and the powerful lift of the engine, the altitude felt plenty high.

Flying together had been their special thing, but it had never been *her* thing. Of course, he'd never known that. His assumption was that she'd come back home after college and he'd give her a "real education" in aerobatics and they would fly the two-plane, father-daughter sequences he'd been choreographing since she could walk. His entire business was already hers, technically. The planes, the hangar, the flight school. Someday—and soon—she would have to sell it all off. She would be selling her father's dreams, and with all the deferred maintenance and debt from the lawsuit, it wouldn't even bring in enough to save the family house.

A lump built in her throat and, suddenly, the height was too much.

With her head spinning, she carefully inched back from the edge and returned to the log where she'd stashed her stuff. She picked the dead leaves out of her hair to distract herself.

Where were the guys? Just *looking* over the side was enough to terrify most people, but her crew was *dangling* from that side. And it had become her nature to assume the worst.

A glance at her watch reminded her that Josh wasn't due for a while. It made perfect sense why the guys wouldn't be answering her radio call: they would be trying to minimize distractions while Josh was climbing. She'd communicated what she needed to—that she was ready—which was all they needed to know.

She sat down and shook out her shoes, and then picked the seeds and thorns out of her socks while her sweaty, blistered feet dried in the sunlight. Relaxing against the log, she gazed out across the lake.

How was it possible for something so beautiful, so untouched to exist? The surface of the lake was perfectly still, giving an unblemished reflection of the upper rim of cliffs, including the waterfall with its thundering muted by the distance. The impossibly bright, bluebird sky was also reflected in the lake, the color shining back on itself like a sapphire.

It was like being in a storybook. An enchanted, fairy-tale storybook. The pure, fresh air and the sun warm like a blanket put her into a trance. She leaned her head back on the log and waited for the radio call that would signal Josh's approach.

Chapter Eight

The airstrip was sizzling hot as her father lifted her into the booster chair on the copilot seat. Her body quivered with happy anticipation. She waited while Dad did the prechecks, then she mouthed along with all the radio calls. Finally, they were at the start of the runway and it was her turn.

"Go ahead," Dad said.

She clicked on the microphone. "Rose Tower, Mooney echo-alpha-alpha ready for takeoff."

"Echo-alpha-alpha, cleared takeoff, runway one left," replied Uncle Hal, who usually ran the tower.

"Cleared for takeoff runway one left, echo-alpha-alpha."

"Good job, April," Dad said. The Mooney Rocket roared and shook as he increased the throttle. He looked over for her thumbs-up, then released the brakes. The plane rumbled ahead faster and faster until they were racing into the nothingness at the end of the runway. Dad increased back pressure on the yoke, and they were floating in the air. Her stomach dropped as they climbed higher and higher, the noise and the vibration of takeoff a tangible force inside the cabin.

She waited for the slight change in speed and altitude that signaled the end of the climb and the landing gear being stowed. "Bumpies!" she cried.

Dad nosed the plane up and down in quick succession, making her stomach drop just like on the mini roller coaster at the fair. She grinned. He made a silly face and played along like the plane was a bucking bronco. She giggled.

"Upside down!"

"The Mooney Rocket doesn't go upside down, honey."

He dipped a wing to the left, then quickly rolled the other to the right as consolation, before banking back to the left. They were going out toward Rose River, which was her favorite route. He lowered as they approached the river, flying over the top of a palm oasis in a shallow canyon. A herd of mustangs burst from the trees, flowing up the sides of the canyon and fanning out across the plateau below them.

She laughed and spread her arms wide like a bird.

Dad nosed the plane higher and then steadied the Mooney Rocket on a course away from the mountains.

"Do you want to drive?" he asked.

She popped out of her seat belt to crawl onto his lap like she did when he let her steer the truck down their driveway, but he shook his head and buckled her back in. He helped her adjust her seat so she was closer to the copilot controls.

"Now, don't make any sudden movements," he said. "Just keep her steady. Like on your bike. Remember what happened when you turned too fast on your bike?"

She fingered the princess bandage on her knee from her crash a few days before.

"You ready?" he asked. She grabbed the leather controls and nodded eagerly.

For the first time in her life, she felt the full power of the Mooney Rocket's 305-horsepower engine responding to even the slightest of hesitation in her hands. The power vibrated through the controls like she was holding the reins of a terrible, mechanized monster. She didn't like it. She didn't like it at all.

She dropped her hands from the controls. "You do it, Dad."

"Don't you want to fly the plane?"

She noted his disappointment and reluctantly put her hands back on the controls.

"See, isn't this fun?" He looked over at her.

She nodded vigorously. She was old enough to know that this was a lie, but his approving smile made her heart swell.

• • •

A shadow crossed April's face, and she had the distinct feeling someone was watching her. Strange. It was probably the dream.

Wait.

Was she asleep?

Her eyes flew open, and there was Josh standing at her feet. Her grimy, bare, blistered feet. She fumbled for her radio.

The power light was green. The volume was still on max. She looked at the edge of the cliff and then back at Josh.

"Oh my god."

She squeezed her eyes shut tight. Maybe *this* was the dream. She hadn't just slept through the top out. She couldn't have.

She opened her eyes again. Josh was still there.

"Do you want me to crawl back over so you can get that on film?" he asked.

Oh, shit. A chilly wave of dread swept over her. She had missed the shot.

Her heart raced. Danny was going to kill her. If he didn't fire her outright, Josh would make sure she was taken off the crew.

"Just kidding," Josh said. "Your crew lost power midway up. They all went back down."

A power problem was a rookie mistake. There was no way it could have happened with a company like Walkabout. And Josh, he wore a harness and rock-climbing shoes, but he didn't have a rope. And his belay partner, Lars, wasn't with him. So how did he get up here?

She was so disoriented.

"The charger shorted or something last night. They ran out of power halfway up. It's not anyone's fault, but Danny's pretty mad."

April checked the light on her radio. Still green. No power problems on her end. But then, she had charged her batteries before dinner last night so that she'd be ready for her early start.

The midday sun was directly behind Josh. The rays fanning out from the sides of his body were almost as bright as the sun itself. She squinted. "How did you—?"

"I hopped over to an easier route and finished it out," he said.

She frowned. He had free soloed it.

"I'm not in the habit of backing off climbs. I don't want to jinx myself."

She relived the drop of her stomach when she peeked over the edge of the cliff. He'd climbed *that* without a rope.

"It's a five-seven," he said. "Barely. Besides, if I hadn't come up here, think how long you'd have been stuck before you realized something was wrong."

"Madigan would have come up and gotten me. Or they would have radioed once they had power again."

"They're probably not even off the rock yet."

She looked down and wiped a stray line of dust off her calf. Even though the debacle wasn't her fault, Josh had still caught her sleeping on the job. Her previous fury toward him was replaced with shame.

What was she supposed to do next? Would Danny still expect footage? Seeing as her equipment was working, she didn't think she could return to camp empty-handed.

"So. What do you normally do when you finish a climb?" she asked.

Josh frowned. "Oh. I see. We're going to have an interview."

She shouldn't have brought it up. She should just be happy he came up to tell her what had happened. Now he was going to think she was an ungrateful opportunist.

"This isn't an interview. I was just wondering what you usually do after a climb." *So you can get on with whatever that is, and I can film you doing it.*

"Hypothetically?" he asked.

He was still standing in front of her, close enough that she was completely covered by his shadow. Anywhere else, the distance would have been fine, but here, with the full expanse of Yosemite all around them and the wide bluebird sky overhead, it was claustrophobic.

"Yes, hypothetically," she answered.

He hooked his thumbs through the side loops in his climbing harness and his frown lifted. "Well, if there was a lake on top, I'd go for a swim."

Was he serious? Josh swimming in the pristine lake on this gorgeous plateau would be amazing footage.

"Are you going to swim in *this* lake?" she asked.

"Why not?"

"It will be freezing!"

"Sure, but wouldn't you rather take a dip in this pristine lake than in the moldy campground showers?"

"Me? I'm not going in the lake."

He looked pointedly at the sweat trails through the dust on her legs and the dried blood from the cut on her thigh.

"You go ahead," she said. "I'll film."

He snorted. "You'll film?"

"Yeah." Danny would be so impressed if she came back with a shot of Josh swimming in the lake.

"Let me get this straight," he said. "You want to stand here warm and dry while I go splash around in the lake like a fool? A big scene of triumphant release here in nature's bounty?"

A little splashing wouldn't be a bad thing, from a visual perspective. "Look at it this way. I'll film you now, and then when we repeat your climb, you won't have to do anything at the top."

"The route I'll be doing isn't easy, you know. After I climb it for real, I'm going to want to rinse off in the lake anyway."

She started to stand, and he reached down to help her. His warm, callused hand was immensely powerful, and he lifted her easily to her feet.

This was getting weird. First he had joked around with her, then he had a conversation like a normal person, and now he was being a gentleman. She didn't know why Josh was entertaining the discussion about filming him in the lake, but she wasn't about to question it.

She released his hand and brushed herself off. Now they were even closer, making all the skin exposed by her jog top buzz. Crossing her arms, she took a little step back. "Come on. You won't even know I'm here."

His eyes shifted, and he seemed to be considering it.

She wasn't going to let this one go. If she had to, she'd pretend to leave, then sneak back and film him in secret. "Please?"

"Okay, here's the deal. You can film me splashing around in the world's most scenic bathtub *if* you go in afterward. And no wading in. You have to jump straight in, just like I'm going to do."

"I am not going to get in the lake."

"Take it or leave it." He sat down on a nearby rock and yanked off his climbing shoes.

"That's completely unfair."

Josh winked. "It's part of the experience, you know."

"I'm not here to have an experience," she said. "I'm here to record *your* experience."

He laughed. "Deal still stands, though."

She eyed the cold glimmer of the lake and the snow along the top of the cliff above it. The water would be more than freezing, especially for someone who thought the ocean water in L.A. was too cold. But the footage of him jumping into that perfect, reflected panorama would be priceless, and she wasn't sure she'd have another chance to get it.

"Okay," she said. "Deal."

He put his climbing shoes next to her pack. "What do you want me to do?"

"Whatever you would do if you were the only one here."

He pulled his shirt over his head. "First of all, I wouldn't be stopping at this."

She blushed. So did he.

"I'm sorry," he said. "It was just too perfect not to say."

Her eyes were like a magnet to his torso. She had admired his body in films and magazines, but that was nothing to prepare her for seeing him shirtless right in front of her in real life. The muscles of his chest, back, and shoulders were perfectly developed, within the lanky profile of an ultramarathoner. Everything about him screamed *athlete*.

April grabbed the camera. "Where are you going in?"

He pointed to a downed tree that hung over the water like a diving board with branches. This was going to be awesome. As he started down the slope to the lake, she worked on positioning the camera. "Don't be so fast," she called. "I need you to do the shirt thing again."

"You mean, like put it back on and take it back off?"

"Yeah."

"Really?"

"Yes, really."

"Are we making a climbing film or porn movie?"

"It's not a climbing film. It's a film about climbing."

"Still, it's a little *Striptease*, don't you think?"

"Yes, but it tells the full story of the scene. We need it."

He scowled, but in a teasing way.

"Come on," she said. "I have to jump in the lake for this. You have to make it worth it for me."

He sighed and then put his shirt back on. She directed him where to stand and told him to face the lake. When he was ready, she began recording. Through the eyepiece, she watched him pull off his shirt. His back was as magnificent as his chest.

He untied the chalk bag cord around his waist and then unbuckled his harness and slid it off, just like it was a pair of pants. He was right about there being a *Striptease* quality to this, but it was only because his body was so sexy.

Josh walked to the downed tree's tangled roots. The tree angled across the water, directly into her right-hand vanishing point. The lake's reflection of the cliffs and waterfall above was as clear as a photograph. It was shaping up to be an absolutely perfect scene.

She silently cheered for Josh as he climbed around the roots and onto the trunk. If he could just make it into the lake without turning around and looking at the camera, the footage would be priceless.

He walked easily down the log. Soon, he was over the water, and the narrowing log was teetering. The farther he went, the more it wobbled, but he didn't seem to notice. When the log began to dip under his weight, he turned to face the water.

April drew in a breath and held it.

Josh leaped into the water with his arms high and outstretched. Perfect!

He disappeared into the crystal-clear reflection, a geyser of white water springing from his entry point. She panned in on the perfect bull's-eye of waves rippling outward. In the background, the log was still reverberating from his jump.

Josh resurfaced in the epicenter of the ripples, gasping for air. He gave a whoop that echoed off the cliffs, and then swam toward the shore at a perfect diagonal through her shot as she zoomed back out.

Yes! Yes! Yes!

She brought the shot to a close as he rose out of the water and stepped onto the narrow ribbon of gravel beach.

"Your turn," he called up to her. He was dripping wet and beaming.

He wiped his feet on a patch of moss and then toweled off with his discarded shirt. "I hope it was worth it."

"Oh, believe me, it was," she replied.

She started to power down the camera but changed her mind when she recalled Danny's advice about catching accidental gems. Instead, she waited for Josh to settle down on the moss and then zoomed in on him as he tipped his head upside down and dried his wet hair with his shirt.

She lowered the resolution, and then started recording just before she walked down to the lake to accept her fate. She stopped at Josh's patch of moss to take off her shoes.

"Are you really going to make me do this?" she asked.

"Of course," he said.

He looked so relaxed there on the moss, lounging back on his elbows with his legs outstretched. It was so unlike the Josh she had previously known.

She walked barefoot along the beach, the gravel between her toes smooth and cold—a chilling foretaste of the lake to come. Using the tree's ancient, twisted roots to climb up onto the trunk, she was surprised to discover it was significantly more unstable than Josh had made it look.

She spread her toes for better grip on the smooth, weathered wood, and then took her first, cautious step. The log vibrated in response. She looked back at Josh, who was still on the moss, now sitting with his legs bent and his arms draped across them.

"You're really going to make me do this?" she yelled.

"It's not getting any warmer," he called back.

April inched forward heel to toe, but no matter how gradually she shifted her weight, the log trembled beneath her. From above, the water was as clear as glass and the bottom of the lake was like a giant's bag of marbles. A school of tiny silver fish darted out from the shadow of the tree. A few steps later, there was a drop-off and the water went deep and dark. At least she wouldn't end up with a smashed skull if the log bucked her off unexpectedly.

The thought of falling messed with her balance. She dropped to a squat and gripped the wood. The log was really shaking now.

She wasn't nearly as far out as Josh had gone, but there was no way she'd be able to make it farther unless she scooted on her butt. Which she wasn't going to do, not with Josh watching. Very carefully she stood and faced the lake.

"You sure?" she yelled.

"I'm sure," he yelled back.

She stared down at the water. It glistened like it was licking its chops to swallow her up. She wasn't afraid of water, but having grown up in the desert, she didn't have experience jumping into anything other than safe, heated swimming pools. It only made it worse that Josh was there, stretching every moment of hesitation into an eternity. She just needed to get it over with.

She took a huge breath, plugged her nose, and leaped from the log.

Even before the falling sensation hit her, liquid nitrogen coated her skin and pressed into every pore. Her lungs collapsed as she catapulted down. Lower, lower, and lower she sank into the lake. Her mind screamed at her to start kicking, but she couldn't pass the signal along to her legs.

Finally, she hit equilibrium and stopped sinking. Her legs found their power, and then she was rocketing upward.

She broke through the surface, but her chest was too tight to take a breath, leaving her to suffocate in the mind-blowing cold. It was instinct alone that kept her head above water and her limbs swimming for shore.

Finally, her breath came in a panicked gasp. As she swam, the cold gave way to absolute, complete numbness, and with it, her breaths slowed and deepened. Only at that point did she notice Josh, who was standing at the shore, clapping and cheering.

She smiled and ice water dripped into the still-warm corners of her mouth. Her stroke was controlled now, and she could feel the ever-so-slight warming of the water as she neared the shore. A few strokes later, her foot brushed against a rock on the bottom. She stood up in the shoulder-deep water. It was warm. Almost.

"It's not so bad," she yelled to Josh.

She reached underwater to scrub the grime off her ankles and feet, and then yanked the elastic band out of her hair. She shook her hair free, then ducked below the surface and swam a few lengths with her hair flowing behind her. When she surfaced again, the water was waist-deep. Even though it felt warmer, her teeth were chattering.

Her feet were numb and clumsy on the uneven, slippery rocks as she waded toward the shore. She rose out of the water, her jog top gripping her waist and her shorts sucking against her thighs.

"Better than a campground shower?" Josh was now reseated on the moss.

"Definitely," she said as she dropped down next to him and brushed her dripping bangs out of her eyes. "But I'm just going to get filthy again on the way down."

"How'd you get up?" he asked.

"The climber's trail."

"Kind of a bitch, huh?"

"That's an understatement."

"There's a different way. It's a lot longer, but it keeps you off those chossy slopes."

Anything. She would do anything to never step foot on that climber's trail again. She lay back onto the soft moss, which had a little spring in it, making it feel a lot like Theo's bouldering pad.

Josh was still being nice. Personable. Normal. She didn't know why he'd decided to be real around her, but she was too relaxed at the moment to develop any conspiracy theories about it.

Overhead, the sun was bright and dazzling. She shielded her eyes with her forearm and watched the puffy clouds against the blue sky, feeling utterly and completely free.

She closed her eyes and marveled at the absence of noise. No cars, no TV, no radio, no footsteps from the apartment above, no voices, no airplanes, no wind. Even the thundering of the huge waterfall on the cliff was perfectly silent at this distance. The only thing she could hear was Josh's soft, rhythmic breathing.

Before she went in the lake, she had been tired and frazzled. Now she felt like she was at a day spa. The moss wicked the water off her skin while the sun above warmed her arms, legs, and face. She could lie in this sweet nirvana all day.

She was so relaxed that when she opened her eyes and drew in the beauty overhead, she wasn't sure if she'd been asleep, not that she cared if she had. She wanted this feeling to last forever and ever.

Josh said something, but it took her a minute to comprehend because she had forgotten he was there.

"What?" she asked.

"I guess we should talk about the gala," he said. "I hear you've been assigned to babysit."

The bliss that filled her deflated a little, anticipating the awkwardness of talking about it. She looked to the sky and squeezed the water from the ends of her hair. "Well, it was either me or Theo, right?"

"I know. I'm glad it wasn't Theo." He smiled.

She rolled to the side and propped her head on her arm. He was less than two feet away. How embarrassing—she must have been so disoriented after the cold water that she'd plopped down way too close to him.

"Theo owes me big-time," she said.

"I'm not *that* bad, am I?"

The closeness amplified the bare skin factor, especially now because they were down to two pairs of shorts and one jog top between the two of them.

"You answered all my questions last week with yes or no," she said. "Dinner conversation is going to be a real pleasure."

She'd meant to be lighthearted, but judging from his silence, he'd heard the truth in her words. Great. Now he would go back to being awful.

He started to reply but hesitated and then swallowed. "I know I'm hard to interview. I'm sorry."

This was certainly unexpected. She avoided looking at his face, afraid that she'd find it stony with sarcasm. "I was just giving you a hard time."

"Still, maybe next time I should take some of your

pointers."

She looked at him then. He was sincere. His eyes—more green now than brown—were so beautiful.

She had to be careful around *this* Josh. Without his ugly armor of hostility, it would be easy to forget her place, especially at the moment as they lay together on this soft bed of moss in a vast storybook landscape. But he was talent and she was crew, and she could never forget that. Crew-talent relationships were taboo, and she would be fired for it. Besides, until an hour ago, this guy had been nothing but a jerk to her.

She sat up and crossed her legs to break the feeling of intimacy. "Did you say you knew a better way out of here?"

"Yes."

"Okay. I'll tell you what. If you get me out of here without getting dirty, I'll give you more pointers before your next interview."

Still lying on his side, he looked at her. "Hmm…" He made of big show of scrunching his face and scratching his head in thought.

"Well?" she prodded.

"Deal." His face broke into a huge smile, bigger even than the ones she'd seen at the climbers' campfire.

Yesterday at the campfire she'd wondered what it would be like to be on the receiving end of one of his rare smiles, and now she knew. It was like being in the beam of a flashlight on a dark night. A beam that was as warm as it was bright. And a beam that made her want to shine right back.

Chapter Nine

An elderly woman with beautiful silver hair in a tight French twist breezed through the doors of the Ahwahnee Hotel. April knew instantly it was Vera. With her floor-length khaki cargo skirt, crisp white safari shirt, and hiking boots disguised as Mary Janes, she could be the cover model for an affluent senior citizen camping magazine. Even the scarf around her neck was a designer version of a red bandanna.

Vera air-kissed April twice. She was in the park for some HSSR business and had asked Danny to have April meet her here for midmorning tea. The maître d' ushered them to their table in the dining room, where a soaring wood ceiling met cathedral windows that gave a spectacular view of Half Dome.

"I can't tell you how happy I am to be here," Vera said. "I used to come four times a year when Vic was still with us. There's just something about this place that makes me feel so alive. Tell me everything that's going on."

"Gabby and I reserved four rooms at the hotel," April started.

"Oh, that! I'm sure you two have everything handled. I want to know about camping," Vera said. "And the film. How is the film going?"

"Good so far," April said. She didn't know how much Vera knew, specifically about the battery debacle on Flying Sheep earlier in the week, so she stuck to something safe. "The guys will be filming Josh on Code for Verity in a few days."

Vera sighed. "I wish I didn't have to be back in the city so soon, otherwise I would stay and watch."

"I can send you some of the footage."

"Yes, please do!"

Vera's phone rang. She silenced it without looking at the caller ID. "I hope Danny doesn't feel like I'm getting in his way, but I like to be involved. This is a very personal project for me."

"Of course," April said.

Vera told her all about what she'd been doing with HSSR on this trip and some of her plans for a temporary funding bill.

"Not many people know this, but Vic's paralysis wasn't caused by the accident," Vera said. "It was caused by the rescue. Or lack thereof. That's the reason I'm so vested in HSSR."

A waiter delivered a tea set and a three-tiered platter of pound cake, scones, and crustless sandwiches. He lowered a basket of loose tea into the teapot to steep.

"HSSR was just a rudimentary first-aid crew back then. It was for tourists—lost children, scraped knees, that sort of thing. Vic had broken a vertebra in his upper back. With proper care, he could have fully recovered, but the crew didn't have the training or equipment to keep a spine immobilized during an advanced rescue."

"I'm so sorry," April said.

Vera waved her hand. "Vic never dwelled on it, and

neither do I. What's important is that we keep HSSR funded. Much of their rescue crew is volunteer, but the operations and training and equipment are very expensive."

The timer next to the teapot went off, and Vera pulled the tea leaves out. She poured cups for them both.

"I have to be honest," Vera continued, "I was a little concerned when Danny told me he had picked a young lady for the internship—not that I think a woman couldn't do it. It's just that Walkabout doesn't have any full-time female employees except Danny's wife, and she's up in Seattle with their kids. The living conditions are rough, and the job is demanding. How are you holding up?"

"I'm getting used to it," April said. "My adviser's worked on films like this before, and he recommended some specialized workouts last quarter."

"Like what?"

"Walking stairs with a weighted backpack. Some upper-body work. Trail running. That sort of thing."

"Good. Then, are you liking it here?" she asked.

"Oh, yeah. It's great!"

Vera beamed.

Living outside in a campground was certainly an adjustment, but now that sleeping was less of a problem and she'd gotten that fantastic footage of Josh at the lake, April was really starting to love it here. Madigan was a good friend, Theo was like a pesky older brother, and Danny was a good mentor. Every day she was learning so much.

"I camped here with Vic and his friends for most of the summer one year," Vera said. "Best summer of my life. Rock climbers are awfully handsome, you know."

April pictured Josh à la *Vertical View* magazine's hunky Redpoint spread. She'd thought about him a lot since the Flying Sheep climb, but she hadn't crossed paths with him except at Walkabout dinners, which he had started attending regularly. Even at dinner, though, she didn't interact with him much because he sat at one end of the table while she sat at the other, in her regular place, across from Madigan.

"Yosemite was so different back then," Vera said. "There weren't as many rules, you know. The sport of climbing was just getting started, and this was the epicenter of it all. It was a bunch of Beats, mostly. Dirty, fearless, authority-hating young men. Imagine Haight-Ashbury right there in your campground."

Vera looked out the window to Half Dome. "I wanted to stay on in the fall and learn to climb, but my parents wouldn't allow it." She turned back to April. "But just think, if I hadn't gone back to college, I would have never met Bill."

She must be talking about her husband, William Smithleigh III. The grandson of the founder of the Smithleigh Company. April knew he had been dead a long time, and they had never had any children. Now with Vic gone, she wondered if Vera was lonely despite all her philanthropies.

April refilled their cups of tea. "How did you pick Walkabout for this project?"

"Vic used to watch Danny's reality series about surfing. He always said surfing and climbing were a lot alike, and he thought Danny had really captured the essence of it."

Vera plucked the last scone off the tray. "There are production companies out there that do nothing but rock-climbing movies, but I wanted a company that could capture the full experience of it. Not all of us can rock climb, but we can be inspired by how climbers live and what they see when they are up there on the walls. For climbers, life is simple but amplified."

April recalled the shock of the cold water as she fell through the depths of Flying Sheep Lake. After, she'd felt clean and refreshed in a way no shower could ever match. Simple but amplified. A perfect description.

She and Vera spent more time talking about Yosemite, and before she knew it, the dining room was filling up with the lunch crowd. A busser came to clear the tea service. Vera tucked a single bill under the flower vase, and she and April walked to the lobby.

"April, before you go," Vera said, "I just want to say how sorry I am about your father."

April froze. Fiery white pinpricks bounced through her vision.

"I knew him back in the nineties," Vera said. "I was on San Francisco's Fleet Week board, and he flew our air show every year. He was such a gregarious person. The life of the party, no doubt about it. And your mother. So demure and elegant."

Hot tears flowed down April's cheeks despite her attempt to hold them at bay. She couldn't believe this was happening in public and in front of the Smithleigh heiress, nonetheless.

Vera squeezed her shoulder. "I know it must still be hard, honey. I didn't mean to upset you. It's just such a tragedy what happened."

It was kind of Vera to use the word "tragedy" when the International Association of Professional Aerobatics investigation had faulted her father for the crash.

The maître d' handed April a thick paper napkin. She quickly blotted the tears off her cheeks. So much for her fresh start in Yosemite. Did Danny know? What if he had only hired her because Vera pitied her?

"How'd you know he was my dad?" April asked.

"I remembered the news articles saying Mitch had a nineteen-year-old daughter. I put two and two together when Danny told me the name of the intern he'd picked and that you were from Arizona."

Variations of "Stephens is survived by his wife of twenty-five years and his daughter, April, nineteen" appeared in every news article for months. Less tactful newspapers used their full names and pointed out that she and her mom were in the audience to witness the crash. The least tactful papers attempted interviews while April was still hospitalized for smoke inhalation.

Her head felt hollow and like it was strung with cobwebs. She gave a nod to Vera that would have to do as a good-bye. She turned toward the doors and smacked straight into Josh Knox.

As in, literally smacked. Her cheek directly into his solid chest, which smelled like fabric softener. She stumbled back. What was *he* doing at the Ahwahnee?

"Hi, Joshua," Vera said, bear-hugging him long and hard. Strangely, he seemed okay with it.

"I'm going to go freshen up in my room," Vera said. "I'll be right back down." She turned to April and squeezed her hands. "This morning was a pleasure. I'll see you at dinner tonight. I hear you guys are having hamburgers."

April's vision was spinning. Vera was coming to dinner at the campsite? Danny hadn't mentioned that. She walked toward the doors, almost plowing into Josh a second time. She noted concern on his face when he looked at her, but she was numb to the embarrassment she would have normally felt about it.

Outside, she went directly to her bike, but her hands were shaking too much to line up the numbers on the lock. She sat on a bench to calm down.

At the Saguaro Butte Airfest in New Mexico, her father had done a tail slide into a dangerous new snap roll sequence. After the investigation, the association had faulted him for two intentional breaches of the code of ethics: the first was for his careless and reckless operation of an aircraft, since he had not sufficiently perfected the sequence before performance, and the second was due to evidence that he had knowingly flown with oil pooled in the engine cowl. Those breaches ignited a lawsuit, which, for almost a year, turned the crash into a national controversy on air show audience safety.

Why, Dad? You had a wife and a daughter.

It was degrading to know that Vera had been following all of that. At least the guys didn't seem to know about it, otherwise they would have said something by now. They might remember the crash being in the news, but they weren't pilots or aerobatics aficionados, so their attention to the subject would have been limited.

The fact that she cared if the guys knew made her feel sneaky and dishonest, like the crash was a dirty family secret. It wasn't a secret at all—thanks to the media coverage. She just didn't want to have to answer any questions about it. She didn't want to talk about it, ever. And she certainly didn't want to be ambushed by someone bringing it up unexpectedly. Like today.

She checked the time on her cell phone and noticed she had full reception, which was rare in the park. Although she didn't feel like talking, she owed her mom a call.

"Hi, April," her mom said. "I'm on shift right now, but I'll be done with rounds in five. I'll call you right back."

Working at a mental hospital was a grueling job for a young person, let alone for someone like her mother, who was practically at retirement age and hadn't worked in the field for decades. Trying to fight the lawsuit had taken all of her savings and the equity on the house, and she needed income badly.

April attempted her bike lock again and this time was able to undo it. Josh walked out of the Ahwahnee as she was wrapping the lock around the handlebars. He was wearing a nice shirt—one that would have been perfect for interviews— and his pants were wrinkle-free. Only the sporty sunglasses pushed up on his head and the water sandals on his bare feet gave him away as someone other than a tourist on a day trip to Yosemite.

She wanted to talk to him but was too afraid. Those moments lying on the moss at Flying Sheep Lake had become sacred to her. Never in her life had she felt so at peace, and he had been part of that experience. He'd been a different person then, and for him to return to being the gruff and dismissive talent around her would break the spell of the lake and that perfect, magical place.

She hurried to pull her bike off the rack and escape around the side of the lodge before he saw her.

Too late. He was walking her way.

He stopped in front of her, real and mirage-like at the same time. Her heartbeats quickened.

Her phone rang. "Sorry, I've gotta take this." She put the phone to her ear and shouldered away from him.

"Hi, Mom," she said. "All done with rounds?"

"For now," her mom said. "It's been one of those days. What's going on?"

Josh walked back to lodge and leaned against a pillar, watching tourist kids play on the lawn. He didn't seem at all sullen or feisty. In fact, he couldn't be Awful Josh, because Awful Josh would never have approached her to begin with.

"…it looks pretty dangerous," her mom was saying. "How are you feeling about that?"

"What?"

"Rock climbing. The things I saw online, anyway."

"Oh. Don't worry. I'm not filming any of the climbing."

April looked at Josh. Why *had* he come over to her? Maybe he actually wanted to talk. Like a normal person. The thought made her warm.

"That's good," her mom said. "Just be aware that even things that seem dissimilar could evoke the same emotional reaction, and that could cause your PTSD—"

"First, I don't have PTSD, and even if I did, it wouldn't matter. I can't run from everything forever."

"No, but you can make sure you're ready before you attempt certain things."

"Remind me not to call you at work. You're in full psychologist mode right now."

"Because I know you don't have *your* psychologist there in Yosemite."

Good thing her mom didn't know she had quit therapy not long after she started. The sessions weren't productive, and she needed to save money. "Once I get a job, I have to be able to film whatever I'm assigned," she said. "I think it's good for me to be around this."

"Yes, but it might be too early. You haven't flown since it happened."

"I had to fly to get here, and I did just fine."

"You know what I mean. The last time you took one of our planes up was when Sophie came out to visit. That was Christmas your sophomore year."

"I will probably never *pilot* again," April said. "Don't you think that would be understandable?"

"It would, depending on what was motivating you to make that choice."

"Ugh, Mom, I really don't want to get into this right now." Not only that, now that she knew Josh was being normal, she really wanted to go say hi before Vera came down.

She looked over at him, dismayed to see she'd already missed her chance. Vera was there, her red bandanna tied around her hair like a kerchief. She and Josh walked toward the valet stand.

"I have your box all ready to go for the gala," her mom said. "I packed some nicer clothes and shoes for the rest of the weekend, too."

"Thanks, Mom."

"The makeup that I put in there is my hypoallergenic stuff, so there shouldn't be any scent."

"Don't worry, I haven't seen any bears yet," April said.

The valet pulled a vintage convertible to the curb just as Vera and Josh reached the stand. Vera got in and the top slid off. Josh said something to Vera, and she laughed and got out of the car. He took the driver's seat.

April kicked herself for not talking to him when she had the chance. She didn't know when she would see him again outside of dinners. Probably not until the next interview, and *that* was guaranteed to break the spell of the lake.

A shrill alarm went off on her mother's end of phone. "It's probably just a drill, but I've got to go. Sorry, honey!"

The phone went dead. April turned it off and put it in her pocket. Over at the convertible, Vera was digging for something in her purse.

There was nothing left to do but go back to the campground. April wheeled her bike toward the road. She glanced over her shoulder at Josh, who was fiddling with the radio. Vera was opening a sunglass case, which was empty. She got out of the car and hurried toward the lodge.

Before she could change her mind, April straddled her bike and coasted the short distance to the convertible. *Just pretend that he's Madigan. The worst thing that could happen is that he'll blow you off.*

In which case she would be devastated.

"Nice car," April said.

Josh looked up with surprise. His face tensed, then softened. "I know. Sure beats a truck-house."

"I didn't realize you were buddies with Vera McWilliams-Smithleigh."

"I knew Vic. He did the first ascent of the Sorcerer."

"I thought that was you."

"No, I was just the first to free it. Vic climbed it in the

sixties using pitons and some other sketchy homemade gear. It was very dangerous."

He clicked the engine off and rested his elbow on the car door.

"Where are you two headed?" April asked.

"Out to the HSSR command center for a tour. Vera's hoping they'll take us up in the helicopter. I'm hoping they won't."

"You don't like flying?"

He shook his head. April laughed aloud.

"What?" Josh asked. His face was flushed and adorable.

"*You*, afraid of flying?"

"I'm not *afraid*. But I only do it when I have to."

Vera returned to her car, and April said good-bye. She took her time riding back, drinking in the beauty of the valley as a warm, gentle wind flowed through her hair. Wildflowers were blooming in the meadows and the Yosemite River was running full and smooth. The bike path dipped onto a gentle downslope and she coasted over it light and free, still deeply happy that her encounter with Josh today had been positive. Perhaps it meant Normal Josh was here to stay? They were too different to ever be actual friends, but there was no reason they couldn't be friendly like this more often.

Chapter Ten

Rockfall. A natural phenomenon where chunks of rock break free and plummet along the face of a cliff. There are no warning signs, and it cannot be predicted.

That's what was happening at Code for Verity, which was out near Curry Village. The rockfall on Code for Verity wasn't big—more like gravel—but even the smallest of rocks falling from Yosemite Valley heights could crack a helmet in two. And, according to Theo, "You never know when a stream of gravel could spit out a suitcase-size killer." She shivered just thinking about it.

She had stayed back at the van to log some footage, but with filming canceled for the day, the guys had insisted she join them for some top roping at Celery Slabs, a popular band of short cliffs not far from the campground. Being midday, the cliffs were striped with neon climbing ropes and bustling with people of all ages, speaking many different languages.

Madigan showed April how to put on a harness, and then they all sat around waiting for a group to finish a pair of climbs that Theo promised were the easiest ones at Celery

Slabs. She was surprised—and pleased—with herself for going along with this so easily. The way Theo had explained it made it seem like top roping was no different from climbing at an indoor rock-climbing gym, and once they arrived, there were a reassuring number of obvious novices on the rock.

Once the group they were waiting on was done, Theo and Ernesto—one of the contractors Danny had hired for the Code for Verity sequence—climbed the cliffs to get the ropes set up on top, with Danny and Madigan belaying them from the ground. Neither Theo nor Ernesto had the fluid grace Josh had when he climbed. Theo put obvious muscle into the rock as he reached and stretched, lunged and balanced. Ernesto moved robotically at a turtle's pace, always scanning ahead for his next move.

Beside her on the pile of rocks where she was sitting, there was a heap of rock-climbing gear. She picked up one of the gadgets, which was surprisingly light considering it was made of metal. Each of the six half-circle discs had teeth on the spine, like bike gears, and they were offset from the center so that when she pulled on the wire tail attached to them, they compressed to a fraction of the width.

"You put that in a crack, and when it expands, it's as bomber as a bolt."

April turned to find Josh next to her. His clothes were rumpled, and his smile was large and genuine.

His friend Lars was with him.

"It's a cam," Josh said, nodding toward the gear in her hand. "A Camalot. Or camming device, if you want to get technical."

She looked at him and nodded. Celery Slabs didn't seem like Josh's kind of scene, and she was surprised that he was here. He grabbed a much smaller cam from the pile, pulled the tail to make it narrower, and then slipped it into a gap between two of the rocks in the pile. He released the lever and the device stayed locked in place.

"Pull on it," he said.

She pulled. It didn't budge.

"Harder," he said.

She yanked. It still didn't budge.

"It's one of Esplanade's newest. It can hold sixteen hundred pounds of force," he said. "An eighty-foot whipper, no problem."

He hooked his pinky finger through the webbing on the end, then leaned back with his full weight. April couldn't decide if she was more impressed by the tiny cam or the strength in Josh's finger.

"Hey, dude, that's Rolf Ruiz over there," Lars said.

Josh pulled himself back to vertical. The two of them looked over at a gray-haired man in purple spandex leggings on the cliff. Lars went over to talk to Rolf's belayer, but Josh stayed with her.

"Rolf's one of the old greats," Josh said. "He used to climb with Vic."

Josh perched on the pile of rocks next to her, and they watched Rolf climb. She was hyperaware of how close Josh was. Madigan kept glancing back over his shoulder at them, making her feel guilty, like she was not supposed to be talking to the talent outside of an interview. She hoped Madigan knew it was Josh who had joined her and not the other way around.

"Did you fly yesterday?" April asked.

"No. They needed the helicopter for a rescue, thankfully. It was cool to see behind the scenes at their base, though."

"I'm sure it will help you out for your speech at the gala."

"Don't remind me."

"You mean you're not excited?" April was already counting down the days. It was a two-night, three-day vacation from the tent. A whole weekend of being clean, wearing normal clothes, having privacy, and good cell phone reception. Not to mention a real bathroom and a soft bed!

Josh shrugged. "I am looking forward to it, kind of. But I would really rather not give a speech."

"Are you nervous about it?"

"It depends. Are we on or off the record?" he asked.

"I'm not a reporter, you know."

He raised an eyebrow, and she couldn't help smiling.

"If it was anyone but Vera putting this on, there's no way I'd do it," he said. "HSSR is a really important cause." His face was serious, but not in the hardened way she was more used to seeing it. "It's the same with the film, you know. I would never let you guys tag along if it weren't a tribute to Vic."

How ironic. He and Danny felt the same way about him being in the film.

"I thought you were doing the Sorcerer *because* of the film," April said.

"No. I was supposed to do it last fall, actually, but the weather never lined up before winter set in."

A small weight lifted from her shoulders. She was relieved Walkabout wasn't the reason Josh was doing this insane feat.

"You're all geared up," he said. "Are you going to climb?"

"I'm going to *try*."

"Ever been before?" he asked.

"Never."

"You'll do well. You're strong."

She wasn't sure how he'd know that, but perhaps all the pull-ups she'd done last term had shown when she wore the jog top at the lake.

Madigan was staring at them blatantly now. "It must be my turn," April said.

"Can't be," Josh said. "Theo's still on the rope."

Madigan wasn't the only person looking at them. A huddle of teen boys were as well. All at once they stopped whispering and walked over to Josh.

"Oh, great," Josh said, looking like he wanted to sprint into the trees.

"It's cute," April said. "You have a fan club. They love you!"

"But *I* don't love them when they take pictures and post them on the internet."

"I bet your sponsors do."

April hopped off the rock as the boys moved in. "Good luck," she mouthed to him. After this, he'd probably bolt, which was fantastic for her. She'd rather not have a professional climber and the star of their film watching her blunder all over the rock.

"You ready for this?" Madigan asked.

"No," she replied.

"Don't worry. I'll help you."

He stepped in close and showed her how to tie the climbing rope through her harness.

"That's it?" she asked.

"That's it. Go for it!"

She stepped up to the cliff. She reached out, and her fingers hesitated. From this view, puny Celery Slabs looked as tall as Flying Sheep Buttress. It was as if having the intention to climb the thing transformed it into something alive and unwelcoming. *Go ahead. Just* try *to climb me. I dare you.*

She lifted her hands to the rock. Just like the big boulder in camp, there was nothing to hold on to.

Madigan laughed and tapped on a minuscule ledge near her knee. It was six inches long and no more than two millimeters wide. "Put your left foot there, and then you'll be able to reach this big knob with your right foot," he said, patting a knot of rock near her elbow.

Theo came over to help, but Madigan shooed him away. He pointed to a spot above her head. "There's where you put your hands." She stood on her toes and felt around. Sure enough, there were two bulbs that she hadn't been able to see.

"Okay," she said. "Here goes nothing."

Madigan stepped back and pulled the rope tight. She gripped the handholds and pressed her foot onto the hairline ledge. Like a miracle—and thanks to the grippy rubber shoes—her foot stuck. She stood up on that leg, but her hands were too low to support her, and she slipped. She gasped, but the rope caught her almost before she knew anything was wrong. With embarrassment, she noted her feet were only a few inches off the ground.

She started over, managing not to slip on the first move, only to find herself in another precarious position as soon as she got past the knobs. Her heart raced. She was only six feet up, but it sure seemed like a lot when all her weight was on a single hand that was moments from giving out.

Frantically, she patted the rock overhead for another handhold.

"Match your hands," Madigan called up to her.

"What?"

"Put your left hand next to your right hand."

Sure enough, both hands fit on the handhold. She worked her feet onto good footholds. Rock climbing was definitely a lot harder than guys like Josh made it look.

She found the next handhold on her own. It was a ledge so thin she had to curl her hands and grip it with just her fingertips. Inch by inch she climbed higher. Every move was a puzzle, with each foot gained a victory, until she reached a place that was completely impassable.

She tried not to think about the fact that she was higher than the treetops. This time, she didn't have a hand free to feel around for more holds. The foot she was standing on started to jackhammer.

She yelled down for a suggestion. Madigan pointed to a

handhold, but it was way too far to reach.

"That's the crux," Theo yelled. "Just get past this and you're golden."

"What?"

"The crux. The hardest part. You're going to have to stand on those nubs to reach it."

"Where?"

Her heart was racing, and she could hardly breathe. Was her harness on tight enough? Would Madigan really be able to stop her fall this high up?

"They're all over the place," Theo yelled. "Smear your shoe on one of them."

He was right; there were little bumps all over the place, but they were only as big as gumballs. The small kind of gumball.

"You're going to have to trust your feet, Hollywood," Theo yelled.

Her forearms burned, and she was a breath away from slipping off. She really, really didn't want to fall.

This was a beginner climb, she reminded herself. Josh climbed stuff infinitely harder, and with a camera crew in his face.

April scraped at one of the nubs with her unweighted foot.

"Are you sure they'll hold me?" she yelled to Theo.

"You're on top rope. Nothing to be afraid of!"

"Get out of here! You're not helping," Madigan said to Theo. "I've got you, April. Go for it!"

She had to make a move. And soon.

She breathed calmness into her jackhammering foot and then hooked the toe of her shoe across a gumball. Pressing her thigh into the wall, she put her weight on the gumball and stood.

Suddenly, the handhold was in reach. She lunged for it.

It wasn't a good hold. Her hand was slipping off it. She threw her foot over to a higher gumball, and before she knew it, her foot was on a solid ledge and her hands gripped a nice, deep pocket.

Down below, Danny, Madigan, Theo, and Ernesto were cheering. She glowed with her accomplishment.

She rocketed up the final section of the route and then sat back in her harness and Madigan lowered her down.

She'd done it! There were high fives and cheers all around when she reached the ground.

The knot through the front of her harness had tightened in on itself from being lowered. Her fingers shook with fatigue, and she couldn't get it to budge. Madigan helped her loosen it. "Take a rest, and then I'll teach you how to belay."

The rock-climbing shoes were pinching like lobster claws, and she couldn't wait to get them off. She grabbed her running shoes from the base of the cliff and started toward the rock pile to put them on.

And there was Josh, sitting on top of the pile.

She continued toward the rocks like it was no big deal. Had he been there the entire time?

He grinned and gave her a high five. She couldn't help grinning back.

"Hollywood, huh?" he said. "That's your nickname?"

"Not by choice."

"I thought you went to UCLA."

"Yeah. The two are totally different things. Theo likes to pretend he doesn't know that."

She pried the climbing shoes off her hot and clammy feet. Worried they smelled, she hurried to get her running shoes back on.

"How'd you like climbing?" Josh asked.

Their eyes met, and the sensation was a little like falling, only euphoric instead of scary.

"It was really hard," she said. "But fun."

"That was a five-eight," he said. "Not bad for your first climb."

She looked down and tied her shoes to hide her blush. The rock pile wasn't very wide, and she was sitting quite close to Josh. Surprisingly, it felt natural. Preferable. She wouldn't mind being around him like this a lot more.

April looked up, and Madigan was watching her with a disapproving look, like she was a schoolgirl caught doodling a boy's initials in her notebook.

"Hey, Josh," Madigan yelled over. "Do you have a second so we can talk about tomorrow?"

April forced herself not to look at Josh as he got off the rocks. Did Madigan actually need to talk to Josh, or was he just trying to rescue her from her faux pas—being too familiar with the talent?

She forced her eyes over to Danny, who was climbing the route she had just finished, but her mind remained on Josh. Surely he had better things to do than hang around here and watch mortals scrape their way up the cliff. Was it possible he had known the Walkabout crew was coming here this afternoon and his being here was not a coincidence?

Mostly, though, she replayed their high five. Unless it was her imagination—or wishful thinking—Josh had squeezed her hand a smidge longer and tighter than everyone else.

Chapter Eleven

When perpetually hyperactive Danny asked April to join him on one of his morning runs, she knew it wasn't just a run but some sort of business meeting on the go. About what, she didn't know, and he wasn't coming right out with it.

They were on the asphalt tourist path at the base of Yosemite Falls. It was still early, but there was a solid stream of camera-wielding visitors making the pilgrimage to the falls. She had worried at first that she wouldn't be able to keep up with Danny, who regularly ran half marathons, but he was older and stockier, and she wasn't having any trouble keeping pace.

Since he wasn't bringing anything up, she gave him updates on gala plans: his wife's flight to Sacramento, the VIP brunch on Saturday morning, and Josh's speech and tux.

"Sounds like you've got it handled," he said.

"I think so."

They stopped to stretch at a falls overlook. The power thundering off the waterfall was tangible, and the air was heavy with mist. It was invigorating in a way coffee could never be, especially with the beautiful symphony of birds all around them and the sun lighting the sky from behind the valley walls.

Danny dipped into a lunge. "I've been wanting to tell you that I've been impressed with your work so far. You're knowledgeable, professional, and you definitely have an artist's eye. You're doing really well keeping up on cataloging the footage and getting everything scheduled for when the other climbers arrive."

"Thanks. I appreciate it," she said.

He didn't say anything else, which made her wonder if the compliment was just a prelude to bad news.

You're doing great, but your lack of climbing knowledge has not turned out to be an asset to this film after all.

You're doing great, but Madigan thinks you might have a crush on our star and we just can't have that.

"Ready?" Danny asked, and they started jogging again. "Your footage at Flying Sheep Lake was remarkable, by the way."

She'd done a trial cut of Josh jumping in the lake, and it came out exactly as she'd hoped.

"I have to ask, how in the world did you get him to cooperate for that?"

"It was his idea, actually. I was just ready with the camera." Danny didn't need to know about her jumping in, too.

"Well, we will definitely use it in the film. Remind me to have him wear the same shirt when we refilm that climb."

April glowed. Maybe there was a place for her in the documentary film industry after all! They rounded a corner that brought them onto a path along the shoulder of the main road.

"There's something I want to discuss with you," he said. "But first, I want you to know that it's perfectly okay for you to say no."

What? Another gala to escort Josh to?

"I'd like to invite you to join our Sorcerer team," he said.

The Sorcerer? She eyed its sharp apex looming over the treetops to their left.

"I'd hate for you to finish your internship without getting into the core of camera work on a film like this. It's not easy, but now that I've seen you on the rock, I'm confident you can handle it. It didn't seem like you were afraid of heights."

She didn't know what to say. It was such a compliment and an incredible opportunity, but she thought immediately of the guy drinking on the roof at that party. To have a front-row seat for Josh's ropeless feat? She did not have the nerve for this sort of thing.

"We use a lot of the same equipment as climbers when we're up there," Danny continued. "You'll have to learn the rope system, but there's still plenty of time for that. You'd be at the highest position on the Sorcerer, which is the easiest to get to. You just walk up the trail and do a quick rappel down to your spot."

There was nowhere else she would be able to learn technical skills like this. If she could do even a fraction of what Madigan and Theo could, it would really make her stand out from all the other new film school grads when she applied for a job. The idea of it was exhilarating, but actually doing it would be terrifying.

"Think about it," he said. "Just let me know soon, okay? If you want to do it, you'll have some long hours ahead with Madigan and Theo."

· · ·

"You've got mail," Madigan said when April got back from her shower after the run.

She was so preoccupied about the Sorcerer that it took

her a second to notice the stack of packages and envelopes on the picnic table. The largest box was hers. It was from her mom, which meant it was her gala dress.

On every surface of the box, her mother had written, *Do not open! Read note first!* There was an envelope taped to the top, and she used the blade of Madigan's pocketknife to cut it open. Inside were a notecard and several pictures.

April, I know you're going to want to see the dress as soon as you get it, but if you're still living in a tent, you should probably leave this sealed up until you get to Sacramento. The dress and the heels are vintage, so take good care of them! Love, Mom

The dress in the pictures—strapless, full-length, empire-waist, apricot in color with a layer of fine silver netting on top—was the one dress in her mother's collection that April had never been allowed to borrow. It was a couture dress, a gift from the designer himself for her mother to wear at a ball following a royal London air show held for Prince Philip's birthday.

In the first picture from that ball, her exquisitely beautiful mother leaned against April's tall, handsome father, with the dress flowing around her like mercury. Tears came to April's eyes. It was that night in London her father had proposed to her mother.

The other photos were of the dress hanging on the closet door, showing it from different angles. April handed the photo of her parents to Madigan.

"She's your mom?" he asked.

"Yep."

"You look exactly like her."

"She was just a little older than me when that was taken."

Madigan handed the photo back. April flipped through the rest of her mail, which was all from UCLA's accounts department. Like she needed a reminder of how little she was making here compared to what she owed.

It was midmorning, which meant most of the people in the campground were off exploring the park. She took a deep breath, smelling sun-warmed pine trees and the juicy orange Madigan was peeling.

He split the orange in two and handed half to her. She pulled a segment off and took a bite.

"Danny wants me to film on the Sorcerer," she said.

"I know," he said. "He asked me about it last night."

"What do you think?"

Madigan's cornflower-blue eyes lingered on hers. "I think it would be great to have you up there."

"Do you think I could be ready in time?"

"Sure. All that's different is that you're filming from a harness instead of on the ground."

"I know it's not *that* simple."

"Okay, so you have to get to your filming spot and then back up."

"Yeah, on a sheer cliff face."

He popped an orange segment into his mouth and thought for a minute. "If you can get past the sheer cliff part, think of all the other places you'll be able to shoot. Rainforest canopies, skyscrapers, canyons, you name it. And it's a pretty rare skill to have, you know."

"I know. But…"

"But what?" he asked.

She pulled a white string off the edge of her orange. There were lots of *but*s. She wasn't going to discuss the main one with him, so she named one of her lesser worries.

"What if I hurt someone because I don't know what I'm doing?" she asked. "I could drop a microphone on someone's head. Or I could get in Josh's way and make him fall."

"You are such a worrier." He gave her a playful shake.

"Although that's a valid concern. We have everything on tethers up there, and we rehearse ahead of time."

She finished her orange and poured water over her hands to rinse off the stickiness. Yes, she was a worrier. A chronic *what if*–er. In this, she had always been so unlike her daredevil dad.

"And something else to factor in—we've got a bunch of projects lined up starting next winter, and we will definitely be doing some hiring for cinematographers. I don't think Danny would be quite so generous in committing to all the learning time unless he were impressed with what he's seen so far and is thinking that you knowing these skills might benefit the company on more than just a temporary internship."

"Wow, really?"

"Just speculation on my part, of course. But if you decide to do it, I know you'll be fine," he said. "You're solid with the camera, you're athletic, you're not afraid of heights. All you have to do is learn to move on the ropes."

Exactly how her dad would have put it. Take some feat that most people would never dream of doing and make it sound as easy as one-two-three. Her mom would have the opposite opinion. She would say it was too soon, that it could lead to flashbacks.

What would happen if she had some sort of episode while filming? Would she be putting the crew in danger? Herself?

But rock climbing was different than an airplane crashing. There's no way a human peacefully climbing a beautiful cliff could compare to metal colliding into cement at five hundred miles per hour.

She'd had a reaction to a bungee-jumping scene in one of the films they screened in her digital effects class, though, breaking out in a massive sweat and having to escape to the bathroom to compose herself. If it had been on an IMAX screen, she might have passed out. But it hadn't been and she didn't.

No. Her episodes weren't like the shocking war veteran rampages that made the news. They were little blips triggered by things that reminded her of how she felt just before the crash: the panic, horror, and gridlock of knowing what was about to happen before everyone else figured it out. Her episodes were ten-second mini blackouts, or confusion about what was real. The blackout in the crosswalk—she had been drinking, and surely the alcohol had been a contributing factor. And that had happened less than six months after the crash. Now, it had been almost three years.

It wasn't every day a filmmaker like Danny Rappaport offered to let an intern tag along on something so big *and* budget the time for his staff to teach her. Furthermore, she *wanted* to join the team. Even though she'd always felt cowardly compared to her dad, the tricks that she knew how do in an airplane would give most people nightmares. Deep down, she knew she had a tolerance for this sort of thing, and this was her chance to use it.

That, combined with what Madigan said about upcoming job openings at Walkabout? Yes. No matter how scary it was, she was going to film on the Sorcerer.

Chapter Twelve

With the Code for Verity climb still on hold for rockfall, Danny had insisted that she do an interview with Josh today. During one of her jogs last week, she'd found a much better location for filming. She'd triple-checked her batteries and had everything staged in the van. Even if she only got one usable answer, she'd be doing better than last time, and with Josh's continued normalcy, she trusted he would keep his word about letting her coach him.

While she wasn't as nervous about the interview, she *was* nervous about being alone with Josh. She was hyperaware of this fact as she sat at the picnic table, waiting for him to step out of the forest.

Today Josh wore a backpack, and when he got to the campsite, he upended it on the picnic table. It was shirts. A whole pile of them. T-shirts, polos, button-ups, thermals, dry-fit shirts. Quite a variety for someone who lived in a truck.

"I'm not going back this time," he said. "Choice is all yours."

Her heart beat faster. Was he being hostile or was he just

joking around?

He ran his hand through his already tousled hair and smiled sheepishly. Joking, thank goodness. Her heart lifted. He sat down across from her at the picnic table, just like at the first dinner. She dug through the pile.

"I hope there's *something* acceptable in there," he said.

"We'll see."

She held up an obnoxious striped polo. "This is perfect."

"That one was a joke."

"It's a great brand," she said. "It'll show our viewers that you can still be fashionable, even if you live in a truck."

It was from an Italian designer. A brand she was surprised to find among Josh's things, even if it was a tad garish.

"So, really, which will it be?" he asked.

For selfish reasons, she was tempted to assign him the thin white undershirt but instead handed him a simple cotton plaid with retro snap buttons. It was the same one he'd worn to the Ahwahnee with Vera a few days ago. He pulled it on over the light blue T-shirt he was already wearing and stuffed the others into his pack. She stored his pack in her tent so he wouldn't have to go back to his truck.

When they left camp this time, he followed her, *and* he offered to carry the tripod and one of the bags. She smiled to herself, silently celebrating these small victories.

The new interview location was a long and narrow meadow surrounded on three sides by stately pine trees. It was an absolutely perfect spot for filming. The trees would hide Josh from the road, while the open end of the meadow would give a spectacular view of the valley. There was even a grove of majestic, white-barked aspens in the near distance, to give perspective to the background.

April positioned a camp stool for Josh at the head of the meadow. He fidgeted with the hem of his shorts as she assembled the tripod and locked the camera onto it.

"I hope you're not nervous," she said. "This isn't the first time you've done this, remember?"

He smiled sheepishly. "I suppose you want me to relax and shake out my hands and all that."

"You're fine like you are," she said. "Just turn your body so you're at more of an angle to the camera."

He turned in the wrong direction, and then angled too far in the right direction.

"Here, like this," April said. She gripped his shoulders and twisted him into position.

His shoulders were rock hard beneath the soft fabric. She let go and stepped back to the camera, embarrassed with the realization that she'd just manhandled him like he was a second grader on school portrait day.

Her palms still burned with the sensation of his shoulders as she rattled off the basics of on-camera interviews: Never look at the lens. Repeat the question in your answer. Be relaxed. Talk like you're hanging out with your buddies. Try not to scratch your face. Be open. Share things about yourself beyond what is asked.

"Okay, are you ready?" she asked.

"I think so."

The chill and stubbornness that had been plastered across his face during the last interview was completely gone. Now, he almost looked scared.

She checked the camera settings one more time and started recording. He'd taped the mic on just right this time. "We'll do a few test questions first while I play with the sound."

"Okay," he said.

She ducked behind the camera. "What's your favorite food?"

"Pasta."

"Okay. More."

"Like what?"

"Get creative. This is for practice. Lie if you have to."

"My favorite food is pasta, but it has to be homemade. Tomato sauce is best, but only if it's made with fresh basil and really good olive oil. The pasta should be hand cut and made the same day. Oh, and some people would disagree with me, but fresh Asiago from local goats is a thousand times better than anything imported from Europe."

April watched the spikes on the microphone data and adjusted the bass intake. "That was perfect, and good job repeating the question," she said. "Did you make that up?"

"I thought you said it didn't matter."

"It doesn't. I'm just curious. You're making me hungry."

"All true."

No wonder he skipped so many meals with the crew. He was probably cooking up plein air gourmet at his truck while they ate tuna mac. She settled into her place on the stool, just to the left of the lens. "Okay, from now on it has to be all truth."

"You got it."

She hadn't made a list of interview questions, but she had a better concept of the project now and what kinds of content Danny was going to need.

"Tell me about the first time you came here to Yosemite," she said.

"The first time I came to Yosemite, it was spring break of my freshman year. In high school. Obviously. I've never been to college."

"Louder," April said. "And more confident. You're talking about yourself. You're the expert."

"The first time I came to Yosemite, it was spring break of my freshman year in high school. Being from Vegas, I wasn't used to this kind of cold."

April nodded in encouragement.

"The guy I came with was older," Josh continued. "I bet

he didn't want to hang out with a kid like me, but it worked out pretty well. I needed someone to drive, and he needed someone to lead the hard stuff."

"Good!" April said. "See, you can do this! That was a perfect little story."

He ruffled his fingers through his hair, which she was glad he had waited to do until he was done answering the question.

"Your last answer, it was a good length," she said. "Just don't go too much longer than that. We want to have nice, concise sound bites."

He nodded.

"What did you think when you drove into the valley for the first time?" she asked.

"I knew it would be big, but when I got here, I was blown away."

He looked at the lens. April groaned silently. She pointed to her eyes until he got the hint and looked at her. She made a rolling motion with her hand for him to continue, which he did, but not before another nervous glance at the camera.

"Me. Look at me," she said.

"I can't help it. It's staring at me."

"I'm staring at you, too. Look at me."

"You have nice eyes. The camera, it's like a Cyclops."

"It's not a monster," she said, laughing along with him. "Try that answer again. And don't forget to repeat the question."

"The first time I saw the valley, I couldn't believe it. Especially El Cap. I'd seen pictures, but to be there in person—"

He glanced at the lens.

"No! Eyes on me!" she said.

"...in person it was so enormous. My first thought was that there was no way anyone had ever climbed it."

His eyes slid toward the lens again.

"Don't look at the camera."

He sighed and rocked back on the stool. "I'm sorry, can we just pause this for a minute?"

She stopped the camera.

"I get really nervous," he said. Indeed, his eyes were large and worried. Very endearing.

"You do fine with the camera when you're climbing," she said.

"I pretend it's not there."

"You can do the same thing here."

"Doesn't work that way. The mind space is totally different."

Poor guy. "I know something that will help," she said.

She ducked into the woods and snapped a branch off a small tree, which she balanced over the lens. It was a trick that had worked well at Kids Are Wee, using blankets or stuffed animals.

"How's that?" she asked.

"Better," he said.

She ducked behind the camera to make sure there weren't any leaves in front of the lens. "Okay, back to the question."

"How did I put it before?" he asked. "That was good. Can you rewind and tell me what I said?"

"Too much work. Picture the moment and describe it. And don't forget to include the question."

He closed his eyes briefly before speaking. "When I drove into the valley for the first time, I couldn't believe it was real. I'd seen pictures, and I knew it was big, but to be on the valley floor and looking at three thousand vertical feet of El Cap—the enormity of it…it's unimaginable to think of someone climbing it. I've climbed it dozens of times now, but when I sit in the meadow and look up at it, it seems like it was all in my imagination."

She gave him a thumbs-up. Maybe Danny would give

her a raise if she came back with a few more sound bites like that. "Did you climb El Capitan that first time you came to Yosemite?"

"It took me three trips to Yosemite before I could find a partner who would climb El Cap with me. Even then, I was only seventeen. I had no idea what I was doing. It's a miracle we made it up alive."

"Perfect," April mouthed to him.

He gave another excellent answer to her next question and really got into a groove after that. The problem was, the less she had to focus on his answers, the more she focused on him.

His eye contact with her was also excellent, and her mind kept wandering back to the lake, but an alternate-reality version where Josh was even closer. Close enough to touch. She could practically feel the soft moss beneath her arms and Josh's sun-warmed, slightly damp skin against her back. They were talking and laughing. His arm was draped over her shoulder, and he was absentmindedly twisting a lock of her hair.

Her breathing sped up even though it was just a daydream.

What is your problem? It was one thing to think the talent was cute but quite another to fantasize. For one, it was delusional for a crew member to think she had a shot with the star, but more importantly, it was unprofessional. Josh Knox was just a rock climber. An attractive and intriguing one, sure, but if she couldn't handle herself around *him*, how would she be in the future on bigger films where she'd be interviewing celebrities, certifiable hunks?

Back in reality, Josh was reliving a magical climb up in Tuolumne high country. Great emotion, vivid detail, fantastic tone of voice. It was the golden footage she hadn't dared to hope for, but at the moment, she was thinking about the gala. She would have the whole evening to do what she was doing now: examining his beautiful, intense, brown-green eyes and cataloging his other nuances, like the slightly goofy turn of his mouth when he was embarrassed, and how he continued to fidget with the hem of his shorts when he was considering an answer.

"Let's talk about the risks," she said. "How does your family cope with what you do out here?"

"What do you mean?"

"It has to be hard for them, knowing what kind of risks you take every day." She thought of her dad. "They must worry."

He frowned. "It's not actually that risky."

He was still looking in her general direction but not making eye contact. The smiles that she hadn't realized were passing between them vanished completely.

"But it *is* risky," she said. "It's dangerous."

"How so?"

He'd done such a good job today. He'd found a way to relax, and he had shared more about himself in this one interview than in five years of accumulated interviews. Was he irritated about how distracted she had been?

"First of all, not many people do this sport," she said.

"It's not a sport."

"Okay, yes, we've been over that. Most people don't rock climb. For a reason. They're scared—"

"I'm not."

"Well, why?"

"I know what I'm doing."

"You BASE jump. That's so risky it's *illegal* here."

"I don't do it for fun. But I need to practice in case something happens on the Sorcerer and I have to use the parachute."

"You wouldn't call that risky? Not scary in the slightest?"

"I'm not going to fall."

Fear, risk, and danger were key elements of rock climbing and, therefore, the film. She had to keep pressing. "Listen, Josh. I know you say you're not scared, but anyone else would be. You say it's not dangerous, but accidents happen. People die. I mean, look at Vic. He was paralyzed for the rest of his life."

She waited to continue until his darkened eyes made contact with hers. "How do you process those kinds of risks? Especially when you don't have a rope. And what makes it worth it for you to face that?"

Josh picked at a thread on his shorts. It was a long time before he looked at her again, and when he did, his eyes were so hard she wished she had called it a day back when things were going smoothly.

"It's different for me than it is for everyone else," he said.

Right. The daredevil factor. Missing the fear gene. People who were truly, inexplicably not scared. Her father had been one of them. He'd thrived on risk and danger. He'd craved it. Needed it. Always pushing the limit. Testing the edge.

But Josh wasn't at all like her dad, in personality, anyway. Where her dad had been gregarious, Josh was reserved and private until you got to know him. Her dad had lived for fanfare; Josh shirked it.

She looked at Josh, who was digging a hole in the grass with his sandal.

"*How* is it different for you?" she asked.

A breeze filtered through his hair. Slowly, he looked up from the ground. His face was softer now but deflated.

"April," he said, "I don't mean to be difficult, but this is different. It's personal. Really personal."

Jackpot. Whatever it was, this was the piece Walkabout needed to tell Josh's whole story. A piece that would make his character complete and genuine in the movie. To tell the story of rock climbing in Yosemite and this climber who represented it all.

He looked so vulnerable. If she pushed just a little more, she knew she could get exactly what she wanted. But *because* of his vulnerability, her heart ached for him in the same way it had that first day in the cafeteria.

Sitting there on the camp stool in the meadow, he wasn't any of the Joshes she'd previously known: Josh the sponsored athlete, Josh the sullen jerk, or the friendly Josh from Celery Slabs. This was a different man. Perhaps it was the true Josh, the one at the core of it all.

She wanted to respect his request, but if she let this moment go, she might never get it back. She would be jeopardizing the film, and for what?

She thought about the lake. That had been different. Special. Their titles and roles had vanished, along with the reason for being there in the first place. They were just two people under wide-open skies, surrounded by unimaginable beauty.

Just like right now.

The hardness in his eyes was completely gone, and they were pools of liquid hazel. He could have ended the interview and gone back to his truck a long time ago. But he hadn't. He was still there, putting his trust in her, and waiting for her response.

"It's okay," she said, stopping the camera. "I understand. I think we're good for now."

Chapter Thirteen

"Pay attention, April," Madigan said. "This is important."

She was on her second day of ascending and rappelling lessons. The problem was, she couldn't stop thinking about Josh. She could still feel the earnestness in his eyes melting her willpower during the interview. What was it he hadn't wanted to tell her? And would he be edgy around her because of it when she saw him next?

It wouldn't be long before she found out. After they were done, she was going to be running sound as Madigan filmed Josh doing something called slacklining out at the search-and-rescue camp.

Trying to focus on Madigan's demonstration was as hard as concentrating in school right before summer break. Except that she wasn't in a classroom: she was standing on two measly loops of nylon with twenty feet of air between her and the ground.

"We're reshooting on Flying Sheep the day after the gala," Madigan said. "You need to get this dialed in before then. After that, we'll be fixing lines on the Sorcerer."

"Okay," she said. "What should I do next?"

"I'm going to stay right here. Go ahead and rappel down to the ledge," he said.

This would be the first she'd rappelled without him doing it alongside her. She didn't feel ready. "Can we go through the steps one more time?"

"You've done this twenty times," he said. "It won't sink in until you do it yourself. I'll stop you if you do anything wrong."

"You'll watch me *really* closely?" she asked.

His eyes met hers. "I will."

He had been so patient with her, not only today but ever since she got here. She trusted him completely, but trusting herself was a different story. She checked each piece of her gear as slowly as she could, giving Madigan plenty of time to catch her mistakes. She paused when she was down to the final step—pulling the lever on the Grigri to start the rappel.

"Does everything look okay?" she asked.

"Don't ask me," he said.

"Then I'm going to pull this little lever here…" She looked at him, hoping for a nod or something.

"That's up to you," he said.

She checked her entire setup one more time, down to the gate locks on every carabiner. She set her fingers loosely on the Grigri and took a breath. "Okay, then, here I go."

Putting pressure on the gate, she slid down several inches. After letting the gate snap closed to make sure it was working, she slid down a few inches more. She gradually put more and more force on the lever until she was walking down the wall at a steady speed.

At the ledge, she released the lever and came to a halt. Five seconds later, Madigan had zipped down his rope and was next to her again, looking proud.

"Nice job, April. How'd it feel?"

"Good," she said. She was proud, too.

She switched her gear to climb back up the rope with

the ascending devices and webbing ladders, and Madigan told her to go ahead without him. Going up wasn't nearly as intimidating, mainly because she wasn't looking at the ground. *Weight onto left foot. Slide right hand. Stand up. Weight onto right foot. Slide left hand. Repeat.*

"See how fast you can go," he yelled up to her. "Have some fun with it."

She zipped up the rope, feeling like she was on the NordicTrack climber her dad had when she was a kid.

She leaned back on the rope and caught her breath while Madigan climbed up to where she was. On the Sorcerer, all she would have to do was rappel down to her filming spot, sit there with the camera, and then climb back to the top when she was done. One complete cycle, which she had essentially just done on her own. She definitely needed practice—to do the whole cycle a hundred more times—but for the first time in two days, the skill felt like it was within reach. She was really going to do this. She was really going film while hanging off the side of a three-thousand-foot cliff.

• • •

The slackline was essentially a tightrope of two-inch nylon webbing stretched between two pine trees, about four feet off the ground. A guy in pastel capris was walking on it, throwing his arms about spastically as he struggled to stay balanced.

The line was in the middle of the search-and-rescue camp, where a dozen other people were hanging out, lounging on logs, camp chairs, and weather-beaten furniture. April circled the group with filming release forms as Madigan unpacked the camera. Josh strolled into camp from the main road, wearing flip-flops, his chalk bag, and carrying his climbing shoes, which meant he had either been free soloing or bouldering without a crash pad.

She finished with the forms and then helped Madigan with the camera. He decided not to use a microphone after all, so she wasn't needed anymore. She found a dilapidated recliner at the far end of the slackline where she'd be out of the way.

Josh stood next to the center of the slackline. Madigan gave him a thumbs-up, and Josh pushed the webbing down and situated his foot along it. He focused on a spot ahead, and then hopped up and straightened his leg, with his arms going out in a balancing T. Under his weight, the lowest point of line was only two feet off the ground. When the line stopped wobbling beneath him, he placed his other foot carefully on the line and stepped forward, making it look as easy as walking on a balance beam.

He pivoted at the end of the line, starting in the opposite direction, toward her. His body was relaxed, yet his muscles were firing like lightning, auto-correcting themselves even before his mind knew what was happening.

At her end, he raised up on his toes to pivot, and as he did, his eyes dropped straight down to her. He lost his balance immediately and had to throw a leg out to the side. As his arms flailed, his shirt lifted up, revealing a thin trail of light brown hair running up his tight, tan stomach. So incredibly sexy. She forced herself to look away. Thank god she was not in the shot.

When she looked back, she limited herself to watching Josh's feet. They were much wider than the webbing, and the outsides wrapped over the side like roller-coaster wheels. With each step he'd match the heel of his leading foot to the toe of his trailing foot, and then smear the ball of his foot down on the line.

Josh reached the middle again, where he stayed in place and bounced on the line like it was a trampoline. Before she knew what was happening, he was back at her end of the line and stepping off.

His cheeks were pink from the afternoon sun, and his hair was windblown and spiked.

"How'd I do?" he asked, gazing down at her.

A flush followed his gaze down her arms and out to her fingertips, making her whole body tingle.

"Great," she said. "I think."

He rested his elbow on the back of April's recliner, making it jerk backward. She gasped and grabbed the armrests. They both laughed.

He was close enough that she could smell his laundry soap, a scent that had lingered in her tent after storing his backpack of shirts there during the last interview.

"Check out this guy," he said, nodding toward a short, shirtless guy who was climbing onto the slackline. "He knows how to flip. Maybe with that camera going, he'll do it."

The camera wasn't going, though. Madigan had put it down and was walking toward them.

"I'm going to give it a try," Madigan said.

"I'll film you," April offered.

"No way." He laughed. "I haven't been on a slackline in two years." He took off his shoes and waited his turn. "Wish me luck," he said when shirtless guy jumped off.

It took him several tries to get on the line, and he couldn't go more than a few steps at a time without the line pitching him off. April watched him faithfully, but her awareness was fully occupied by the buzz that radiated from Josh, less than a foot from her. They weren't talking, and she was afraid if she didn't think of something to say, it would be awkward and he would leave.

"Did you think about those suggestions I made on your speech?" she asked.

"I finished last night," he said. "You can look at it whenever you want."

"It will have to be tomorrow. We're leaving first thing Friday morning."

He didn't respond, and an uncomfortable silence drifted in.

"Hey, I'm sorry you're going to be stuck with me Saturday," Josh said.

She looked over at him. His cheeks weren't pink anymore, and he didn't look as huggable.

"Josh, it's totally fine," she said. "Don't worry about it. We all have to go anyway."

"I hope Madigan's not upset about it."

"I don't think he cares."

"No? You'll be hanging out with me all night."

"Why would he care?"

"I would if I were him."

"We're talking about Madigan?" she said. "Madigan who's on the slackline right now?"

"Yeah."

"He's my boss."

"I know, but you guys are a thing."

April laughed. "A thing? Madigan and me? Like *that*? No."

"Really?"

"Really!"

"You two are always together."

"Uh, yeah. He's my boss."

"And you're always wearing his clothes."

"I was borrowing his jacket for a while because mine wasn't warm enough. I have a better one now."

They both looked at Madigan wobbling his way down the slackline. Yes, Madigan was cute, and, yes, he was a friend in addition to being her boss, but there wasn't anything more than that.

"You're serious you guys aren't dating?" Josh asked.

"Yes!"

Out on the slackline, Madigan lost his balance and jumped off. This time he stayed on the ground. "April, you should give it a try," he called.

"Yeah. Come on, I'll help you out," Josh said.

She would really rather not, but before she could refuse, Josh was at the center of the line, waiting for her. Was she desperate enough to touch him that she'd take a turn looking like a drunk circus performer on that damn line?

She rolled the bottoms of her jeans up and kicked off her sandals. Apparently she was.

Josh pushed the line down and held it there while she put her foot on it. She clasped the hand he was holding out for her, and the powerful buzz from before zipped through her body like a delicious electrocution, making the backs of her knees weak.

"Just stand up on that leg," he said. "I've got you."

She started to shift her weight, then hesitated. Her knees were literally, physically, going to give out.

"Give me a second," she said.

Her eyes met his lovely brown-green ones, and he smiled ever so slightly. She blushed and the faintness went away.

She pulled hard on Josh's hand and stood up on the line. It wasn't just wobbly, it was a 7.0 earthquake!

Josh eased the slackline back to its full height and took her other hand. His palms were callused and his grip powerful.

"Hang out here for a minute," he said. "Wait for all the motion to settle."

When the line stilled, she let go of his far hand, gripping the remaining one like her life depended on it as the line vibrated beneath her feet. It felt very inappropriate to be touching him with all these people around, but at the moment, she didn't care. There was a perfectly good excuse for them holding hands, and she was going to take full advantage of it.

She took one step on the line and then another. With each shift of her weight, the line shot from side to side, trying to buck her off. But with Josh steadying her, she made slow, deliberate progress, eventually reaching the tree trunk at the end.

Carefully, she turned around. She'd planned to get off the tightrope as soon as possible, but when she got back to the low spot in the middle, where it would have been the easiest to step off, she let Josh guide her on. It felt so good, so natural, for them to be touching and working together like this. From now on, it would feel *wrong* not to be touching when she was near him.

Josh looked up at her. "You're doing awesome."

He was so handsome, and not only on the outside. There was something about him that radiated comfort, excitement, and caring, all at the same time.

He was still looking at her, his face reflecting some of the same intense focus he had while he balanced on the slackline and when he climbed. Just a few minutes ago, he had triple-checked her relationship status. And now he was helping her in a very intimate way, even though it would have made a lot more sense for her coworker—the same guy he had been convinced she was dating—to do it.

Had his appearance at Celery Slabs truly not been a coincidence? What about how he was now a staple at Walkabout dinners? And his sudden cooperation during interviews?

She stumbled on the slackline, and it threw her against him. He grabbed her waist to steady her. They locked eyes. His hand stayed warm and firm on the narrowest part of her waist.

What if…?

Her skin tingled.

What if her attraction to him was mutual?

Chapter Fourteen

April wrung her washcloth into the bathroom sink. The water that came out of it was alarmingly brown. She rinsed it again and wiped her other leg. A month ago, she never would have imagined that anyone besides a homeless person would take a sponge bath in the sink of a public bathroom. Now she was doing it, and she wasn't even embarrassed.

She had just finished another ascending lesson with Madigan. She was really getting the hang of it, and her confidence was growing. What she was *not* getting used to was all the sweat and grime that went along with a day on the cliffs.

A shower would have been great, but there wasn't time before she was supposed to meet Josh at his truck to go over his speech.

The prospect of being alone with Josh on his turf felt dangerous. Not exciting-dangerous, but dishonest-dangerous. That's because reading Josh's speech would only take a few minutes, and to buy more time she had swapped dinner duty with Madigan and told Danny she was going to get some

B-roll of Josh hanging out in his camp.

She finger brushed her hair that was limp from sweating all day and pulled it back into a ponytail. Outside, the light afternoon breeze refreshed her damp skin, but it did nothing to ease the tightness in her chest. What was she about to do? Josh was the talent, and she had no business crossing that line. And for what? Her own curiosity? Even if she confirmed that he was interested, he was still a man who risked his life for a living, and because of that, she would never allow anything with him to be more than a quick fling. And to jeopardize her entire career in film by getting fired from this internship for a quick fling? No way. It made her sick just to imagine Madigan catching her with Josh in a situation that even bordered on inappropriate. She was just an intern, but she was filling a significant role on this film, and she'd never do anything that would let Danny and the guys down.

She made a quick stop at the Walkabout site to put her bathroom kit in a bear box and pick up the camera she'd temporarily stowed in her tent. The problem with the excuse she'd given about filming Josh's truck was that she'd actually have to get some footage to show when she got back.

The guys were sharing a newspaper over at the fire ring. Her camp chair stood empty next to Madigan's. Their two chairs were practically touching, whereas the others were spaced out around the ring. Someone—probably Madigan— had put a beer in the cup holder for her.

No wonder Josh had assumed she and Madigan were dating.

As if he sensed her thinking about him, Madigan laid his newspaper over the back of his chair and joined her at the tent. "What are you up to?" he asked.

He held the camera for her as she zipped the tent back up. "The B-roll, remember?"

Concern flashed across his face. "Do you want me to go

with you?"

"No, it's okay. I also have to go over Josh's speech one last time. He's made some changes."

Theo looked at them over the top of his newspaper section.

"Well, grab a radio and call me if you change your mind," Madigan said.

As she walked through the woods, she thought about how much had changed since her first visit to Josh's camp, not only her comfort level with living on location in a campground, but with him.

When she reached the front of his truck, she crouched and unpacked her camera. She was glad the truck had one of those extra-tall canopies, because it helped her stay hidden as she tiptoed along the side of it. She peered around the corner. The hammock was weighted and swaying. Bingo! She could catch Josh before he realized she was there, get a quick pan, and be done with filming.

When the camera was ready, she pressed her shoulder into the side of his truck and pivoted around so that only the camera lens poked out. Josh was in the hammock all right, and he was sleeping. Double bingo! She could get in closer and take her time. They might actually be able to use this footage in the film.

She crept wide around his truck toward the tree at the foot of the hammock and then hid behind a tree to collect herself. Without a tripod, she would need to be absolutely steady for this shot. She took a huge breath, stepped out from behind the tree, and then started her pan.

The scene was magnificent. Josh was the epitome of relaxed and natural, with his head resting gently on the side of the hammock and a textbook collapsed across his chest. A beam of yellow light drifted through the branches, making the particles in the air sparkle above his face.

She panned past him to where a clothesline stretched between two trees, his bright T-shirts and several pairs of khaki shorts swaying in the breeze in time with the sway of the hammock. Next, she panned to his camp chair at the fire pit, where he had been using a log round as an ottoman and another for an ax rest. She finished the pan into the open back of Josh's truck-house, where there was another book facedown on the tailgate, along with his harness, which was all bunched up, with his shoes sitting on the peak.

April lowered the camera and turned it off. Mission accomplished.

She peeked at Josh. He was still asleep, his eyes flickering beneath his eyelids. The sunshine was warm on her shoulders, and watching him unguarded like this made her unguarded, too. If only she could curl into the hammock and drift to sleep alongside him.

"Josh," she whispered.

He didn't stir, so she tried again, louder. This time he blinked and looked around, eventually seeing her at the foot of the hammock.

"Hey, April," he said.

"Sorry for waking you," she said.

"It's okay. What's up?"

"Do you still want me to look over your speech?"

He yawned and stretched. "Yes. Definitely."

He set the book down and sat up. He swung his feet to the side of the hammock, and then noticed the camera. He froze.

"How long have you been taping?"

"I'm done. The camera's off."

"You taped me sleeping?"

"It's just a quick shot for B-roll."

"April! My god! How about some warning?"

"It was less than ten seconds. And was just a pan of your camp."

"You got my truck? It's a total wreck in there!"

"You can't tell from here. It looks pretty clean to me."

"But there are clothes over there," he said, pointing to the clothesline.

"It's just shirts and shorts."

"Still, you should have asked."

"You were sleeping. Think of it as the easiest scene you've ever had to do."

He scowled, but the smile in his eyes canceled it out. "Good point."

"You can watch it if you want. You'll see, it's just a short little clip."

"Okay, show me," he said, standing up.

She turned the camera on, and he stepped behind her shoulder to see the screen. She'd done pretty well keeping it steady, which was a relief. To Josh, the shot would look like a simple recording of his campsite, but in film language, all the details delivered a powerful and intimate image. Danny would be thrilled when he saw this.

"It's fine, I guess," he said when it was over. "But no more filming back here until my truck is clean."

The breath from his words flowed across the side of her neck, making her skin prickle with excitement. He smelled fresh and clean, but not in a typical soap-and-shampoo way. She knew he'd spent most of the day climbing, so perhaps he had bathed in another pristine Yosemite lake afterward.

A gust of wind rippled through the pages of Josh's book, sending his bookmark flying across her feet. She picked it up, discovering that is wasn't a bookmark but a photograph of a very large family—presumably his. They were posing at one of the hotels on the Las Vegas Strip, the one with the jungle safari theme.

She handed the picture to him, and he tucked it back into the book without comment. It was kind of cute that even though his family lived in Las Vegas, they still hung out at the Strip like tourists.

He went to get his laptop from the truck cab, and she waited at the tailgate.

She looked inside, trying to figure out what he had been so embarrassed about. The only thing messy about his truck was that his bed wasn't made. Otherwise, it was impeccably organized. A plywood platform raised his thin mattress two feet above the truck bed, and below it were clear plastic bins of gear, each neatly labeled in his symmetrical handwriting.

There was a rustling in the bushes behind her that was much too loud to be a squirrel or raccoon. She gripped the tailgate.

"What's wrong?" Josh asked.

"Shh!" she hissed. "Bear."

"Where?"

She turned around cautiously and, of course, there was nothing there.

"It was probably just the wind. It's been shifting directions today," Josh said. "Don't tell me you're scared of bears."

"Have you seen those signs in our campground? Who wouldn't be?"

He laughed. "Bears are like cats. Just clap your hands and they'll run away."

Easy for him to say.

"Your truck isn't messy at all, you know," she said, changing the subject.

"If you're going to live like this, you've got to be very organized," he said. "Otherwise it's like being in a dog kennel."

"Is that so?"

"Seven years ago, you wouldn't have gotten within twenty feet of this truck. Nasty stuff gets stuck everywhere, and it really starts to stink."

He'd been living on the road like this for seven years?

He was only two years older than her. That would mean he'd been doing this since he graduated high school.

Josh sat on the tailgate and logged in to his laptop. He handed it to her.

"The glare is really bad," he said. "You might want to sit up here so you can read it."

Her arms, sore from back-to-back days of ascending lessons, screamed as she pushed up onto the tailgate. She sat cross-legged with the laptop balanced on her thighs. It was a tailgate, but it was also his bedroom, which was subtly thrilling.

His eyes were on her as she started to read, and she was thankful she'd taken the time to clean up in the bathroom. The speech was quite good, actually. Much better than the last version she'd read, which he must have thrown together just to prove to Danny and Vera that he wasn't procrastinating.

"It's great," she told him. "Right on target."

"Good."

Dread crept through her heart. He didn't need any help, which meant she didn't have a reason to stay there with him for much longer.

"You have everything ready for tomorrow?" she asked.

"I think so."

"The tailor will be waiting for you at the hotel as soon as we get there."

"Okay."

He was giving her clipped answers. Weren't they past this?

"We'll probably leave around ten," she said. "Does that work for you?"

"Sure."

Maybe they weren't past this. Her body was as heavy as lead as she handed the laptop back and slid off the tailgate.

"Well, I guess if you're all set, I better head back."

She went to the hammock to get the camera. The disappointment was like a vise ratcheting tighter and tighter around her lungs.

She shouldn't have filmed him. She'd known he wouldn't be happy about it. Or maybe his previous friendliness had all been exaggerated in her head. Some sort of psychosis of wishful thinking. She'd have to ask her mom about that.

Josh was still over on the tailgate, pressing his fingers along the top of his laptop like it was a ledge on a climbing route. The wind whipped her ponytail and blew her bangs into her eyes.

It was all for the best, she reminded herself. Seriously, what did she think would happen here today? That he'd push her against the side of his truck and kiss her like in *Gone With the Wind*?

"Okay, well, I'll see you tomorrow," she called.

His fingers froze on the edge of the laptop. His eyes were large and troubled.

"I have the pictures that go with the speech," he said. "Do you want to see them?"

She'd already seen the pictures, last week, when she mailed a CD of them to Vera. He had to know April would have checked them over before sending them.

Hope rose up and filled her chest.

Yes. He had to know she'd already seen them, but he had still asked. This was a good sign. Maybe he wasn't mad. Maybe he wanted her to stay as much as she did.

If she was smart, she would leave now. She would go back to the Walkabout campsite immediately.

"You're right. I guess I should take a look."

She climbed back on the tailgate, this time letting her legs swing free. He set the laptop between them, and she had to scoot closer to support her side of it.

Although she'd seen the pictures before, tonight she saw them in a new light. These weren't at all like the action photos that dominated climbing magazines. These were pictures of sunbursts behind jagged rock-and-ice Sierra peaks, pristine alpine rivers, and vistas from the eastern reaches of the park down into wide deserts, breathtaking views of the park as it could only be seen from the sides of its trademark formations, thousands of feet in the air. Views she had gotten a taste of only because she'd been to Flying Sheep Lake. His photos were of solace, beauty, and peace. Freedom. Reverence. Challenge. Commitment. Exploration.

As Josh arrow-keyed through the pictures, his arm was floating above her bare thigh. He stopped clicking, and she prayed it wasn't because he could hear how fast her heart was beating.

"What happened to your hands?" he asked.

She looked down at them, wondering if she had been fidgeting.

"Looks like you crawled through razor wire."

Indeed, her palms were a patchwork of torn blisters and fiery splotches. Her fingertips were hatched with scratches.

"Madigan is teaching me how to ascend," she said.

He raised an eyebrow.

"I'm filming on the Sorcerer."

He looked surprised. "You are?"

She thought he knew. "Are you okay with it?"

"Might be kind of a distraction."

Danny should have asked Josh before changing up the plan on the climb!

He elbowed her. "I'm joking, April."

She laughed like she had known it all along.

As they looked at a few more of his pictures, she was grateful for the warmth of the laptop on her leg. She was still dressed for the daytime heat, but it was getting chilly with the approach of sunset, and the winds were stronger than usual. Josh grabbed his gray hooded sweatshirt from the back of the truck and held it as she slipped her arms into the sleeves.

The softness of the sweatshirt and the intensity of his familiar scent weakened her knees. It was almost as if she had *him* wrapped around her.

He cocked his head. "It's a little big."

She pushed the sleeves up and connected the zipper at the bottom. It got stuck midway up.

"Sorry, it's really old," he said. "But there's a trick."

He carefully reached for the zipper pull, tugged down twice, wiggled it, then yanked it the rest of the way up. Her goose bumps from the cold refreshed themselves with goose bumps from his touch.

It occurred to her that he had probably hooked up with all his camerawomen. The romantic gesture with the sweatshirt could be a practiced move, and she was the village idiot who was falling for it.

She looked at him, and his eyes glowed with warmth in return. She didn't really believe that about him. Besides, she'd never seen a woman's name in any of the cinematography credits in the dozens of climbing films she'd watched since she got here, so hooking up with camerawomen wasn't a likely scenario.

He took a half step toward her and lifted the soft hood over her head. His fingers lingered on the edges of the hood, adjusting it around her face.

"Better?" he asked.

She nodded. He lowered his arms to his sides, leaving a tangible emptiness between them. She longed to close the gap, to be near him once again. To have his hands back on the hood framing her face.

"Just out of curiosity, how come Theo isn't teaching you to ascend?" Josh asked. "He has a lot more experience than Madigan."

"He will, later, but he's been so busy with rigging."

Josh cleared his throat. "Okay, well, maybe you should

try wearing gloves next time. Mind if I take a look at your hands?"

She opened her palms toward him. He placed one of his hands beneath hers and lifted it closer to see. Her cheeks burned, and she struggled to mute her shallow breaths, which roared loudly in her ears.

"I have some lotion you can put on them," he said.

He grabbed an unlabeled plastic tub from the shelf above his bed.

"A friend of mine makes this." He twisted the lid off the tub. "It has beeswax and lanolin in it. It'll heal your hot spots really fast."

She expected him to give her the tub, but he reached for her hand instead. She was afraid to look at him as he glided the light-as-air lotion across her torn skin. His hands were hot on the backs of hers while the lotion sent cooling tingles into her palms.

The sweatshirt and now this? What did it mean and where was this going?

Josh set the lotion down. He cupped her hand in both of his, using his thumbs to gently rub the lotion in. Damp heat rose from his skin and surrounded her.

The dizziness was heady. Intoxicating. They were on the verge of something. Something big. *This* was what she came here for. And now it was about to happen.

He lowered her hand, and she gave him the other one. It was just hands. Her one between his two, but it was more intimate than anything she'd experienced.

How could she ever force herself to see him platonically again? How would she be able to finish the interviews? How would she manage to keep her sanity when she filmed him on the Sorcerer?

Really, this was serious. She needed to consider these things.

He lowered her hand but didn't let go. She wanted to freeze this moment forever, the feeling of his hand soft against hers.

"Thanks," she whispered. "I think that's really going to help."

His breath mingled with hers in the space between them. A magnet-like force was pulling her toward him. She wanted to touch him so badly. To kiss him. Another millimeter and she wouldn't be able to stop.

But this was not okay. They could not do this. She would not jeopardize her career. Space. She had to put some space between them before something happened that they could not take back.

Reluctantly, she let go of his hand and slid off the tailgate. "I've got dinner duty. I have to go." She unzipped his sweatshirt and handed it back. The night was cold and harsh.

She grabbed her camera bag, and he walked her around to the front of his truck.

"See you over there in a bit," she said.

"I'm not coming tonight," he said quietly. "They're having a big cookout here."

"Well, then, I'll see you tomorrow at the van."

He nodded. There was a trace of confusion in his eyes.

She forced herself to get moving. The pull between them was still there. Like a rubber band, the desire to return to him intensified with every step in the wrong direction.

It would have been much better if she had never come.

"Hey, April?"

She turned.

"I'm really looking forward to the gala."

He was leaning against his truck, so strong and solid yet deeply vulnerable.

Something snapped. All she wanted was to be near him, to understand him. To *know* him. There was something more going on between them. And two nights from now, at the gala—and just for the gala—if it continued to happen, she wasn't going to stop it.

Exactly like the first time she'd come out to his truck, his eyes burned not into her but *through* her. She held his eyes. "I am, too."

Chapter Fifteen

The aesthetician spun April around to look in the mirror. She hardly recognized herself. Vera's team had somehow managed to get some curl in her hair, which was piled on top of her head. Her skin was radiant from the facial Vera had arranged for her earlier in the day, and the blush made her look like she was keeping a wonderful secret. The carefully applied raspberry lipstick with the melon gloss layer on top had turned her mouth into a perfect cupid's bow.

But it was her eyes that brought the whole look to the next level. Five shades of shadow, three eyeliners, and a thick set of falsies added five years of sexy and made her eyes as bright as a lap pool in the sunshine. Vera wasn't exaggerating about having the best hair and makeup people in California. They had transformed April from a mosquito-bitten, low-paid film intern into a full-blown fairy-tale princess.

"Thank you," April whispered. "This is amazing."

The aesthetician winked at her in the mirror and squeezed her shoulders. "Vera will be so excited when she sees you."

It wasn't Vera's reaction April was imagining. It was Josh's.

She would be knocking on his door in just a few minutes. What would he think? He'd never seen her wearing anything but jeans, T-shirts, and workout clothes. He'd never seen her with makeup, either, and she was wearing a lot of it. If she'd attempted even a fraction of this amount of makeup on her own, she would have come off looking like a geisha.

Vera's stylist followed April down to her room and helped her into her gown so she didn't mess up her hair and makeup. Her mom's vintage dress was heavy and smooth against her bare skin. An extra three inches of fabric pooled around her feet. The stylist helped her into the vintage Marketto sandals, and the delicate gray lace points of the hem skimmed the floor exactly as designed.

April waited for the stylist to leave, and then dashed to the full-length mirror for an in-depth examination.

The whole effect was incredible. The empire cut of the dress enhanced her chest perfectly, while the hidden heels boosted her out of the petite realm. The muscles in her arms and back were defined from hauling equipment around Yosemite and accentuated by the sparkle dust bronzer Vera's team had brushed across her skin.

She took a step back from the mirror and then another. With each, she looked more and more like a stranger, like a ghost of her mother twenty-five years ago.

Thinking of Josh again, she smiled. With the smile, her reflection ceased to be a stranger but a fancier, dressed-up version of herself. She twisted around to see the back of her dress, then spun in a circle until the heavy fabric lifted around her. When she halted, it swung tight around her legs before swishing back around and hanging straight.

"Thank you, Vera," she mouthed toward the penthouse.

April glanced over at the clock. There were exactly fourteen minutes to stall before walking across the hall to his room. She took a selfie and texted it to Sophie and her mom, then looked at the view of the city out the window while she waited for a reply.

She hadn't seen Josh since his tux fitting yesterday afternoon. The CEO of Esplanade was in town for the gala, and he'd occupied all of Josh's time that Vera hadn't already reserved. It was the longest she'd gone without seeing him since they'd jumped into the lake, and it felt like an eternity.

Closing her eyes, she felt his hands around hers, rubbing lotion into her palms. She relived his powerful hand on her waist, keeping her steady on the slackline. She saw him trusting her during their second interview, laughing with her at the lake, and his attentiveness while he adjusted the hood around her face.

What would it be like to be around him at a formal function like this? In every way, it was the opposite of all their previous time together in Yosemite. It could be really awkward.

Argh. She was starting to psych herself out.

No one had responded to her text yet. *Come on, guys, talk to me!*

Her phone beeped. *Amazing, April. Gorgeous*, her mom wrote. *That dress is perfect on you. Have a wonderful night, okay?*

I'm nervous, she wrote back. *I really like him.*

Finally she admits it. :)

Mom! He's the talent…it's like dating a patient.

Except you guys are already friends, right? Just take it easy, enjoy his company. Don't do anything unsafe. If you know what I mean.

Mom! I'm 22!

Like that's so old. Have fun, honey!

There were still eight minutes left before April was supposed to meet Josh, but she was too antsy to wait any longer. She went across the hallway and knocked softly on his door. He answered quickly and then stood there for a second without saying anything.

"April! Oh my god, I—"

He took a step back. She held her breath.

"You don't look real," he said. "You look like a doll or something. Sorry. That didn't sound right." He stepped aside so she could come in. "What I meant to say is that you look really beautiful. Like you were born to wear dresses like that."

The warmth of a blush crossed her face. It was exactly how she was hoping he'd react. "Thanks, Josh."

The room was heavy with the freshness of a recent shower, as evidenced by Josh's darkened, wet hair, which he was scrubbing with a towel. He was wearing a white T-shirt with his tuxedo pants and his feet were bare.

He pulled his dress shirt off a hanger and put it on. He was getting dressed, not *undressed*, but she averted her eyes anyway. There were two textbooks on his night table, *Macroeconomics* and *Introduction to Statistics*, the same ones he'd spent the whole van ride to Sacramento reading.

"You do some pretty heavy reading," she said.

"It's for classes."

"You're a student? You never told me that."

"You never asked."

She peeked over her shoulder and watched him button his shirt.

"I'd have to know a little something about you to ask," she said. "And you're pretty mysterious."

"Am I?" He smiled naughtily. "I take a class a term, when I have a good internet connection," he said. "And time."

"I'm surprised you're doing a class now. You kind of have a lot going on," she said. "Starring in a major documentary and all."

"And being grilled by a ruthless reporter in the meantime."

"Filmmaker."

"Okay, a ruthless *filmmaker*."

"Sounds awful."

"You have no idea." He was looking down as he shoved his shirttails into his pants, but she could tell he was grinning.

There was something about this guy. She had such an affection for him. So much so that her nerves were tight. Just because she thought she'd detected interest two nights ago at his truck didn't mean he actually felt the same as her.

She handed him the belt that was lying on his bed. He threaded it through his belt loops.

"What are you studying?" she asked.

"Guess."

"No."

He looked amused. "Why not?"

"It's a trap."

"How so?"

"You'll accuse me of domicile discrimination," she said.

"Because of my truck?"

"Yes."

"Okay, then. I'm majoring in business," he said.

"You're right. That's surprising."

"So what would you have guessed?"

"Philosophy. Outdoor recreation, maybe."

"Sheesh. You do have a bad case of domicile discrimination. And coming from a film major, on top of it!"

She laughed, which loosened her nerves a little.

He grabbed the cuff links off his desk. She was hoping

he'd struggle with them so she could lend a hand, but he poked them through his sleeves like he'd done it a million times.

He pulled his jacket off the hanger, and April held it for him while he put it on.

"Where's your bow tie?" she asked.

He pointed to a slim box in the closet.

"How are your bow-tying skills?" she asked.

"Do I look like I know how to tie a bow tie?"

"You definitely do not look like you know how to tie a bow tie."

"Is this about my truck again?"

"Pretty much. Need help?"

"That would be a good idea. Vera will thank you."

April pulled a beautiful gray silk tie out of the box.

"Vera told me how well you did at the VIP brunch this morning. She said she has checks for six hundred and fifty thousand already. Thanks to your charming alter ego."

Josh leaned forward, and she popped his collar up and laid the silk across the back of his neck. Their faces were all but touching. "Alter ego?"

She stood on her toes to pull his collar down over the tie. He leaned farther down and their cheeks brushed. Her pulse picked up. "You're not always charming, you know."

"No?" His smile pushed against her cheek. "I'll be charming tonight, I promise."

The air from his words drifted across her neck, making goose bumps rise along her arms.

With her heels planted on the ground again, she began the bowknot she had tied for her father ever since he taught her once on a whim. When she was finished, she stepped back to get a good look. Like her, Josh had been transformed.

He always carried himself tall and straight, but wearing the perfectly tailored tuxedo, he looked truly refined. And he appeared to be comfortable in it, which was surprising. When

Madigan and Theo had tried on their budget rental tuxes earlier, the effect hadn't been the same. Theo, in particular, who was between sizes, looked a little like a hobo clown with his greasy hair and the too-big jacket.

"You look fantastic," she told Josh.

He smiled sheepishly. "Handsome?" he asked.

"Yes. Very," she said, wishing she could take a photo of him and send it to her mom. Perhaps Mom was wise to have given her the safe-sex reminder.

Josh's hair was flat from the towel drying. "Do you have any hair gel?" she asked.

They went into his bathroom. She flicked on the light, and he squinted in the brightness. His lashes were long and thick, the kind she wished she had. The shadows falling from them made his eyes look more green than brown.

There was a bottle of expensive men's styling gel sitting on the counter, undoubtedly another of Vera's foresights. April rubbed a dab of it between her hands and stepped much closer to him than necessary, running her fingers through his hair and mussing it until it looked just right.

When she was done, their bodies were not only close but pressed together.

She rinsed and dried her hands and joined him back in the bedroom, where he was tucking the pages of his speech into his breast pocket. The clock read 5:55.

"I guess we better get going," she said. "Are you ready?"

His eyes reached into hers with the same intensity as when he'd asked her not to push during the second interview.

"I've been ready for a long time," he said.

Her heart raced as she walked across the room to him. His eyes were resting on her as she brushed a piece of invisible lint off his lapel and straightened the lay of his jacket. She rose on her toes to tuck a tiny section of hair behind his ear.

She was already off-kilter from her nearness to him, and

she leaned against him for balance. As a reflex, his arm lifted across her back. He exhaled softly, and she closed her eyes.

Yes, for this one night, she wouldn't worry about *couldn't*s or *shouldn't*s, or what was ahead for them back at Yosemite. All that mattered in the world was that they had the whole night ahead of them, together.

Slowly, she lowered off her tiptoes, letting her cheek slide along his neck. He leaned in slightly, and suddenly it was the side of her lips against his shower-fresh skin. Her legs were going to give out. He pulled her in tighter before releasing her.

"Shall we?" she asked.

Instead of taking her arm, he took her hand.

Chapter Sixteen

The elevator dinged when it reached the lobby. Josh released her hand just before the door slid open. Gabby was waiting in the foyer and whisked them to the ballroom.

April stopped in her tracks as they stepped inside. Vera hadn't just decorated; she had recreated Yosemite. It was magnificent.

High-resolution canvas panels of trees, waterfalls, meadows, and rock formations ran floor to ceiling on all four walls for an overall effect of being in a windowed room with 360-degree views of the park. The ceiling itself was a work of art, with soft strips of blue fabric floating among layers of sheer white.

The tables were covered in spring-green linen with a weave that looked like blades of grass. The centerpieces were impressive arrangements of pine branches, birch bark, and wildflowers. The background music was mellow American folk, the kind of sound that wouldn't be out of place if someone played it on speakers back at the campground. Even the stage was in costume, with a lodge-like facade of skinny logs and river rock. The live, potted pine trees near the doors added to the overall effect.

They walked to the stage, where Josh pulled his speech from his pocket and handed it to Gabby. She three-hole punched it and clicked it into the binder on the podium.

"Are you *sure* we can't put this on the prompter?" she asked.

"No way," Josh replied.

Gabby ushered Josh up to the microphone and waved a technician over for the sound check.

April and Gabby waited to the side of the stage.

"He sure cleans up nicely," Gabby said. "Are you guys a thing?"

April coughed. "I'm on the film crew."

"Better you than one of those climber girls," Gabby said. "They are all over him."

"Really?"

"Yeah. When he was staying with Vic at Vera's one time, this girl randomly showed up at the gate. She was totally grungy. Full dreadlocks and everything. I don't care who the guy was, I'd never just go up to the Smithleigh mansion like that."

"What did Josh do?"

"Told the guard to ask her leave."

Josh stepped off the stage. "Thanks for waiting," he said to April.

"You two should get some drinks before the receiving line starts," Gabby said. She ushered them over to one of the bars, also decorated lodge-style. "Elderberry martini for the lady, Tioga Pale Ale for the man."

Gabby disappeared into the hotel kitchen.

The bartender, who was about their age, kept staring up at them as he prepared the drinks. "Excuse me for asking, but are you Josh Knox?" he finally asked.

"I am," Josh said.

"I heard you're going to free solo the Sorcerer."

"Free BASE, but yes. I'm going to try."

April shivered.

"That's so ballsy," the bartender said. He put their drinks on the bar. "I'm looking forward to your talk. It's the whole reason I'm working tonight. Half the waitstaff, too."

April and Josh took their drinks over to a cocktail table. His cheeks were red. "Jeez, no pressure or anything."

"The Sorcerer or the speech?"

"The speech!"

"And you said you weren't nervous." She playfully nudged his arm. He caught her hand and only let her pull it slowly out of his grip.

"You're going to do great up there," she said.

"Coming from the person who had to give me speaking lessons."

"That was an on-camera interview lesson, and there aren't any robot cyclopes in here, so you'll be fine."

"Yeah, but everyone will be doing videos on their phones for Facebook. Or worse."

"So? Wouldn't that be a good thing?"

"I'm going to be talking about stuff that is really important to me."

"Even better!"

"Maybe you should have gone into marketing."

His brows were pinched with worry, and she felt bad for him. "If it helps, the light in here will be too low for cell phone video cameras to work once they dim the lights and turn those lanterns on."

"But they have flash. They can still take pictures."

"Cell phone flash won't work that far away."

"What about the waiters? You heard what the bartender said. Some of them might try to sneak up close."

"If Gabby sees a flash go off, I guarantee she'll get a name. The staff knows not to mess around during an event like this."

Josh sighed. Somewhere very close by, a bird chirped.

"Did you hear that?" April asked.

"What?"

"A bird. A pigeon must have gotten in here."

The bird chirped again.

"That?"

"Yeah."

Josh laughed and pointed to a speaker on the wall. "Have you noticed that a stream and crickets have gotten in here, too?"

"Don't tell me the air in here is damp on purpose."

"I wouldn't put it past Vera."

"She doesn't miss anything, does she?"

"Never. Vic would have loved all of this," Josh said. "It's too bad he couldn't be here to see it."

Gabby was over at the doors to the ballroom. She waved at them to join her in the lobby.

"That was quick," Josh said. "We better drink up."

They chugged their drinks as they walked. The delicious martini was no problem at all to swallow down fast.

Gabby introduced Josh and April to the other people in the receiving line, who included the superintendent of Yosemite National Park, the director of High Sierra Search and Rescue, and a U.S. senator who was championing the cause. Vera joined them, looking as royal as Queen Elizabeth in her frosty blue gown. She gave Josh a gentle squeeze, and then April.

"You two make a magnificent couple," Vera whispered before releasing her.

Vera took her place at the head of the line next to Josh. "It's nice to have some young faces here with all of us old codgers. Joshua, there are at least two dozen guests who have personally told me they are dying to meet you."

The Walkabout crew passed through the line early on.

"You look amazing, April," Madigan said, with a hug that lingered a little too long. "I'm sorry we're having you work tonight." There was the faint smell of tequila on his breath.

Theo wolf whistled and gave her a high five. "You clean up nice, Hollywood. Hey, do you know if the drinks are free tonight?"

She nodded.

"Score!"

Once the Walkabout crew was safely inside the ballroom, April drifted closer to Josh, until her bare shoulder was grazing the smooth fabric of his tuxedo. She stayed anchored to him through the blur of smiles and handshakes in a stream of perhaps three hundred people, each of whom Gabby announced by name as they arrived. If they didn't have a title of doctor or congressman, then their last name was recognizable. There were even some San Francisco–based movie stars and one Academy Award–winning director who passed through the line.

The receiving line disbanded just before dinner. Josh took her arm properly, and they reentered the ballroom like guests.

The head table was in the center of the room. April scanned for the Walkabout crew, finding them at the far end, in seats that faced the wall. She and Josh would have relative privacy. Not that anything was going to happen in the middle of the ballroom, while sitting at a table with the film's benefactor and a bunch of millionaires.

The speeches began after the last of six delicious dinner courses. The lights dimmed, and the fabric of the artificial sky glowed with sunset oranges and yellows. The waiters made rounds to light the candles in the lanterns on all the tables, and the sound effects changed to peaceful nighttime Yosemite noises, like the gentle crackle of a campfire.

Josh leaned over to April. "Do you hear that? I think the ballroom's burning down," he whispered. "And this place might be infested with crickets."

"Not funny," she said.

Wisely, Vera's staff had not included any bone-chilling branch snaps or wild animal howls on the soundtrack for the gala.

The early speeches were short ones from search-and-rescue stakeholders who showed a lot of slides April would have rather not seen: images from the harrowing rescues and bar charts of injuries and deaths in Yosemite. Climbing-related accidents led in both categories.

The superintendent's speech was next, which was Josh's cue to go to the front. He downed the rest of his beer.

"Wish me luck," he whispered. She felt for his hand and squeezed it.

He pushed her fingers open and laced his between them. Time slowed and flowed by in milliseconds as his eyes burned into hers.

Josh slipped away to wait his turn at the side of the stage, stepping into the spotlight as the applause from the superintendent receded. A complete transformation had taken place. Gone was the guy who grimaced at video cameras and hated talking to anyone who didn't rock climb. In his place was a man who could easily be the son of one of the VIP guests, standing tall and confident on the stage in his custom-tailored tuxedo.

Somehow, Josh was as comfortable speaking to the crowd as he was talking to his climbing buddies around the campfire. His voice was calm and deliberate. He was hardly looking at the pages in the binder in front of him, and he definitely wasn't looking at the teleprompter, where Gabby had loaded his speech just to be safe.

It was the first time in real life April could blatantly stare at him. She watched his every gesture, every shift in expression. She listened to the words she had read on his laptop come alive in his familiar but amplified voice.

Suddenly, the words were ones she knew had not been in either of the versions of the speech she had read. Josh's eyes cut directly to her.

"I climb because there's nothing else in this world where you can so fully live in the moment and be completely at peace. Especially in a place like Yosemite. It's magical to be up among the formations, to be at their level and at the same time dwarfed by their immensity."

His eyes were raw and vulnerable as he continued to look in her direction. It was the million-dollar question no reporter had ever wrangled out of him. The question she herself had been pushing to get: *Why do you do it?*

"All the continents have been discovered, the West has been won, the wilderness has been mapped. To climb new routes is to explore a final frontier, and it's one of the few things left in this world where your survival is based solely on your skill. It's deeply satisfying. Climbing an old route a different way is also a new frontier. It's a new frontier of skill. An evolution of what is physically possible."

Climbing wasn't something Josh did. It was who he was. She understood this because it had been the same way for her dad and aerobatics.

Josh returned to his written speech with a story about HSSR rescuing one of his climbing friends last year. He finished to uproarious cheers.

When he finally made his way back to the table, April threw her arms around him. "That was fantastic!"

He squeezed her hard, the damp skin on his face a giveaway that the speech hadn't been as easy as he'd made it seem.

The waiters delivered dessert and coffee as Vera took the

podium. Vera was an amazing public speaker, and she was unabashed in encouraging the guests to take both monetary and political action to keep HSSR funded permanently. She walked off the stage to a standing ovation as the sunset overhead cooled into a starlit night sky. The waiters delivered more candlelit lanterns to the tables.

When the stage lights came back on, there was a band in place, ready to play. It was Jackal Legs, a bluegrass band that had hit the mainstream top twenty a few years back.

"What do you say we take a spin?" Josh asked.

Dance? With Josh? They were in public. Did she dare?

She glanced over at the Walkabout table, where the guys' chairs were facing the back wall again, and it looked like someone had just delivered a round of drinks.

"Okay," she said.

She followed Josh through the tables to the dance floor and kept nudging him onward until they were at the farthest point from the Walkabout table. There were a lot of couples dancing, making the floor fairly crowded. They should be safe from any notice by Vera or the Walkabout crew.

Josh set one hand loosely on her back and swept her into a casual, peppy step that matched the song exactly.

"Another hidden talent, Josh Knox?" she asked as they turned in a circle.

"One of many."

"How'd you learn?"

"My mom." He grinned. "Where'd you learn?"

"My dad."

"I thought you were going to have to stand on my feet."

"*I* thought I was going to have to lead."

When the song ended, Josh clamped her lower back and dipped her almost all the way to the floor. Her cheeks were hot when he pulled her back up, and her ribs were straining against the dress.

The lights above them dimmed, and a mirror ball flung prisms of white across the sea of couples. A slow song was about to come on. This would definitely be too much if anyone caught them. It was too dark to see the Walkabout table, and for all she knew, Danny and his wife, Michelle, were out on the dance floor with them right now.

Josh seemed to sense her hesitation, because his face was serious and his eyes concerned. She let him take her left hand, and he gathered her in close with his right.

The song was one she'd never heard, soft and melodic, with Celtic undertones. The rest of the world, the couples all around them, faded away. She no longer cared who saw them.

April rested her cheek on the breast of Josh's fine tuxedo. He twisted their clasped hands inward until her hand rested against his chest. Beneath it, his heart beat rapidly.

She was completely surrounded by a man with whom she was entirely consumed. How could she ever go back to a world where she couldn't be with him like this all the time?

Her body screamed in protest as the song slowed and faded.

"Do you want to get some air?" Josh whispered.

She nodded, following him blindly along the perimeter of the ballroom and through the open French doors onto the balcony. The night was warm, and city lights and car motors replaced the twinkling stars and chirping crickets. He took her hand and led her to the corner, where a sculpted cypress in a massive planter hid them from view.

Josh turned to face her. Her ears buzzed, and her body trembled.

He reached forward, brushing her bangs to the side with the backs of his fingers. Although he was smiling slightly, his eyes were infused with melancholy. She leaned into his hand and stepped closer. Everything was happening fast, but also in slow motion. Her face tipped up as his head lowered. Her whole body was in a free fall.

Their lips touched and melted together like warm butter. It was not like embarking on something new, rather, returning to what always should have been. This was Josh. Hunky, enigmatic Josh. For the moment, *her* Josh.

His lips stretched into a smile, and he pulled her tightly against him. The sensation of falling hit her again.

Then, without warning, Josh's body went stiff. She pulled back and followed his eyes toward the ballroom.

Madigan had just stepped through the doors.

Chapter Seventeen

Madigan stood in front of her. He was disheveled, and his eyes were bloodshot. Her chest was still heaving from kissing Josh.

"I'll see you back inside," Josh whispered, then drifted away.

What had Madigan seen?

She glanced back at the corner, where it was completely black. From the doors, he would have been too far to see anything, but even so, the mere fact of them being tucked away in that corner together was suspicious.

"You didn't have to dance with him," Madigan said.

Her shoulders relaxed. If he was bringing up dancing, then surely he hadn't seen the more serious offense.

His eyes locked on her boldly, which was something she wasn't used to from him.

"It's beyond what we would have expected of you tonight," he said, his words slurring a little. If he wasn't drunk, he was well on his way to it.

"It's okay. I didn't mind. I like dancing."

His eyes softened, and he looked more like himself. "Still.

I never liked that Danny asked you to do this. Josh is talent. And there is a line."

A lump of guilt formed in her throat.

He pulled a pack of cigarettes out of his pocket and thumped it sloppily against the heel of his hand.

"I didn't know you smoked," she said.

"I don't. Usually."

He offered her one. She shook her head.

Madigan swayed as he focused on lighting the cigarette. He and Theo getting a head start on the drinking this afternoon had been a really bad idea.

"You look really nice tonight," he said. "You do always, but tonight..."

There was longing in his eyes. Josh had been dead-on.

"We should get back inside," she said.

He took a long draw of his cigarette. "I'm sorry, April. I shouldn't have said that."

"It's fine. You've had a lot to drink. I know that."

She put her hand on his shoulder and guided him toward the door.

"Wait," he said.

"We should get back." She nudged him forward.

When they reached the Walkabout table, Danny and Michelle were still congratulating Josh on his speech. Madigan collapsed into his chair and grabbed a nearly full pint of beer, which sloshed all over his rental tux.

"You need to cut him off," she whispered to Theo.

"Fine by me," Theo said, snatching Madigan's beer and taking a gulp.

By one a.m., couples were drifting toward the lobby, picking up Vera's Yosemite-themed gift bags on the way out. April had hoped that she and Josh would be able to steal away together, but the late hour and the alcohol had brought out the amateur climber in every middle-aged man in attendance.

There was a line of them at the Walkabout table, waiting to ask which climbing gym in San Francisco was the best, what Josh's favorite brand of cam was, and if he was really going to climb the Sorcerer without a rope.

When the line of men finally petered out and Michelle put on her wrap, April's hope of escape rose again.

"Where are we going next?" Michelle asked. "Better be somewhere with dancing."

No way. April threw a frown to Josh.

"I'm actually pretty tired," he said. "I was going to head up and—"

"Josh!" a man yelled, slapping him on the back. It was the tan, fit, white-mustached CEO of Esplanade.

"Barrett! We're going out. Join us," Michelle said.

"Good thinking," Barrett said. "Let's do it."

"I was just saying I'm pretty tired—" Josh started.

"Oh, please," Barrett said. "You, tired?"

April trailed behind the group with Josh. She couldn't bear to go with them. It would make her too sad to be around him in a group, while she watched the only minutes they would ever have to be alone together drain away.

"I have a headache, guys," she said when they got to the lobby's rotating front door. "I'm going to head up to my room."

Michelle gave a disappointed groan.

"Oh, come on, April," Madigan slurred. "Come with us."

"He really shouldn't drink anymore," April said to Theo.

"I agree with Madigan," Theo said. "You need to come."

"Sorry. My head." She turned toward the elevators, hoping that Josh could find an excuse to sneak back to the hotel later.

"I'm actually going to bail, too," Josh said.

No! That was too obvious.

"I don't think so, bud," Barrett said. "You owe me a beer from last night, remember?"

April glanced back. Barrett was steering him through the rotating door. Josh looked over his shoulder, his eyes searching for her. She walked calmly to the elevator, trying to hold her composure until she was safely inside. But once there, she wasn't alone.

"Hey, you were the one with Josh Knox tonight?" said an older man in a half-undone tux. "He's an *amazing* climber."

Correct. She *had* been the one with Josh Knox, but she wasn't with him any longer. She nodded to the man, keeping her eyes forward as she swallowed back tears. Would she see Josh again tonight, or was this the end of it forever?

At the door to her room, she fumbled with her clutch and then dropped the key card. She scooped it off the floor and impatiently slid it in and out of the reader, getting a series of red lights. Her frustration mounted. Finally, the light turned green and the lock rolled off. She pushed into the room.

This couldn't be it with Josh. Surely he would come to her room as soon as he could get away. But how long would that be? A couple of drinks? It was already so late, and they were driving back to Yosemite in the morning.

Danny's wife was a stay-at-home mom with their two kids and probably never got out like this. Between her and Barrett, they'd probably keep Josh hostage all night.

April desperately wanted him to show up at her room, but for the sake of her pride, she couldn't expect it. Besides, he didn't know her room number. Or her cell phone number.

She slithered out of the beautiful dress and changed into her purple pajama boxer shorts and a polka-dotted tank top, both things her mom had mailed to Yosemite with the dress.

In the bathroom, she pulled the pins out of her hair and it flowed down to her shoulders in deep waves. She washed off the makeup and then brushed her teeth and spread gloss on her lips, just in case.

She flopped onto her bed. The air puffed out of the down

comforter, and then refilled, floating up around her body. It would be great to talk to someone right now, but who did she know who would be awake at this hour and not in a crazy-loud bar or in the middle of a hookup?

Staring at the ceiling, she told herself that she had been blessed with a chance to cool down and think things over. Her chance to stop a messy situation with serious implications before it happened.

There was a light rap on her door, and her heart leaped. Who cared about any of that? This was *her* night.

She walked to the door and peeked though the peephole. Her heart plummeted. It was Madigan.

She cracked the door. "Hey, Madigan. What's up?"

"I just—had to make sure— Are you okay?" He was swaying badly, like he was going to come crashing down at any second. She pulled the door open, ready to catch him.

And there was Josh, right next to him, ready to do the same thing. Her heart soared.

His eyes crinkled as he smiled at her.

"Madigan wanted to come check on you," Josh said. "But I thought he might need a little help getting back to the hotel."

"I'm fine," April told Madigan. "I took some aspirin and the headache's almost gone. Thank you for checking. Let's get you back to your room before you pass out."

She and Josh guided Madigan down the hall to his room and laid him on his side with pillows stacked against his back so he couldn't roll over. Josh made a funny face at her from the other side of the bed. She choked back a laugh.

Madigan grabbed her hand and looked at her like he meant to say something, but the call of the comfortable bed was too much and he was asleep and snoring softly in seconds. April took his shoes off, and Josh left a glass of water on his night table.

They sneaked back down the hallway to her room. She

undid the deadbolt she'd used to prop her door open and then let it fall closed. Finally, they were truly alone.

She turned, and Josh was right there. Gone was the jovial camaraderie from helping Madigan. His face was dead serious, his eyes yearning. Before she knew what was happening, she was pinned between his body and the door. Their mouths were together, their tongues hot, deep, urgent. She couldn't breathe, but she'd rather die than stop kissing him.

His tuxedo jacket was open, and his rock-hard abs pressed against her. She reached up the back of his jacket, grabbing his shoulder blades and pulling herself even closer. His hands were in her hair, sweeping tight along her scalp.

She needed more of him. More, more, more.

He gripped her shoulders and straightened his arms. The sudden space he'd created between them was like a wave braking on top of her head. The freezing water crashed all around her, sucking at her shins as the sea called it back.

She looked up, fearing he would say it had all been a mistake, but his eyes were dancing with happiness. "Do you know how long I've wanted to kiss you?"

"How long?"

"Since the very first time I saw you."

"At the cafeteria?"

He bent his arms, drawing her near again, and then closing the sides of his jacket across her bare shoulders. His stomach expanded into hers with every breath.

"No," he said. "Since you fell out of your tent, and when you were at the bathroom watching me climb, and *then* when Madigan introduced us in the cafeteria."

The blood in her body surged all at once. Her knees would have buckled if she were not still leaning against the door.

But— Oh, no. The tent?

"Please tell me you didn't really see that." A goofy smile crept to his face, and she buried her face in his lapel.

"How could you have seen that? You were over on the boulder!"

"Yeah, a boulder that has a great view of the whole campground." He put his fingers under her chin, forcing her to look up. "It was the most adorable thing I've ever seen."

He tightened his grip across her back and lifted her off the ground. Her feet dangled in the air as he slowly spun her in a circle, like they had all the time in the world together.

The carpet was soft against her feet as he gently lowered her down. He took off his jacket and folded it over the back of the desk chair. She studied his face across the small distance. They'd kissed twice, yet, in a way, she was just as intimidated by him now as she had been that very first night at Walkabout's candlelit picnic table. Her fingers, itching to fiddle with something, found the lace on the hem of her boxer shorts. He was just so gorgeous, and those eyes of his, so intense.

He held out his hand and she took it, their eyes never straying as he pulled her closer. She placed her palm square on his chest, in the slight dip between his pecs beneath his smooth white dress shirt. This ability to just reach out and put her hand on him—it was like being able to touch an impossibly beautiful, lethal jaguar straight from the pages of *American Geographic*.

She unknotted his silk bow tie and pulled it slowly out of his collar, noting the new-fabric smell of his tuxedo, the citrus from the hair gel, and a trace of night air from his walk back to the hotel. Raising onto her toes, she popped open the top button. Just like in his room before the gala, he laid his arm across her lower back to steady her, only now, her tank top had lifted with her arms, and his hand landed on bare skin, igniting sparks through her body.

For a moment, neither of them moved. Then his fingers bent around the narrowest part of her waist, making her heart race. His rumpled hair fell across his forehead, and his eyes were dark as his mouth lowered to hers, tasting faintly of the spearmint gum he always chewed. In his kisses, and in the tight hold he kept on her waist, was something distinctly reaching but also yielding. Like he wasn't just kissing her but giving over a piece of himself and trusting her to keep it safe.

"Come here," Josh whispered, guiding her toward the bed, where he propped pillows against the headboard.

She sat next to him, but he nudged her closer, and she slid over so that her back was against his chest. He bent his knees and slid his face alongside hers, his breath flowing down her neck. His lips followed his breath, grazing her skin in kisses that were as light as a down jacket. Her eyes floated closed for a beat as she tipped her head to the side to expose more skin.

The dim lamp next to the bed cast a ghostly reflection of her and Josh against the window and the night lights of Sacramento. Her blond hair looked white, fanned across his black pants.

She watched in the window as he lowered his head to kiss the place where her neck met her collarbone. Her lips parted, and she inhaled. Heat spread through her body.

They stayed like that for a long time, his lips against her neck as his fingers traced lines slowly up her forearms.

"April?" he asked.

"Yeah?"

"Why do you like film?"

She ran her thumb across a faint scar on his knuckle. "Film? I don't know, it's just always been my thing."

"Well, what about it makes it your thing?"

"I guess it's because in movies, you can live in someone else's world for a while. And when you have the ability to give that experience, viewers come away with this complete sense of empathy that can't be matched in any other medium— especially not in print advertising or marketing. With film, you can help to influence so many good changes in the world."

"What was the first movie you made?"

It was a sappy short about a wild cat that lived in one of the airstrip hangars. She laughed. "Let's just say it's a good thing I accidentally deleted that movie a long time ago."

"Can you expound on that?"

"Wait a minute, this is sounding familiar."

"Don't forget to repeat the question in your answer."

"Are you *interviewing* me?" She whipped around. Sure enough, there was a goofy grin on Josh's face.

"We can start with something easy," he offered. "Like your favorite food."

"Josh!"

"You know everything about me, and I barely know anything about you."

"I wouldn't call two short interviews *everything*."

The grin faded from his face, leaving her swimming in the intensity of his eyes, in the heat of his body wrapped around hers. "April, I'm serious. I want to know everything about you."

She relaxed back against his chest. He picked up one of her hands, lacing their fingers together.

"Okay," she said. "Ask me a question."

She answered all of his questions, telling him how she was a film fanatic as a child, watching every documentary and art film at the library and on her parents' streaming service. She told him about Christmas when she was eleven, the year her parents bought her a video camera, and how her favorite food was her mom's buckwheat waffles. She told him the kinds of films she hoped to make someday, and how three of the seven teens in her sample film to Walkabout were now in permanent foster care because the county of Los Angeles had uploaded her film to their YouTube page.

It seemed like no time at all had passed, and suddenly the sky out the window was lightening at the lowest reaches of the horizon. She and Josh were still lying on the bed, talking.

She studied his face. The lines at the corners of his eyes and the heaviness of his eyelids gave away his deep fatigue, but he managed a small smile. She ran her fingers along his jaw, and he closed his eyes.

"I'm sorry I made you cry at the first interview," he said when he opened his eyes a moment later.

Her body stiffened. He had seen her tears!

He pulled her into him, softening the impact of what he said. "I was scared of you," he whispered. "I wanted to keep you at a distance, but I overdid it."

"I'm five foot one. How could I possibly be scary?"

He swallowed. "Because I wanted you to know the answers to the questions you were asking me."

Her heart crumbled. She nudged him onto his back and laid her head on his chest exactly where her palm had been while they danced. "What made you decide to be nice?"

"After I realized I made you cry, I knew I had to shape up or you'd never talk to me again. And that made me more afraid than of anything you might ask me."

She found his hand and threaded her fingers reassuringly though his. She closed her eyes and listened to his heartbeat.

· · ·

Sun warmed her face, and she opened her eyes. The sheets and pillows were unbelievably soft against her skin. She was adrift in happiness.

Josh. It was like it had all been a dream, except he was still spooned behind her with his arms holding her tight. She twisted within his warm embrace to face him.

"Good morning," he said.

She lifted her head off the pillow, and they kissed deeply.

"Just so you know, we don't have much time before we

have to be downstairs at the van," he said.

"How long?"

"Twenty minutes."

"Oh my god!" She sat straight up. "I hope you were planning to wake me up at some point!"

"Not until we were a half hour late."

She smacked him. He tackled her back down to the bed with him, covering her jawline with kisses.

"You are not going to make me miss my last chance for a real shower for the next two months!" she said as she kicked to free herself.

She got as far as her knees before pausing to look at him. This was *Josh* in her bed, the king-size pillow they'd shared still under his head and his thin white T-shirt doing an inadequate job of concealing his tan, chiseled chest. He snatched her up again, logrolling, with her shrieking and him laughing, all the way across the bed. They rolled to a halt right on the edge. She scooted closer, examining his face up close in the natural light, where the laughter still sparkled in his eyes. Lowering down on top of him, she kissed him, playfully at first, but then, remembering that their allotted time together was now over, she kissed him with all the longing that was still in her heart.

Chapter Eighteen

Everyone but Theo, who was driving, slept the entire way back to Yosemite. But naps — and any relaxation whatsoever — were over the second they pulled into the campground parking lot. Josh went off to climb, Danny rushed over to the Park Service office, and April helped Madigan and Theo set the camp back up.

They would be reshooting Flying Sheep in two days, and now that she knew Josh's secret route to the lake, she would not have to use the dreaded climber's trail for filming the top out. *Hallelujah.* Code for Verity would come next week, since the rockfall had stopped, and they'd be prepping for the Sorcerer in between.

April went to her tent to change her clothes for rappelling practice with Madigan and took some extra time there to be alone with her thoughts about Josh. It had been the most beautiful, intense night of her life. But it had been just that. One night. Now they were in Yosemite, and it was over. To break the rules while they were here on the job was a whole different level of wrong, and she had to put space between them so she'd mentally be able to handle filming him on the Sorcerer. Not that she was presuming Josh would be interested in more. Besides, he'd be leaving for Utah to shoot an Esplanade Equipment commercial as soon as he climbed the Sorcerer.

You knew this was the way it had to be, and you did it anyway. Now you have to get on with things just as they were before.

She forced herself out from beneath the weight of her sadness and walked to the parking lot to meet Madigan. He was at the van, chugging from a huge bottle of water. She prayed he was too drunk to remember any of the things he'd almost told her last night.

Theo joined them, and they followed the trail well past Celery Slabs to a lesser-used top-roping cliff. While Theo went around to the top to fix an anchor for the ropes, she and Madigan got into their gear. He wasn't joking around with her like normal, which wasn't a good sign, and she could really use the distraction right about now. He carefully avoided eye contact when he handed her the backpack with the camera in it, making her cringe. It was going to be a long afternoon.

They clipped into the ropes, but Madigan made no attempt to start ascending. He sighed. "I feel like I need to say something here."

Shit. Couldn't they just pretend it never happened?

"I was pretty drunk last night," he said. "I vaguely remember coming to your room. I think I might have said something—"

"Oh! Nothing. You didn't say anything. You're right. You were *really* drunk. Josh and I just helped you back to your room."

"I really feel like I said something, though. Something I shouldn't have."

April pretended to think it over. "Not that I can remember.

But, you know, I was drinking a lot, too."

He looked at her like he didn't know whether to believe her or not. "Well, I want to apologize anyway. I'm sorry if I said something to you that was out of line."

"Don't worry about it. It happens to everyone. It's happened to me, too."

Actually it hadn't, because that would require her to have feelings for somebody. Which hadn't happened since the crash. Until, well, Josh.

Madigan looked at her strangely, and she realized she'd just given it away that he *had* said something—or had at least tried to.

"I want you to know that it was the truth, April," he said. "But we work together and I would never put you in a position like that."

Madigan had stunning blue eyes, and there was no doubt that he was a cute guy. It was strange that she had never considered this before. It was probably because she'd known he was her boss from the moment she met him. Not only that, he was five years older and lived in a completely different world than her. He owned a house. He had a golden retriever named Tucker. He'd probably had girlfriends who'd lived with him.

He swallowed. "I thought, maybe after we're done with this film…"

Then he burst out laughing. "I totally did it again. I'm really, really sorry, April. Can I blame it on my hangover this time?"

She was laughing, too. She gave him a friendly bear hug.

His eyes were a smidge wistful when she pulled away, but he got right back to business, checking their harnesses and gear. "Okay. Are you ready for this?"

She knew he would be true to his word. He would not broach the topic until she was no longer an intern. Perhaps by then, knowing it was a possibility, she'd feel differently about him. Someone who was *not* a risk-taking, free-soloing professional rock climber *and* who was as passionate about filmmaking as she was? That would be a definite improvement on her current situation. But for now, she was just thankful she had her friend back. She grinned. "Let's do it."

They ascended the side-by-side ropes until they were twenty feet off the ground.

April practiced switching her gear, rappelling, and climbing back up. To her relief, her fingers remembered the movements perfectly after the weekend away.

When they filmed on the Sorcerer, she would be wearing a chest harness to help stabilize the camera, but today she was just holding it on her shoulder. She was already familiar with camera technique at vertical angles such as this, though shooting while being harnessed in was all new. Madigan gave her a quick lesson on cliff-side filming stances. He clipped a tether to her camera in case she dropped it, and then rappelled down so she could film him ascending.

"Let's see," he said when he returned to her. She handed him the camera, and he reviewed her work.

"You did well overall, considering how close the ropes are," he said. "Can you see the importance of the correct setup?"

"Definitely."

"Same with knowing where the key moves and most cinematic backgrounds will be. No one wants to watch a guy yawning up an easy section when you could have him sweating it out on a corner with a great panorama in the background."

Madigan kept hold of the camera and settled into a filming stance. "You go down and I'll film you coming up."

She completed the ascend-rappel cycle without any prompting or intervention from Madigan. She watched what he filmed, finding it hard to believe the small blond woman in the red helmet operating all that crazy gear was her. Madigan's camera work was better in a number of subtle ways that added up to a completely different effect for a nearly identical shot.

There was a whistle from the ground. Theo was back at the base of the cliff, ready to be a climbing model for April. She stayed in place on the rock while Madigan rappelled down to belay him.

Theo pulled himself up the rock until he was about fifteen feet below her and then stopped. "Ready?" he called.

April situated the camera on her shoulder. "Go ahead."

He climbed up to her, then past her, stopping when his feet were above the level of her head. He repeated this section of rock over and over. At first, he kept her entertained by acting out different emotional themes. Determination, frustration, fury, elation, exhaustion, fear, focus, pain. But after an hour, she was too uncomfortable to be entertained by his antics. Her stomach was growling from not eating breakfast or lunch, her shoulder ached from the heavy camera, the balls of her feet were sore from the pressure against the rock, and her harness had transformed itself into a torture device.

The many physical discomforts made it impossible to focus. And made it impossible for her to stop thinking about Josh. She'd do her best to avoid him for the rest of the time until the Sorcerer, but they would inevitably cross paths. When they did—

Her heart grew granite hard just thinking about it. It would kill her to be around him, pretending to be nothing but an acquaintance after all their time together last night.

But what if Josh assumed she would keep sneaking around with him here in Yosemite? If that was the case, she'd have to explain the crew-talent rule and why she couldn't risk it. And to say no to Josh if he *was* still interested? How could she possibly turn away from his kiss? Or the opportunity to wrap her arms around him? Would she physically be able to?

Through the camera, she watched Theo look down at Madigan and wink. She was out of patience for his games. There had to be a bylaw in the Cinema Guild about being forced to film without a tripod for this long.

Theo screamed and plummeted from view. She gasped and then screamed along with him. The camera rolled off her shoulder and almost slid out of her hands.

She made herself look down. Theo's head was only six feet lower than it had been. And he was grinning at her like the Cheshire cat.

"Okay up there?" Madigan asked.

"Fine," she snipped. They'd done that on purpose.

"That's enough for today," Madigan said. "Let's head back and get dinner started."

"Good," Theo said. "My arms are about to fall off."

No kidding.

April put the camera in her backpack and rappelled down. She helped the guys pull the ropes, and they started back to camp.

"Let's talk about Theo's fall," Madigan said as they walked.

A debrief? She had very little energy left to concentrate. Was this really necessary right now?

"How'd you feel when it happened?" he asked.

"I wasn't expecting it."

"You screamed," Theo said.

"So did you!"

"So might one of our climbers," Theo said. "But you don't want to be screaming if one of them really falls. You have to keep your head. Always."

"We're working with the top climbers in the U.S. on this film. These are guys—and girls—who are tackling the hardest routes there are, but they don't succeed without failing hundreds of times first. They have great control of their fear, but you'll be able to tell when they're on something that scares them. As the cinematographer, you're praying to see that emotion, but when it happens right next to you, a thousand feet in the air, it can be hard to keep your cool."

April thought of Josh. There's no way she'd be able to keep her cool if something bad was happening to him. She wasn't sure she'd be able to keep her cool even if everything was going normally. To her, the mere fact of him doing the climb *was* something bad happening.

This was yet another reason her time with Josh at the gala had been a bad idea and why it was crucial that she avoid him now: to be emotionally capable of filming him on the Sorcerer, she had to be able to lock away her feelings so deeply that she didn't feel any differently about him than she did any other rock climber. She wasn't sure how she was going to manage that, but she had to. Otherwise, it could be a very dangerous situation next week on the Sorcerer.

Back at the van, they stowed their gear away. The guys were still going on about the nuances of rock-climbing cinematography.

"You'll be sweating and shaking," Theo said. "But hopefully not shaking too much, otherwise you'll ruin the footage. I almost puked once."

"When was that?" Madigan asked.

"Filming Barbara Gregory. She missed a hand jam and took a sixty-foot whipper."

"See, April?" Madigan said. "You have to separate yourself from what the climber is going through but still be engaged enough that you can capture the scene."

"Yeah, like with Barbara, I saw what was going to happen a split second before it did," Theo said. "Even if I had the time to react, there's this line you can't cross. You're just the cameraman. Or camerawoman. You can't tell the climber where to put her hands. That's her skill. Her talent. Her risk."

"Not that you wouldn't say anything if you saw something that was blatantly unsafe," Madigan said.

"Was Barbara okay?" April asked.

"She broke three ribs, but otherwise fine," Theo said.

Danny was on his laptop at the picnic table when they got to the campsite. "There's weather moving in," he said.

April and the guys gathered behind him and looked at his screen. She didn't know much about satellite imagery, but the red and yellow gob in the middle of the Pacific Ocean didn't look good.

"The big concern is the routes getting wet," Madigan explained. "It can take a long time for them to dry. It could really affect our filming schedule, and it would definitely delay Josh's Sorcerer climb."

"We've been lucky with weather so far, and we might stay lucky," Danny said. "It's hard to tell where this system will go once it hits land."

Theo got some beers out of the bear box and handed them around. April and Madigan started dinner. Tuna mac, but mixed with salsa to change it up.

As April started opening the cans of tuna, she subconsciously scanned the woods for signs of Josh. Would he walk through the campground on the way back from wherever he was today? Would he come to dinner tonight? She was dying to see him, but she knew she couldn't.

"April!" Madigan called. "You just drained the tuna into your beer!"

She looked down. Indeed she had.

"Want it?" she asked. "It's the new big thing in L.A."

"You should drain those over in the fish-cleaning room. We don't need any *Ursus americanus* visiting tonight."

She gathered the can opener, tuna, her tuna-juice beer, and dish soap and headed for the scullery room where she'd filled the five-gallon water container her first day on the job.

She unloaded her arms and poured the tuna beer down the sink.

"Hey, there," Josh said.

She whipped around, and there he was, leaning against the doorframe. She was going to explode with happiness and relief.

He kicked the door shut behind him and kissed her. She longed to wrap her arms around him, but her hands were still covered in tuna juice.

"Just a second," she said. She squeezed dish soap onto her hands and scrubbed them under the faucet.

"I should do the same, thing," he said. His hands were dusty from climbing, nearly black in places, and his knuckles and nail beds were caked in white chalk.

Their hands mingled under the stream of water as they rinsed the soap off. She shook her hands dry while he patted his on the underside of his shirt. "I wish we could have spent the day together."

He wrapped his arms around her and looked into her eyes. "I wish we could spend every day together."

Her heart raced in response. This was very much not over. Not yet.

He scrunched his nose and frowned. "You know, it really stinks in here."

She laughed and pushed the door open. They stood outside next to a big pine tree.

"Are you coming to dinner tonight?" she asked. "We're having tuna—obviously—with mac and cheese and salsa."

"I already told some of my buddies I'd barbecue with them, but you should swing by later."

Yeah, right, she was going to hang out with the biggest climbing celebrity in Yosemite National Park in front of a bunch of other climbers. The gossip would reach Danny before morning.

"I have an econ test coming up. I'll just be studying at my truck after dinner," he added.

Meeting Josh alone was a different story, but she needed to give herself time to think about what she was doing after her heart slowed down and she had a straight head.

"I'll see if I can get away," she said.

Chapter Nineteen

It only took April halfway through her bowl of tuna salsa mac to decide there was no way she was *not* going to see Josh tonight, even though it was the opposite of what she *should* do. After dinner, she went into her tent and changed into running clothes so the guys would think she was going for a jog.

"I'll be back in a bit!" she called to them as she started toward the main road.

"If you wait just a minute, I'll join you," Danny said. "A run sounds great right now."

"I'm just going on a quick one. Probably only two miles." Two measly miles wouldn't be worth the effort for Danny. She didn't wait for his answer before jogging away.

"Light's getting low, watch for bears!" Madigan called.

Even though she didn't have much time, she took the longer, more concealed way to Josh's camp, which was a fire road on the opposite side of the search-and-rescue camp. Her whole body was throbbing from filming today, and the jostling from the jogging was almost unbearable. She rounded the back side of the camp and there was Josh, swinging in his hammock and reading a textbook.

"Hey," she said, brushing up alongside him.

He smiled as he closed his book. He stood and wrapped his arms around her.

"I'm so glad you came." He buried his face in her hair. "You smell like raspberries."

"It's my shampoo. Pomegranate."

There was a ridiculous turquoise jar candle burning atop the grill on his fire pit. "I see Michelle hit you up at the gala, too."

"What'd you get?" he asked.

"The citronella bullfrog. It's on back order, though."

"Danny would just die if he knew."

"For sure."

He hugged her tighter against his body.

"Josh, I have to tell you, I'm not allowed to be doing this."

He took a quick breath and held it. She pulled back so she could see his face. His brows knit together in concern.

"Why?"

"I signed a contract."

"A contract for what?"

"Employee conduct. It's standard for crew. To prevent *this* from happening." She motioned between the two of them. "I can't get fired. I have so much school debt, and getting a job after my internship is going to be practically impossible as it is."

"It's not because *you* don't want to?"

"Want" wasn't the right word. The contract was only the tip of the iceberg in terms of why she *couldn't*. But he looked so impossibly sad…and she did *want* to. Badly. "No."

His body relaxed a little. "What if no one knew? What if we made sure?"

"How could we possibly? Everybody knows who you

are."

He turned her hands over, a frown on his face as his thumbs smoothed the new calluses forming on her palms from this afternoon. "Come on, get in." He tugged her forward.

She hesitated. "In the hammock?"

"What, you don't trust my knots?"

"It doesn't look very sturdy."

He sat down in it to prove otherwise. When she didn't move, he yanked her hand and she fell into his lap. He kicked his feet up and pivoted back, pulling her down. She clung to him as the hammock swung wildly, sure it was going to flip and dump them both on the ground.

Soon, the swinging slowed to a gentle rock, with the sides of the hammock pressing them into each other. Their mouths were instantly together, and she was pouring her whole heart into the kiss.

I wish we could spend every day together.

"My god, April," Josh said, gripping her arms and pulling her in for another one.

She kissed him until her bottom arm went numb, and then she twisted around, wrestling for space in the tight cocoon of the hammock until they were both lying on their backs with their shoulders overlapping. Josh slipped his arm beneath her and grabbed her hand. "I promise you I'll make sure no one sees us. We can be careful."

She rested her head in the perfect cradle of his shoulder. "Okay," she whispered. *For now.*

The sky glowed orange and yellow behind the darkening profiles of the pine trees. The hotel had been supremely luxurious, but she'd missed Yosemite. In the openness and beauty of this landscape, she felt free in a way she had never been before.

If she had her way, she'd stay in the hammock with Josh all night, but she was already well past the seventeen minutes it would have taken her to jog two miles. The light was low, and she hadn't brought her headlamp.

"I have to go," she said.

"Already?"

"They think I went jogging."

"Next time, tell them you're using the internet in the cafeteria or something."

She gave him a half smile.

"Are you shooting tomorrow?" he asked.

"I'll be on top like last time."

He squeezed her hand. "That's what I was hoping."

• • •

At the top of Flying Sheep Buttress, the sun was shining brightly. There was just enough breeze to ripple the surface of the lake and destroy the reflections, and thus, the lake was a solid sapphire gem under the endless dome of the sky.

She'd gotten up extra early so she could take the secret—but much longer—way to the top. With her camera all set up, she sat next to the same log she had last time, but this time she was prepared to stay awake with a twenty-four-ounce can of Horsepower Juice she'd taken from Theo's stash in camp. She cracked open the lid, frowned at the menacing purple foam around the spout, and then drank it all down.

The guys were on the radio constantly as they got ready for the climb. She followed along as they moved into their filming positions and counted down to Josh's start. Her stomach fluttered each time they mentioned his name, even though it was a roped climb that had been selected more for its aesthetics than its difficulty. Once Josh started climbing, the radio chatter was much less frequent, with all focus on capturing the climb. April got ready behind her camera when she heard the call that Josh was nearing Theo, who was in the highest position. She ran a test clip, just to make sure the lighting was still okay.

Josh's fingertips appeared first, followed by a tuft of hair, then his eyes, face, shoulders, and the rest of his body. He stood at the cliff's edge and shook out his hands. He put them on his hips and looked into the camera lens. "Well, what now?" he asked.

April groaned. He'd totally ruined the sequence, and she wanted to give him a hard time about it, but the guys would be watching this later, so she just said, "Whatever you'd normally do."

He walked in from the edge about ten feet, sat down, and started pulling the excess rope up to the top. "How'd it go?" she asked him.

"Do you want me to look at you when I answer?"

"Whatever feels natural."

"There isn't anything natural about having a camera at the top of my climb."

"Well, how'd it go?"

"Fine."

"Josh!"

"Can't we do this later?"

"Let's just get it over with."

"Fine."

"What were you feeling when you got to the top?"

"I was excited to see you."

She made a mental note to cut this section out before Danny saw it. "And what else?"

His bangs were clumped into little points from the sweat on his forehead. "Nothing else."

"Did you feel relieved to be finished? How about a sense of accomplishment?"

"Just you."

"You cannot say that on camera!"

"Oh, come on," he teased. "Wouldn't it show my personality? Isn't that what you people are always hounding me about?"

"Give me two good sound bites and I'll turn off the camera. We don't have much time up here."

"Just tell me what to say and I'll repeat it."

"No way. It wouldn't sound right."

"I am completely serious. If said I was thinking about anything other than you when I was climbing, it would be a lie."

He untied the rope from his harness, and before April knew it, he'd pulled her in front of the camera and was kissing her.

"Josh! I'm recording right now!"

He laughed.

"I'm going to have to cut this footage out of my log, and it's not that easy. And where's Lars? Don't you need to belay him up?"

"Lars wouldn't be able to do some of the moves on that last pitch without aid gear. I told him to just rap down with your crew."

Josh held her at arm's length and examined her. Deep breaths moved her breastbone, which was exposed in the low neck of her jog top. His gaze was unnerving and energizing at the same time.

He bent his arm, bringing her in close to kiss again. Under the huge, blue sky, with the breeze slipping between the bridges of their noses and across her back, it felt like the whole world was watching, and she liked it. She wanted everyone to see her like this, with him, but of course that could never happen.

"Why did you say we don't have much time up here?" he asked when they pulled apart.

"Well, first, I'm going down the long way, so that's an extra hour, at least, and I have to meet the guys back at the van at three o'clock. And now, thanks to you, I have to get there extra early to fix this SD card before they ask to see any footage."

"Why don't you just rappel down with me?"

"I don't have a harness."

"Don't you?"

He opened the front compartment of her backpack that she had prepacked last night. He pulled out a harness with a Grigri attached.

She shook her head. "I don't think anyone has any idea how crafty you are."

"It's probably better we keep it that way."

She looked at his coil of rope on the ground. It was only a fraction of the height of Flying Sheep Buttress.

"I don't understand how we can get to the ground with a rope that short."

"It's a multipitch rappel."

"I don't know, Josh. I'm new at all this. I've only done the kind where there's one rope that goes all the way to the bottom. Maybe it's better if I just walk down."

"This is the same thing, it's just that we do it several times in a row. We're going down over there," he said, pointing to the side of the buttress that was shorter and less steep. "There are belay chains and nice big ledges all the way down."

Still, she was skeptical.

"Two hours to walk off, or thirty minutes to rappel," he said. "Take your pick."

The rappelling option would give her ninety extra minutes alone with him. How could she argue with that?

"I'll race you to the lake," he said.

"Oh, no. I'm not going in the lake again."

"You big baby."

She groaned. "It's *so* cold."

He was already unbuckling his harness. "Loser owes the

winner a whole box of Loftycakes."

"Hey! I don't even like Loftycakes."

He was completely ignoring her as he tore off his shirt and wiggled free of his harness. She popped the camera into its padded case and zipped it closed.

She sprinted down the granite ramp, her body screaming from the work on the cliff yesterday as she closed the distance to Josh. They hit the gravel beach at the same time, but she was first to have her feet in the water.

"Yes!" she yelled.

They climbed up the roots of the downed tree, and he followed her out to the middle.

They turned to face the water. "Ready?" he asked.

She grabbed his hand, took a huge breath, and they leaped from the log. She knew what to expect this time, so the freezing water didn't make her panic as she kicked to the surface. They bobbed in the water, gasping for air, and then swam for shore.

They slowed where the drop-off ended and the water was warmer. Josh was able to stand there, but it was still too deep for her to touch. He pulled her to him, and she wrapped her legs around his waist. They were still breathing fast from the cold water, and their warm bellies fought for space to expand.

He lifted her and spun her slowly in a circle, like he had in her room after the gala. But then he picked up speed and flung her into the lake. The deeper, colder part of the lake. She came up sputtering and swam up to him from behind, making him lose his balance and slip underwater.

"Brr! Truce! Let's go back," Josh said when he surfaced.

They waded the rest of the way to shore and stood on the same patch of moss as before, pressed together for warmth.

"Let's go over there," Josh said. He pointed to the pile of boulders that rose from the water on the narrow end of the lake. One of the boulders near the top had a flat top that glistened white in the sun.

Soaking wet and barefoot, they picked their way over to the boulder and climbed on top. The granite was as sun warmed as it looked, and the taller rocks behind them radiated heat and blocked the wind. She sat cross-legged in front of him, and he massaged her shoulders with hands that spanned as wide as her back. His fingertips were magical, pressing deep into her aching muscles and melting yesterday's soreness away.

When he finished, she leaned back and he lowered his head to kiss her shoulder. The two of them stayed there on pause, his eyelashes leaving a butterfly kiss on her cheek each time he blinked.

"It feels like I've known you a long time," he said.

"Must be my face," she said. "I get that a lot."

"No, really, April. I feel very close to you. And it's been a long time since I've felt that way about anyone."

Not only did she feel close to him, she felt *safe* around him. It was ironic, considering his profession, but it was true. Ever since the crash, she had been on guard. Even in her happiest moments, she could still feel that edge, deep down. But when she was with him, there was nothing but joy. Was that how it used to be, before? Before she knew nightmares could—and did—come true.

He lowered onto his back, his torso stretching long as he clasped his hands behind his head as a cushion. She couldn't take her eyes off his body. It was the exoticness of him being so at home against the granite, and the intricate furrows of the muscle beneath his deeply tanned skin. The jaguar effect.

"You look so serious," he said.

"It's just—"

She reached out, laying her fingertip on his sun-warmed skin, slowly tracing the side of his oblique, then letting her fingers drift over the crosshatch of muscle above his belly button. She flattened a bead of lingering lake water on his lower stomach, pulling it like paint through the valley of one of his V muscles.

Josh's lips parted. She laid her hand along his jaw, running her thumb across his lower lip before leaning in to replace her thumb with a featherlight kiss.

He curled into her as she lay down on the rock, tucking his forearm under her head and resting his cheek on her shoulder. He swept a lock of her damp hair back from her temple before trailing his fingers down her arm to find her hand.

In the sky above, a single hawk drifted through the puffy white clouds. The heat from the rock and Josh's body made her delirious. She was so relaxed that she would have fallen asleep, if not for the Horsepower Juice.

The hawk's whistle echoed against the amphitheater of rock surrounding them. Even when Walkabout's film played on big screens, there was no way they'd come close to communicating all that surrounded them: the impossible vastness, pure silence, warm granite, the breathtaking valley, sunshine, the stunning cliffs, hair damp with pristine lake water, not another human in sight.

"I wish this, right now, could last forever," he whispered. His words flowed over her neck like silk.

"Me, too," she whispered.

Would it really be so bad if it did last a long time? If they could keep their relationship a secret until after filming was over, perhaps she could find a way to live with the daredevil part. Her mother had managed just fine for twenty-five years. Her mother, though, hadn't started the relationship already having had her worst nightmare come true.

No. There was no way April could film him on the Sorcerer while emotionally connected to him like this.

But if Danny's storm hit and Josh's climb was delayed,

she would have a smidge longer before she had to face the reality that what they were doing could not continue.

Please, please, please, please let the storm come right over Yosemite.

April twisted beneath Josh's arms so they were face to face. As they kissed, the valley and the surrounding cliffs spun and toppled upside down. The saturated greens of the grasses, the stark white of the waterfall, and the warm grays of the cliffs merged and streamed past them in ethereal ribbons, like barely blended paint. Then the blinding blue sky bobbed back into place overhead, and the world was open and free, bursting with sublime majesty.

• • •

The wind started picking up after dinner, and by the time April made her last trip to the bathroom before bed, it was strong enough to be Halloween spooky outside. She was more at ease once she was zipped inside her tent, which Madigan had assured her was well staked and designed to withstand not only a spring rainstorm in Yosemite but 140 mile-per-hour winds in the Himalayas.

April changed into her pajamas and snuggled into her sleeping bag. Her tent wasn't anything fancy, but it was familiar and as much of a home as she had right now.

She reached for the brand-new issue of *Vertical View*, which she'd bought from the Yosemite Village Market after she and Josh got back from the lake that afternoon.

She flipped to the photo feature on Josh's Indonesia trip. Most of the pictures were hunk-of-the-month style except one: a black-and-white portrait of Josh sitting at the base of one of the climbs. He wasn't looking at the camera, and from his relaxed expression, he probably hadn't been aware the photographer was taking it.

This was her Josh, with the slight crinkles of concern at the corners of his eyes, the wild hair, the strong jaw, and the subtle amusement playing across his lips.

She hugged the photo to her chest and clicked off her headlamp to go to sleep. Closing her eyes, she reflected on their multipitch rappel, which had been much more sexy than it had been scary. It was amazing to have the opportunity to be with Josh directly in his element like that, especially each time they were at the tight quarters of the belay anchors, hanging from the side of the cliff together with the breathtaking views all around them.

Sometime later in the night, she awoke in the darkness. A wet splat sounded on the tight nylon roof above her head. She held her breath and looked upward. There was another splat and a third before the wind blew a handful of splats into the side of the tent.

The raindrops picked up pace until they sounded like a drummer setting the beat for a band. Then, all at once, there were a dozen drummers, all around.

It was the music of an answered prayer. She and Josh would have a little more time together. Still clutching the magazine, she flipped over and fell back asleep, dreaming of Josh.

Chapter Twenty

The downpour had stopped sometime during the night, but it was still drizzling. The rains had turned the campground into a giant mud puddle, and the cafeteria was more crowded than April had ever seen it. She grabbed the last unoccupied window table.

She had a bunch of stuff to do for Danny, but she had all day because of the weather, so she started an email to some of her college friends, who had recently been making fake missing-person posters of her and posting them on Instagram. *Eaten by a bear?* was the heading on one of them. An instant message pinged in.

JKnox@EsplanadeEquip.com: *Morning, Hollywood.*

April@WalkaboutFilms.com: *What are you doing up so early on a rainout day?*

Josh: *Early? I've been up working since six.*

April: *On what?*

Josh: *My overdue econ test.*

She pictured him sitting cross-legged on his bed in his cozy truck with the drizzle all around.

"Awesome!" said a guy behind her. "You got a window seat." It was Theo. And Madigan, Danny, and Ernesto. And the two contractors who had arrived yesterday—brothers Rick and Russell.

They pulled a second table against hers, unloaded their trays, and started up their laptops. Suddenly she was sitting at a cybercafé. She finished her cup of coffee and bit into a streusel-topped blueberry muffin.

"The rain will clear by this evening, and the sun will be back tomorrow," Danny said over the top of his computer. "Looks like we only got the edge of the storm, thankfully. This shouldn't delay us more than a few days."

April's IM dinged, then dinged again. Theo looked over with a raised eyebrow. Like he never IMed. She muted the sound.

Josh: *You there?*

Josh: *Want to know how I knew Madigan had a thing for you?*

April: *No.*

His next IM popped up silently.

Every time I used to look at you, he'd be looking at you, too.

She squirmed in her chair. Madigan was sitting across the

table from her.

Josh: *It's never fun to look at a cute girl and lock eyes with a dude instead.*

April: *Stop! He's right here!*

Josh: *I know.*

April: *How would you know that?!*

Josh: *Turn around.*

A hot blush spread across her face. She whipped around, and there he was in his gray sweatshirt with the hood up, sitting behind a laptop five tables away.

April: *You're horrible!*

"April, are you okay?" Madigan asked.

The rest of the guys looked at her.

"Your face is all red," Theo said.

"I'm fine. I just need more coffee." She was going to kill Josh. She stood up with her mug. "Anyone else want anything?"

Josh: *You're adorable.*

She rolled her eyes and closed her laptop screen so no one accidentally saw the conversation.

"Can you grab a bunch of saltines?" Theo asked.

"Sure."

"I'm not talking just one or two. A big handful, please."

"I'm not going to steal crackers for you," she said.

"It's not stealing. They're free."

"Yeah, for people who buy chili."

"Who cares?"

"You're being low-class, Theo."

"Fine then, I'll get them myself." He snatched her mug and disappeared.

She sat down and shot a nasty look to Josh, who grinned while avoiding her gaze. She lifted her screen back up.

April: *How long have you been here?*

Josh: *The whole time. I was going to come join you, but you got six handsome guys instead of just one.*

April: *Who said you were handsome?*

Josh: *You did. At the gala.*

Memories of that night came rushing back. His fresh-from-the-shower smell, the buzz from the elderberry martinis, the proximity to him in a public setting, her dress brushing against his pants leg under the table, dancing, kissing, the knock on her door.

Danny had forwarded her the link to the official photos from the gala so she could pick a few to post on the Walkabout blog. She clicked through them now, surprised to find two of her and Josh. Vera was right about them making a nice couple.

In one photo, she and Josh were standing arm in arm in front of their table, smiling at the camera. Josh was movie-star handsome, and when she looked at herself, she saw her mother, twenty years younger and glowing with happiness. Josh's face was relaxed in a way she'd rarely seen it before that night, except when he was hanging out with other climbers. Now it was that way around her whenever they were alone.

In the second photo, she and Josh were in the same

position, only they were looking at each other and laughing. His hand was draped lightly across her back, like he was about to guide her somewhere. Perhaps away from the camera. Funny. She didn't remember anyone taking a picture of them. But then, she hadn't been aware of much else besides Josh. Hopefully there hadn't been too many of these intimate moments in front of other people.

April: *Have you seen the gala photos?*

Josh: *I thought you said no one was taking pictures.*

April: *No one except the official photographer.*

She IMed him the link.

Danny was loading a blank DVD into his laptop. "April, there are some clips I've been wanting you to watch. Some good examples of climbing cinematography, some classic climbing scenes, that sort of thing."

"Be sure to give her Scotty Knight on Godzilla Returns," Ernesto said. "It's sick."

"Definitely," Danny said.

April sneaked a glance at her computer screen. Josh had IMed her a thumbnail of the laughing shot. *This one's a keeper!*

The photo or the girl? she replied, feeling bold.

Josh: *Both.*

"Who's got an outlet?" Ernesto asked. "I'm out of juice."

It was no wonder: his enormous laptop had to be at least a decade old. Everyone searched the floor. The only outlet was next to her chair.

"Me, too," Danny said, handing her the end of his power cord.

Josh: *How 'bout we get out of here?*

April: *I can't. Not with everyone here.*

Josh: *:(*

Danny popped the finished DVD out of his computer and slipped it into a sleeve. "This is good stuff here," he said.

She put it into her bag and then scanned the cafeteria, trying to think of an excuse to leave. People were disproportionally crowded around the edges of the room. Near outlets. Bingo. Their outlet was already at capacity. There was her excuse.

April: *Actually, maybe I can.*

Josh: *That's more like it.*

April: *You go first.*

Josh: *Yes, ma'am! I'll be in my truck.*

Josh stopped by their table on his way out. His laptop was in a duct-taped messenger bag slung over his shoulder. His hood was still up.

"Vera's treating the whole crew to dinner tonight at Tall Pines," Danny said. "You free tonight?"

"The Tall Pines? I am now," he said.

It was torture being this close to Josh and not being able to look at him properly. Dinner tonight would be torture, too, being around him without being able to touch.

"My battery's almost out," she announced fifteen minutes after Josh left. "I've got some clothes to wash, so I can finish my work over in the Laundromat."

· · ·

April took her rain jacket and shoes off and crawled into the truck. The curtains were drawn on the side that faced the search-and-rescue camp but open to the forest and the misty drizzle on the other. The radio was on low to a classical station. They sat cross-legged across from each other with their knees touching.

She ran her fingers through Josh's hair, chasing the droplets of drizzle away. "So what's the deal with your hood?"

"What about it?"

"You had it on indoors, but your hair's wet, so you must have taken it off when you were out in the rain."

"I had bedhead," he said. "I had to hide it."

"You must have bedhead all the time, because I never see you without that thing up."

He looked off in the distance. His eyes returned to hers, beautiful and deep but troubled. For someone who lived such a carefree life, he seemed to carry so many burdens.

"I've never thought about it," he said. "But I guess it's because I don't want people to recognize me."

He forced his face into a lighter expression. "I know exactly what you're thinking. Don't say it."

"What am I thinking?" she asked.

"That I'm turning down free publicity. But do you know all the things I do already? Magazines, ads, movies, websites, climbing workshops—"

"Galas?"

"Yes, that was the worst of all."

She pushed him over on his back and pinned him down. "Dare to say that again?"

He flipped her over and kissed her. The truck rocked on its shocks and came to a rest. She wiggled out from underneath him.

"No distracting me," she said. "I have some videos to watch. Danny's going to ask me all about them at dinner."

Josh sighed and then folded the mattress back at the cab end of his bed to pull a bouldering pad out from the trapdoor. He rested it against the canopy. Voilà, they had a couch. Josh leaned against it. She sat between his legs and pulled his comforter around them.

She popped the DVD into her laptop. The one *Danny Rappaport* made for her. In the cafeteria, it seemed so normal for him to hand her the DVD, but she didn't take this simple action for granted. She was so lucky to be in a position where an accomplished filmmaker like Danny personally selected files off his computer for his intern to watch.

The first of twenty clips followed a climber for several months as he failed over and over on a short, overhanging cliff.

"Do you know him?" Josh asked.

"No, but it looks like a Crank It production."

"Not the director, the climber. He's a buddy of mine. Scotty Knight. Ever heard of him?"

"Oh, is this the Godzilla climb?"

"Godzilla Returns. Out in New Hampshire. He'd been working on it for two seasons before they came out to film."

Not only was she watching Danny Rappaport's hand selections, she was watching them with one of the best climbers in the world. Perhaps *the* best. It was like watching a football game with Tom Brady.

"Does he make it?" she asked.

"Yes. It was the hardest route in the world for years. The first five-fifteen ever."

On-screen, Scotty's whole body was shaking as he inserted a cam into the overhanging crack. It certainly looked impossible.

"The camera work here would be hard, too," she said.

"How so?"

"See how the camera is moving right now? They wouldn't be able to get a boom all the way in there, so they must have made a trolley or something."

Some people burned out on watching movies once they started making them, but she would never be like that. She loved everything about film, how all the parts came together to sweep you completely out of your world. If it hadn't been for movies, she would not have survived that first year back at school after the crash.

On the screen, Scotty Knight reached the top of his climb. "Yes!" he yelled, throwing a hand into the air. He bent over, trying to catch his breath, and after he did, he stood up with an ear-to-ear grin.

"Take note," she said to Josh. "That was perfect."

"You want me to do a victory dance at the top of my climbs?"

"That was hardly a victory dance."

As the next clip started, she laid her head against his collarbone. He wrapped his arms around her and slipped his fingers in between hers. Her chest lifted, and she felt like she was floating.

It was such a perfect way to spend a rainy day. Watching movies with Josh. It felt so *normal*. Like they did this all the time, and like they'd do it hundreds of times again.

"Do you know what I regret?" he asked her.

"What?"

"That it was your crew who took you climbing for the first time. I wish it had been me."

"The second time could be really special, too."

"You'd go again?"

"Yeah. It was fun."

The fifth clip started with a breathtaking bird's-eye view of Monument Valley from a red sandstone tower. A woman about ten years older than April with a long black braid was clinging to the corner of the needle, desperation on her face.

April paused the video. This looked like it could be the sequence that had terrified Theo. "Let's skip this one."

"Wait. This is good. It's Barbara Gregory's famous whipper."

April thought about the bungee-jumping scene in film class. Her stomach cramped. Decision made. She closed the file and double-clicked on the next one in line.

"What?" Josh asked. "You only want to see the triumphs and victory dances?"

"No. I just don't want to watch someone take a nasty fall."

"She doesn't get hurt that bad."

"I still don't want to see it."

"Falls are a fact of life in climbing. It's okay. We all appreciate a good one."

Her skin was clammy. "That's terrible, Josh."

"If you're not falling, it means you're not taking risks."

Anger filled her. She was glad her back was to him so he couldn't see her face. "So why do you *need* to take risks?"

"You'll never go anywhere in climbing if you don't."

"Oh, so it's totally worth it."

"It's not just a climbing thing. It's the same with any other athlete. It's a life thing, really. If you're not taking risks, you're not really living."

The hairs on the back of her neck stood straight up. Her father used to say the same thing. He had said that to her over coffee on the morning of the crash. *What good is life if you're not living it?*

She hardened herself to the memory. The rain extended her vacation from reality for a few days, and she wasn't going to waste it thinking about her dad, or bickering about the very reason this thing with Josh would never be more than an interlude.

April played the next clip on the DVD, instantly recognizing the looming profile of the Sorcerer, where a big-eyed, light-haired boy was putting chalk on his hands.

"Aw," she said. "It's you."

"Oh, no! We're not watching this one."

"You were so cute! How old were you?"

"Eighteen," he said. "Okay, moving on."

Eighteen wasn't all that long ago. He'd changed so much in the last seven years.

"You skipped one, I get to skip one." He reached over her shoulder and paused the clip as his younger self stepped up to the dark rock.

Neither one of them had a problem with the next clip, and they made it through the rest before her battery died. But when the distractions were over, there was a lingering sense of gloom in her body.

Josh was watching her, his brow furrowed. "Is something wrong?"

"Are you sure you're okay with me filming on the Sorcerer?"

"Of course. Whose idea do you think it was in the first place?"

Her mind fumbled to understand. "You told Danny to assign me to the Sorcerer?"

"No, not like that. I just asked him one time why you never filmed on the rock, and he said, 'You know, there's really no reason she can't.'"

Even if it had happened in a casual sort of way, it still stung that the invitation to join the Sorcerer crew had been initiated by Josh rather than being Danny's idea first.

"You *will* be a distraction, you know," Josh said.

He was smiling. He meant it as a compliment. He was just teasing her. Flirting. She knew these things, logically, but it didn't matter. Her presence messing with his mind space on a life-or-death climb? That was not okay. Invisible plates of armor slammed up around her, locking into place. Her breathing was getting heavy, and she pulled her hand out of Josh's. This wound from her dad, it would always be open, always affecting her. Her brow was drenched in sweat. She had to get away.

"April?"

So much for a rainy day vacation from reality. Not with stakes like this.

"April, look at me."

She didn't want to, but she did. His eyes were pleading.

"You have to understand, I only asked Danny about the filming because I was so desperate to know more about you. I would have done anything. I even messed with the charger that day on Flying Sheep so I could have some time with you when you weren't working."

Her sweaty body went cold. It was worse than she thought. He'd messed with their equipment? Because of her?

"I had no idea that anything would actually happen with us," he said. "I thought you were dating Madigan, remember? Even if you weren't, I didn't think there was any way a girl like you would be interested in a guy like me."

This had all been such a mistake, and now everything was irrevocably tangled up. But it hurt to see him miserable like this. She fought her urge to run and reached under the blanket for Josh's hand, threading her fingers between his. "You underestimate the attraction of a truck-house."

"April, I'm really sorry that I meddled with your guys' equipment."

If only she could disappear into him and have the peripherals go away. Like at the gala, where it was the two of them, adrift together within the rest of the big, wide world.

But she couldn't, because that was not the reality of their situation. Those things out on the peripherals had the power to kill one of them. The danger was right there beyond reach, looming, closing in. She'd always feared that her father would be killed in a plane crash, but when it actually happened, she'd been caught completely off guard. She would not be caught like that again.

"It's fine," she said. "I overreact sometimes. This internship is really important to me."

Josh looked relieved, but she could also tell he didn't quite believe her.

"I'm fine, I promise." She smiled to prove it. "But I have to go do some footage logging in the van."

She slid to the edge of the bed and put on her shoes.

She was so *not* fine.

Chapter Twenty-One

April heaved her backpack off her shoulders and dropped onto the nearest log. Three thousand feet of elevation gain in six miles, with a pack that weighed almost as much as her. This kind of exhaustion they did not teach in film school.

Other than the dampness in the air, it was impossible to tell it had rained in Yosemite just yesterday. The sun was shining, the sky was bright blue with puffy white clouds, and birds were chirping all around.

Theo the mountain goat had arrived long before the rest of them and had already built a safety line along the Sorcerer's spine with rappelling anchors off the far end. He dug through April's discarded pack for the rest of the equipment he had been waiting for.

"Want any help?" she asked.

He snorted in response. April put on her harness and helmet while trying not to look at the fin, which extended into the valley like a diving board of the gods.

It was all happening so fast now. Josh's practice run of the Sorcerer was in just a few days, when he would climb it with a rope and Lars belaying him. After that, the Walkabout crew would be doing a dress rehearsal with everyone except Josh. Then they'd just be waiting for a go from Josh. After the climb was done—assuming Josh survived—he'd be leaving for Utah.

Over on the end of the fin, Theo motioned for her to clip into the safety line and come join them.

From below, the Sorcerer's fin looked as thin as a knife blade. In reality it was ten feet wide, but with the sheer drops on either side that were three times as high as Flying Sheep Buttress, ten feet wide was terrifyingly narrow. The extreme exposure made her dizzy. Walking down the fin was like being drunk on a balance beam. If her boss wasn't right there watching, she would have gotten down on her hands and knees to crawl.

She reclipped her line to the anchor at the end and sat down with the guys. Theo opened his sequence board to reveal a remarkable 3-D pencil drawing of the top third of the Sorcerer. Josh's route and key moves were in bright red, and the rest of the crew and their position shifts were color coded and labeled.

"April, you'll start here," Theo said, pointing to the lower of two magenta Xs. "After Josh passes through his knee bar, you'll move up to here."

Danny had told her that she was just rappelling down to her spot and would stay there. Now she had to make a move on the rock, during filming? Her stomach heaved. Theo's words were garbled and warped as he discussed the orange Xs, which belonged to one of the contractors.

Her butt, hands, and feet were planted securely on the rock, and her daisy chain hooked in securely, but she felt no more stable than a toy top careening along the rocks. The air around her was alive, like she was inside a cloud that was sizzling with lightning.

"Ready?" Madigan asked her.

The guys already had moved over to their lines and were prepping their gear for the rappel. "You're over here," Madigan said, pointing to the line between him and Danny.

To stand took a herculean effort, and to walk the five steps to her anchor required every bit of focus she could muster. She grabbed a length of the rappel rope and pushed the Grigri gate open, but her hands were shaking too much, and it snapped closed on her fingers.

Madigan backed over the edge and waited for her. She wiped her clammy hands on her pants and tried the Grigri again, this time successfully curving the rope through the device.

"Everything look okay?" she asked.

"Yep. You've got this. It's exactly the same as Celery Slabs, just higher off the ground."

You've done this a hundred times.

But you've only known how to rappel for a few weeks, her devil's advocate replied. *The Sorcerer is not for beginners, you idiot.*

She exhaled and unclipped the daisy chain. Now her life was officially in her hands. She inched backward over the lip of the cliff. Her stomach rolled and then rolled again.

There had been no wind in the valley when they started hiking up this morning, but over the edge, it made its presence known, pushing through her clothes and finding its way beneath her helmet. It was loud and scary, exactly like a sound effect for a doomed party in a blizzard.

Her eyes were so unfocused that she could barely see, but she forced herself to keep pressure on the Grigri lever and continue her baby steps down the side of the Sorcerer. Way, way below, the loose ends of her rope skipped and waved along the rock, a taunting reminder that it was possible to rappel herself right off the ends and into oblivion.

Her body responded with a shudder, and then she thought about the cliff edge up at the top. It had been sharp. A sharp edge could sever a rope, like she'd read in the *Yosemite Deaths* book in the gift shop. She thought about Theo, and how he'd downed four pints of beer at Tall Pines last night. It was very possible he hadn't hooked up their ropes right.

At least she had a rope. How could Josh possibly be up here without one?

One wrong move will mean certain death.

Goose bumps rushed up her shins. She was falling. No, it was her dad falling. There was smoke from the engine, and he was starting to spin. Spinning wasn't part of a tail slide. Wait! Stop! Something wasn't right!

"April!" Madigan yelled.

He was just five feet below her, looking up. "You coming?"

Her eyes were wild, and she knew it.

His words from their first rappelling lesson echoed through her head. *Even if you get scared and let go, the lever snaps back and you're not going anywhere.*

She had, in fact, let go of the Grigri. Guiltily, she sneaked her hand back onto the lever.

"You okay?" he asked.

She'd let go of the Grigri, but, yes, she was okay. She nodded. Sweat was pouring off her like a fever that had broken. The fuzziness and swirling were gone.

"Just keep on going to where Danny is. He'll walk you through your positions."

Her hand was steady on the lever now. She looked straight ahead, pretending the rock in front of her was a section of Celery Slabs. She reminded herself that she'd done the whole multipitch, loose-end-rope rappel with Josh on Flying Sheep without so much as a thought other than how sexy he was.

"That's good right there," Danny said when she was next to him.

He waited for her to lock off. "This is your first spot," he said. He pointed to a hairline fracture in the glass-smooth rock, seven feet to the left. "That's Josh's route."

"There's nothing there," she said.

"Which is exactly why Josh is the only one in the world who can do it."

Josh. The guy with those vulnerable hazel eyes. The guy who was taking a correspondence course in economics and kissed really, really well.

"I want you to keep the camera on him at all times," Danny said. "Even when the angle doesn't look good. He's only doing this one time. There are no retakes. We want to document everything."

"Okay," she said.

"After he's moved through here and you get to eighty degrees, he'll be in Ernesto's camera." Danny pointed to a bulge on the other side of the fracture. "You'll want to get moving right away so you're in place in time. But don't hurry. That's how people get hurt. Let's go to your second spot."

April switched her gear and followed Danny upward. "Josh will be doing a knee bar here, and I really want that shot, especially if he goes hands-free and reaches back for his chalk."

She and Danny rappelled farther down to go over some other things with Theo. Afterward, all four of them ascended back to the top. The guys ate lunch at the end of the fin, but she needed a break from the exposure and took her food back to solid ground near their pile of backpacks. She settled onto a nice patch of grass with a boulder as a backrest.

"Mind if I join you?" Madigan asked. She hadn't realized he had followed her off the fin.

"Sure," she said, taking a bite of her PBJ.

He sat cross-legged in front of her. "I think we need to talk about what happened to your dad."

She choked on her sandwich. How did he know, and *what* did he know?

"It was such a terrible thing, and I'm so sorry for your loss."

She couldn't talk about this. Not with him, not with anyone.

"I know you were there when it happened," he continued. "Do you ever have any flashbacks or anything like that?"

She had a flashback then, but not of the crash. She saw her dad walking through the door at home in his flight suit and felt the surge of happiness that followed, from the lift of that barely perceptible worry she'd carried all day that he might not ever come through that door again. She felt the heat from the Arizona sun radiating from his flight suit as her young arms squeezed all six-foot-three, 250 pounds of him. He was her rock. Her big, strong, boisterous rock that was perched so tenuously on the edge of a cliff.

"I'm just asking because it seemed like you had a little trouble on the rappel today. I was wondering if it might be related."

It was so unfair that her job was in jeopardy because her dad decided to be a stunt pilot instead of having a normal, safe career.

"April?"

She couldn't speak.

"I'm sorry, I know this is a terrible thing to talk about, but you let go of your Grigri out there. It has a safety, but there are a thousand other things that could happen up here where there isn't a safety."

She had to find a way to answer him. If she didn't, his fears would be confirmed and he would take her off the shoot.

"I'm worried about you," he said. "You have to have your head at all times for this kind of work. Really, it's my fault. I should have asked you about this a long time ago."

She swallowed hard. Her dad was a selfish asshole jerk for putting her and her mom through this.

"It was horrible," she said, "but it's been almost three years. I've had plenty of time to process everything."

In reality, she'd *never* be able to process everything. How could she ever forget the smell of the Pitts's charred wreckage? Aircraft fuel, burning metal, and things too grotesque to acknowledge, she had smelled.

"My buddy who went to Afghanistan is still a little jumpy sometimes, and it's been eight years," he said.

"Thanks for bringing this up," she said. "It's a good reminder to control myself if I start to get nervous out there. I'm sure I'll be fine next time. I'll practice more at Celery Slabs."

"You sure? I was pretty worried about you back there."

She was still angry he had brought it up, but she also knew his concern was coming from a good place. She, of all people, knew what it was like to worry about someone.

"I'm sure. I'll be fine now that I know what it's like up here." She gave him a kind smile.

Over on the fin, Theo and Danny had finished their sandwiches and were hooking into the safety line to walk back.

"Just curious," she asked. "How did you know about my dad?"

"The internet. I do a search on anyone we're going to hire."

"Does Danny know about the crash?"

"I told him, but you know how he is when he's focused on other stuff. And it was nine months ago."

Her secret was probably safe. But was it safe from Josh, too? Thankfully, Stephens was a common last name, and with a calendar month for a first name, unless somebody had access to the kinds of personal details Madigan did from her

Walkabout application, it would be almost impossible to link her to *that* combination of April Stephens.

• • •

April put her pack in the van parked at the base of the Sorcerer. "I'm going to stay here and stretch out," she told the guys. "I'll catch the bus back."

Between the incident on the tower and Madigan's confrontation, she needed some time alone to feel stable again. She pulled out her phone, swiping to the very first picture in her photo gallery. It was a picture she'd taken a long time ago of one of the framed photographs hanging in the house in Arizona. It was of her in late elementary school, hugging one of the Mooney Rocket's propeller blades. Back then, she didn't know that everybody's dad didn't have an airplane—or five of them. She also didn't know planes could fall out of the sky.

Her smile in the picture was so happy and carefree. Would she ever get back to that place?

From the road, she took a faint trail to the base of the Sorcerer, which was fully in afternoon shadow. From this perspective, she couldn't see the tower's jagged peak until she'd craned her head so far back that her skull touched her shoulder blades. Even from the ground, looking at the heights of the tower made her feel a little queasy.

She walked to the start of Josh's Sorcerer route and put her hands on the strange black rock. It was cold and slick. Just like her father's coffin had been when the undertakers pulled it out of the air-conditioned hearse.

The coffin had just been for show, of course. But it was a good thing they did it. Even at the burial, he had an audience that packed his section of the cemetery.

Why had he tried that new sequence before he'd fully

perfected it, especially when he knew about the oil in the engine cowl? Why had he even gone up at all? How many other times had he done that type of thing?

Her father flying with a known engine problem was no different than Josh climbing the Sorcerer without rope. Who did Josh think he was? He was a mere human challenging this menacing force of nature to a duel. It was a duel he could never win, and he'd pay for it with his life.

And the lives and sanity of the people who love him.

She leaned against the frigid rock. Tears stung her eyes.

Last night in her tent, she'd watched the twenty-minute segment of Josh's first Sorcerer climb. Instead of admiring how young and adorable he was, all she could see was the terrifying magnitude of the feat. Right from the start, she knew why he hadn't wanted her to watch it. He had been reckless on the climb, to the point of being sloppy. He lunged for holds, his feet slipped off nubbins, and he took several falls that rivaled Barbara Gregory's. It had seemed like he was in an angry race to the top and he didn't care what happened to him along the way. But he'd had a rope to catch his falls then; this time he wouldn't.

Josh couldn't die. He just couldn't. She pictured his large, soft eyes, and a knot broke loose in her throat.

Madigan was right: she couldn't do this. She couldn't sit there on the side of the Sorcerer and wait for Josh to fall to his death.

She'd helplessly watched one man she loved fall to his death. There was no way she could watch a second. A human being only had the capacity to handle so much. There was an emotional trauma ward at her mother's hospital. She would end up there.

She slid down the rock and buried her face in her hands.

What if it hadn't been her dad who'd crashed that day? It would have been awful to see, but her dad would still be alive.

What if she hadn't been in the audience when it happened? The pain of losing him would still be there, but she wouldn't be nearly as physically affected by it.

Perhaps if she could get rid of one half of the equation, she might survive this. But which would it be? Caring about Josh, or filming his stunt?

Even if he survived the Sorcerer, there would always be another Sorcerer, bigger and more dangerous than the last. It was just a matter of time until he died the kind of gruesome death that was the very reason people had paralyzing phobias of heights. Besides, Josh was leaving for Utah soon, but her internship would go on in Yosemite, then she'd be in Seattle, and after that, she'd live wherever she could find a job. This thing between them wasn't going anywhere.

Film was her passion, her career, her livelihood. And the other day, Danny had hinted at the job openings Madigan had told her about. There wasn't even a choice to be made: Josh was the half of the equation that would have to go.

Tears flowed down her cheeks. She had to cut herself off from him, and she had to do it now. As it was, she only had one week to transform Josh into a stranger. One week to train herself to look at his beautiful face and feel nothing.

She hugged her legs and pressed her eyes against her kneecaps, her chest tight with her decision. The shadows were getting blacker and closing in. Cold air flowed along the ground, and she shivered.

Tomorrow she was scheduled to interview Josh in the meadow. And after, she would break it off with him.

Chapter Twenty-Two

April had to get over to the meadow quickly. Josh was due to show up any minute, and she needed to make sure they didn't end up walking over there together. The less one-on-one time they had before the interview, the less chance he'd pick up on something being wrong.

"I'm going to go set up for the interview," she said to Theo, who was sitting at the picnic table, BSing with the contractors. "Can you tell Josh to meet me out in the meadow? He knows where to go."

"No prob, Hollywood," Theo said.

She practically jogged to the meadow, trying to burn off her nervous energy on the way. It was crucial that Josh not notice anything was wrong. It was her last chance to get everything they needed for the film. After she put a halt to their relationship, he would most certainly put a halt to her interviewing him.

He walked into the meadow just as she finished setting up her equipment. Her skin bristled with every second that she held herself back from what would have otherwise been her natural reaction: running to him like in the movies. She couldn't do that, knowing the unhappy ending that was about to happen. As he got closer, she could see that he was not smiling and his face was tentative.

She couldn't stand it. She walked over to him, meeting him halfway, and squeezed him hard.

"April," he said, burying his face in her hair.

What she had to do after the interview was impossible. In this one, single way, dying was a better way to say good-bye. At least there wasn't a choice involved. At least it wasn't personal.

She wiggled out of Josh's tight grip. He grabbed her hands. "Is everything okay?"

"Yeah. Of course."

"You weren't at dinner last night, and then you didn't come out to my truck."

What was she supposed to say? She couldn't promise him nothing was wrong, just to break it off with him once the interview was over. She would be no better than a scoop-happy reporter. Not that she wasn't that already: in switching the order of the interview and the personal conversation they needed to have, she was essentially using him.

"I thought you might be upset about something," he said.

"I'm not. It's just harder to get away now that we have all the contractors here."

She rose on her toes and kissed him. She wanted to lose herself in the kiss, but she was too aware that it was their last, and her eyes filled with tears beneath her lids. She lowered off her toes, and he squeezed her like he might never let her go. Like he was sensing what she was about to do—that if he let her go, he'd lose her for good.

They walked hand in hand to the camera. He sat on his stool, and she checked her light meters and turned on the microphone.

"Are you ready?" she asked.

"Yes, but make it fast so we can get over to ice cream happy hour at the snack shop."

If only life was that simple.

She looked at him through the camera, and the sharp eye of the lens gave him away. His lighthearted comment was an act. There were faint lines at the corners of his eyes, across his forehead, and on the sides of his mouth. Worry lines. Worry lines that had probably been there all morning. He had indeed detected something was off.

She should ask him if *he* was okay, but she didn't. She needed this interview, and then she needed out. *God, I'm a terrible human being.*

"Okay, then," she said. "Here we go. First question. What initially attracted you to the Sorcerer, back when you decided to free-climb it?"

He sighed.

"What?" she asked.

"Can't we start with something easy?"

"That *was* one of the easy questions. Just remember, all you need is a short little sound bite. Just like last time."

She shifted on her stool. "So, the Sorcerer. The first time. What made you want to climb it?"

He looked exhausted, like he'd hardly slept at all last night. "April, I was young. It was impossible. That's why I did it."

"But there are other impossible routes out there. Why this one?"

"One, it's Yosemite. Two, it's a classic."

"Josh, you have to do better than that."

"Honestly, that's all there is to it."

His first Sorcerer climb was what put him into the spotlight of the international climbing community. He went from being an unknown teenage prodigy to a rock star overnight, and he hadn't disappointed yet. He would shock the world again if he succeeded in free soloing the Sorcerer. She had to have more.

"Listen. I know the gear placement is bad. It's impossibly hard. It's dangerous. There's a reason no one had been able to free-climb it before you. How did you do it? Why did you do it?"

"You watched the video, didn't you?"

"Yeah."

"It wasn't pretty, was it?"

"You were insane, Josh. I'm glad you don't climb like that anymore."

She was talking too much. This was an interview, not a conversation. "Josh, you've gotta help me out here. The sooner you give me some good answers, the sooner we can be done."

Literally.

He rubbed his temple and nodded.

"We'll come back to that question later, okay?" she said. "Tell me about the crux and how you've prepared for it."

He took a breath. "The crux is on the tenth pitch. The crack disappears and it goes to a blank-face climb. It's the longest runout I've ever seen."

"What's a runout?"

"April, are you sure you want to talk about this?"

Of course she didn't! "Yes. Please. No holding anything back."

"A runout is the distance between the protection. The gear. Like cams. When a runout is really bad--like this one— it gets an X rating. An X for death if you fell on that section."

"So it's basically free soloing?"

"In that one place. But, remember, I'm not using a rope, so for me, all of it is X for death. Except if I fall near the top, then I have the parachute."

Adrenaline burst through her body. She took a controlled breath.

"But don't worry. I've rehearsed everything a hundred times on a rope. I was here for six months last year, just working on this one route. I've been on it a lot this spring, and the moves are still there."

"Have you ever fallen on the hard parts when you practice?"

"Never."

"Will it be different when the rope's not there?"

"Of course. Those hard spots become hard on a whole different level."

"How do you handle it, mentally?"

"Once you commit, there's no going back."

"It can't be as simple as that. You've got three thousand feet below you. One wrong move…"

"It doesn't matter what's above or below. There's only what's right there in front of you."

"But how do you control your fear? Try to explain it, Josh. I have friends who won't ride in a glass elevator. How can you climb a skyscraper without a rope?"

He shrugged.

"Tell me what you feel when you look down from the side of the Sorcerer."

"I would never look down. I'm not even thinking about that when I'm up there."

She could keep pressing, but she wouldn't get anywhere. And it wasn't because Josh was being difficult. It was like asking a dolphin why it preferred to be in water. Josh was not like other people when it came to fear. It had been the same for her dad. It was almost a genetic thing, like they were born without fear. They were energized by things that would make a normal person vomit with terror.

"Okay," she said. "Let's switch gears. Why do you free solo?"

He studied her face. "April, I can tell something's wrong.

Are you okay? Are *we* okay?"

Yes, something was wrong. That *something* was that she had completely fallen for a man who was preparing to play a game of roulette with the Grim Reaper.

"This interview is really important to the film, and I just want to get through it," she said.

Josh looked beyond her to the grove of aspens. When he looked at her again, she felt the sudden presence of the shadowy cloud that often followed him.

"What was the question?" he asked.

"Why do you free solo?"

"I'm not free soloing the Sorcerer. I'm free BASEing. With a parachute."

Yeah. An unreliable, untested backup method that only works on the top third of the route.

"You know what I mean," she said. "Why do you have to push it like that?"

He was quiet while he considered his answer. "It's like I said at the gala. It's a new frontier of a skill. There's nowhere else in this world you can find that kind of peace."

Again with the western frontier comparison! Not everyone on Lewis and Clark's expedition made it back home, but at least Lewis and Clark were on an important mission. For Josh to take such a deadly risk for something ridiculous like rock climbing was totally different. Who cared if a person climbed the Sorcerer, and furthermore, what method they used to do it?

It was the same with aerobatics. Who cared if her dad did a tail slide or a beginner loop? Hardly anyone in the audience would have known the difference. Her dad couldn't stop himself from doing it, even at the risk of widowing his soul mate and abandoning the daughter who worshipped him. He hadn't deserved their devotion.

April looked at Josh, who was waiting for the next

question. His eyes rose to meet hers, and she realized that he hadn't been making direct eye contact since they started. She didn't care.

"Ten free soloists have died in the past two years," she said. "That's not very good odds, considering hardly anyone does it. The average age at death was twenty-three. Have you ever considered your family? There are people who love you. Have you thought about what it would do to them if *you* became one of the statistics?"

"Why would you ask me that?" he said. His voice was sharp.

"It's not personal, Josh. In a week, all the media who are coming here will be asking you the same thing."

"What do you mean, it's not personal?" His eyes were furious. "The only reason I'm even sitting here is because of you. You think I'd do this for Madigan or Danny? And answer questions like that for some newspaper?"

"My question is legitimate," she said. "And everyone else *will* ask."

He clearly cared only about his own selfish pursuits and didn't even have the guts to admit it. "I'd like to know, Josh," she said. "Personally."

"You don't understand."

He was seething. Good. She couldn't wait to break it off with him. He deserved it for his lack of regard for any of the people who cared about him.

"What's there to understand?" she said. "You're going to die up there. I mean, you could die. You just say 'F you' to your family and up you go?"

"You want to know the real reason I got to the top of the Sorcerer and no one else could? I didn't care what happened to me. And no one else did, either."

He deflated like a balloon, hunching onto his elbows and pressing his fingers to his palms. "My entire family disowned me the day I left home to climb."

In an instant, her anger was gone. She stopped the camera.

"In June, it will have been seven years," he said, his face twisted with the memory of something. "There, you have it. I hope you're proud. You got it out of me. No one — and I mean no one — has ever managed that. I hope Danny gives you a big bonus and you go on to do great things in the film industry."

She collapsed to her knees in front of his stool. She wrapped her arms around his waist. He pushed her away.

"I'm so sorry for what I said," she whispered.

For an eternity, he was silent.

"They got me a sports car for graduation," he said. "I traded it in for the truck. I was out in the driveway, loading up to come to Yosemite, and my dad came out and told me that if I left, I would no longer be part of his family."

Josh's body clenched. "He wasn't kidding."

April's tears flowed thick and fast.

"Brothers, sisters, nieces, nephews, aunts, uncles, cousins, second cousins," he said. "None of them will have contact with me. To them, I am already dead."

He lowered his forehead to hers and closed his eyes. She'd lost only one person, and it hadn't been by choice. His entire family was actively shunning him. She enfolded him in her arms. This time he didn't push her away. She pressed her cheek against his thigh.

The problem of the Sorcerer was still there. But knowing about Josh's family made the situation completely different. If she pulled away from him now, after he opened up to her about his family, it would be a double blow. He would be as reckless on the rock as he had been the first time he climbed it, but this time without the rope. Now, it was her career or his life, and she knew exactly what she had to do.

Chapter Twenty-Three

April was someone who could be counted on to hold up her end of the deal. She didn't back out of things she promised to do, and she'd never broken a commitment, especially not one this big.

She pushed her oatmeal around in her bowl with her spoon. Danny had adapted the entire filming plan to squeeze in a beginner, and now it would seem like she was flaking out on him. She glanced at Theo and Madigan across the table. They weren't just a coworker and a boss. They were friends, and they had spent so much time getting her ready for the Sorcerer. She felt worst of all about disappointing them.

At the end of the table, Danny took his last bite of oatmeal and walked over to the dish tub. She stood up on wobbly legs.

"Danny, can I talk to you for a minute?"

"Sure," he said. "What's up?"

"I can't film on the Sorcerer. I'm really, really, really sorry, but I just can't do it."

Danny frowned deeply, making the blood rush out of her limbs. She grabbed the table for support. Madigan looked over with alarm.

"If you don't mind me asking, why is it that you think you can't do this?" Danny asked.

"This isn't something we want to push April on," Madigan said, suddenly standing next to her. "If she doesn't feel that she can do it, that is her decision."

Danny blinked several times. "I wish I'd known you felt this way a few days ago. Your role at the top is necessary, and it's much too late to get a replacement out here."

She was frozen with fear. He couldn't fire her for not consenting to the extreme filming, but he could let her go for waiting until the last minute to back out.

"April, it's fine," Madigan said. "You're making the right choice. If you have any sort of doubt, you would be putting the whole crew in danger up there. We appreciate you were able to recognize that."

Danny looked at her. "All true. I know it was a lot to ask in the first place."

"One of my film school friends works at the climbing gym," April said. "I'm sure he knows all the rope stuff, and he's a great cinematographer. We have a whole week, I can give him a call—"

"It's looking more like three days now," Danny said.

Only three more days? Only three more days with Josh?

"The west face of the Sorcerer was protected from the rain. We looked at it again this morning. It's dry enough to climb right now."

Her throat constricted, and she could barely muster enough breath to speak. "I'm so sorry. I wish I could, I just—"

"April, really, it's fine," Madigan said.

She'd never been so humiliated. If only there was a legitimate excuse she was willing to share. It only made it worse that Madigan, in trying to help her back out, was unknowingly facilitating her secret relationship with another guy.

"There are tons of things you can help us with on the ground," Danny said. "You can go pick up Michelle at the airport first thing tomorrow morning and give her a hand with the media."

Danny rinsed his oatmeal dish. He wiped it dry with the dishcloth and put it back in the bin in the bear box. "Speaking of, I have a conference call with some of the media in a few minutes, but let's talk more when I get back."

As soon as Danny was gone, April walked toward the parking lot. Once she was sure Madigan wasn't tagging along, she swerved onto a trail in the direction that would take her to Josh's truck.

Josh was sitting in his camp chair, waiting for water to boil on his backpacking stove. His eyelids were puffy, and his hair was wild from sleep. There were pillow lines across his cheeks.

She sneaked up behind him, sliding her arms over his shoulders until her chin rested in the crook between his neck and shoulder. "You know, you'd be a lot warmer if you put your hood up."

He twisted around and kissed her. She tousled his hair and sat in the camp chair next to him.

"What are you making?" she asked.

"Grits."

"Grits?"

"They're big out in New River Gorge."

"Where's that?"

"North Carolina. Lots of southerners climb there. Want some?"

"Hmm. Instant grits? I'll pass."

"Don't get all highbrow on me, Hollywood. They stick with you longer than oatmeal. And they're not instant, by the way. You insult my camp-cooking skills."

He slid his chair closer and wrapped his arm around her

shoulder. Being here with him, she knew she had made the right decision about the Sorcerer. The humiliation of her conversation with Danny was already fading.

"I'm not going to be filming on the Sorcerer," she said.

"Why?"

Because of you. Because of my dad.

This would be the perfect moment to tell him about the crash. But he didn't even know her dad was dead. And surely if she told him *how* her dad died, it would reveal her true feelings about men who risked their lives in such a manner, especially after how she'd acted during their last interview. If her goal was to get Josh through the climb without messing with his mind space, then it was better not to tell him anything about her dad or the crash.

She cleared her throat. "I'm not going to do it because I don't feel comfortable enough with rappelling."

"You did great on Flying Sheep. Just practice some more. You'll do fine."

"No. I think it's better this way."

"I hope this doesn't have anything to do with me."

"Of course not," she said. "So what's up for today, after the grits?"

"I'm climbing the Sorcerer, top to bottom, with Lars."

"Lars can climb that route?"

"With aiders."

She pictured the young Josh from Danny's clip scrambling desperately up the black rock. It had looked like he was trying to run up a down escalator, his sheer determination being the only thing that was keeping his momentum going.

There was a rap on the side of Josh's truck. April shot up from the camp chair. It was Lars.

"Don't worry," Josh whispered. "He won't say anything."

"Morning, Lars," she said loudly. "I was just on my way back to log some footage."

She walked past him like it was no big deal to run into him at eight o'clock in the morning at Josh Knox's campsite, but Lars winked, and her subsequent blush ruined her act.

She took the long way to the Walkabout site, during which she should have been panicking about Lars discovering her and Josh, but instead she was proud they had been seen together. It made them real. Official. Something that existed outside of just the two of them. For a few days, anyway, until the Sorcerer and Josh's departure to Utah, he was hers and she was his.

• • •

There was a scratch on her tent, light but deliberate. The kind of scratch a finger might make.

She lowered the magazine photo of Josh she had been ogling through the beam of her headlamp.

"April," Josh whispered. "Are you awake?"

"Yes," she whispered back.

"Meet me at the road, okay?"

She slid slowly and silently out of her sleeping bag. She put a hat, jacket, and shoes on over her pajamas, and then unzipped the tent noiselessly.

It was surreal to be going anywhere besides the bathroom this late at night. She crept out of the campsite with her headlamp off. Not a soul was awake, and the only evidence of this evening's campfires were the glowing goals in the fire pits.

When she stepped out of the trees onto the main road, the full moon glowed white like it was laser cut from the silk of the black sky. It was so big and bright that craters were faintly visible, as if they had been sketched on the surface with pencil.

Josh was on the sidewalk on the other side of the road. The air puffed out of his down jacket as she hugged him, and she breathed in his scent mixed with the cool night air.

"I'm glad you were still awake," he said as they latched hands. He guided her into the forest, picking up the trail that led to the meadow she'd picked for his interviews.

There, the moonlight colored the pine trees inkwell blue, the grass dusky gray, and the familiar shapes of the Yosemite rock formations shadowy violet. The trunks of the white aspens shone like lanterns.

He released her hand to take off his backpack, and then stood behind her with his arms wrapped around her waist. It was perfectly silent but not silent at all, with the steady conversations of crickets and bullfrogs and the babble of a creek she hadn't realized was close by.

"It's so beautiful," she whispered.

Josh kissed her softly on the neck and pulled an MP3 player from his back pocket. Her skin tingled as he slid an earbud into her ear and then the other into his own. The song playing was quiet, but she instantly recognized it as the beautiful Jackal Legs song from the gala.

She twisted within the circle of his arms, and they danced to the music only they could hear.

"I didn't know you were so romantic," she said.

"I'm not. You're an exception."

She rested her cheek on him and closed her eyes. The rise and fall of his chest was steady and comforting.

The song faded to an end, and April slipped her hand inside Josh's pocket to restart it on the player. There wasn't anything in the world that could be more perfect than this.

They danced to the song twice more.

"Look," Josh said.

He turned her toward the open end of the meadow, and there was a bear walking across the valley in the distance. It was big, but nothing like the superbear on the campground signs, and it didn't pay them any attention. She felt no fear, only awe of the beautiful animal that was bathed in moonlight.

They watched the bear until it disappeared into an island of trees, and then Josh spread a small tarp on the meadow grass and topped it with a soft blanket. After the rain, the grass had sprung up to midthigh. When she and Josh lay on their backs to stare at the sky, the grass was like four walls around them with a blanket of stars for the ceiling.

"Vera's Yosemite was nice, but she could never recreate this," he said.

Everything about their meadow was unimaginably peaceful. How would she ever be satisfied living in a city of cement and obscured skylines after this?

"Just so you know, after the Sorcerer, I'm going to kidnap you," he said.

"Yeah?" she asked. "And where will you take me?"

"Tuolumne. Since you've never been. We'll pick up some champagne and a pizza at Smith Lodge and have a picnic at Tenaya Lake. And after that, I know a great secret camping spot near the east gate."

It sounded amazing, and it made her so sad knowing it would never happen.

"All the media are going to want to do interviews afterward, you know," she said to deflect the idea.

"When have I ever cooperated with the media?"

April rolled to her side and studied him. Lying there with Josh was just like being back at their lake, alone together in incredible vastness. She wanted to memorize this moment, how the peacefulness of the meadow reached into his face, and how his eyes were magnificent, even in the low light.

He ran his fingertips lightly across her forehead and temples, eyelids and nose. She pressed in closer, and he repeated the route with kisses so light they made her shiver. His mouth moved across hers, and he kissed her with a depth that had no end. The warmth of his lips lingered as they watched the shifting moon shadows in the meadow.

"Do you think it's weird?" he asked. "About my family?"

She thought about the picture that had fallen out of his book. There had to be thirty people in that group. "It's really extreme. I don't understand it. How everyone is playing along like robots."

"We're Italian, for starters, and they all work for my parents. When it comes down to it, I guess they'd rather have their cushy jobs than another relative."

"But, still, if you were my brother, there's no way I'd ignore you, no matter what my dad said."

She was such a hypocrite. Just yesterday she was going to break up with him for the same reason his family disowned him.

"It's not like you were leaving home to be a drug dealer or something," she said. "All you wanted was to live in your truck and climb."

He snorted. "They'd probably rather I dealt drugs. More lucrative."

April pulled the blanket tighter around them. Far in the distance, coyotes howled.

"Do you miss them?" she asked.

"I try not to." He took a breath like he was about to say more, but then he didn't. Instead, he fiddled with her jacket sleeve.

"The worst is my nieces and nephews," he said eventually. "The little ones. I used to be really close with them. They've probably forgotten I exist."

"I'm sure that's not true. If they're young, they wouldn't have the means to contact you."

"They would by now."

"Then they're probably afraid. Maybe they think *you* don't remember *them*."

"Afraid, maybe. They could be working summer jobs for

my parents. That's how everyone starts. Everyone but me. My parents always hated that I was never interested in anything but sports."

April pictured her father's stunt planes gathering dust in the hangar. She was going to have to sell the empire that had been his life's passion. Even though he was dead, it didn't make it any easier.

Josh reset his chin on her shoulder. "Sometimes, when I check messages after I've been gone a long time, I get my hopes up, but there is never anything from them. I used to try to call them, but at some point you have to have some pride about the whole thing."

That explained his melancholy the first day in the cafeteria. "Even after all these years, they still can't let it go? Don't they know how successful you've been?"

"Successful? Living in a truck is not my family's idea of successful."

"You know what I mean. Do you think they've seen any of your magazine covers or movies?"

"I don't know. I certainly hope not. Knox isn't my real last name."

"You're hiding from them?"

"April, they forced me to make a terrible choice. Of course, at the time I didn't know I was making a choice. I had no idea how literal my dad was being when he said that. Maybe it's insensitive of me, but I don't want them following the very career they disowned me for. That's the reason I hate doing interviews. Whenever I'm in front of the camera, I can't stop imagining the awful things they'd be saying if they got their hands on the finished movie. It's like I'm doing the interview live in front of all the people who betrayed me."

Poor Josh! She squeezed his hand. Even though he hadn't seen his family in years, they were still managing to make him ashamed of his greatest passion in life. No wonder he was so enigmatic in films. To protect himself, he had to guard everything personal, but to keep the sponsorships he needed, he had to live in the spotlight.

"The climbing community is my family now," he said. "They appreciate who I am *and* what I do."

She flinched.

"I just remind myself that, in a way, I've been successful *because* of my biological family," he said. "See, I was my parents' youngest child, and by the time they had me, my oldest brother already had two daughters. So I was between generations. They were all busy with their own lives, and I did whatever I wanted. If it had been any other way, I wouldn't have been able to essentially grow up at the climbing gym. I wouldn't have had the base of strength and skills to climb big stuff like the Sorcerer."

The images of young Josh scrambling up the Sorcerer's hardest sections flashed through her mind. Her mouth went dry.

"Once I left home, I had nobody," he said. "I was living for myself. I could do whatever I wanted. I took risks I shouldn't have and got lucky. I got sponsorships, and now I make enough money to climb full-time, which was my dream all along."

"You don't think you could ever reconcile with them?" she asked.

"I don't know. Even if they came around about my climbing, the damage is already done. I know their love is not unconditional."

He wrapped his arms tight around her. "That's what scares me about you," he said. "Ever since I left home, I haven't let myself get close to anyone, but I care about you too much already."

Tears wetted her eyes. It was the same for her—she hadn't gotten close to anyone new since her dad died. She valued

Josh's words like a treasure, but she couldn't let them mean anything. They implied a level of seriousness that she had no intention of returning.

"Do you ever think about after?" he asked.

"After what?"

"After this. Filming."

Yes. After filming he would go shoot his commercial in Utah, and then he would disappear back into the world of unmapped camping areas and exotic crags. Their good-bye would be difficult. Once she could stand it, she would track his progress through the internet and magazines. Maybe after a long time had passed, she would stop mourning him and she'd remember the whole thing fondly and credit it for breathing the passion back into her life.

It was getting late and very cold. She put her hat back on and folded up the blankets, which he stuffed into his backpack. Instead of putting his backpack on to leave, he took both of her hands and pulled them into his warm pockets.

After all this time in the moonlight, her vision was as clear as day. The look he was giving her reached into the farthest trenches of her soul, causing a shift—a deeper level of connection—that could not be taken back, even if she wanted it to.

"When we're done here in Yosemite," Josh said, "I don't want us to be over."

Chapter Twenty-Four

Last night, she'd lied to Josh. "I don't, either," she had said.

Technically, it wasn't a lie. She didn't *want* it to end, but that part was irrelevant. It *would* end.

I don't, either. She could have left it at that, but there was an empty space between them yawning for more, and she filled it with, "We'll find a way to make it work."

She hadn't ever been forthright with Josh about her intentions, but it seemed okay, because neither of them had brought it up directly. But now, he had opened up and told her the truth, and she had responded with a lie. A blatant, outright, dark, and malicious lie.

Now, she was somewhere in the Sierra foothills, driving to Fresno to pick up Michelle from the airport. The road was curvy, and her turns were too sharp. Everything was coming together too fast. The weather report for Friday wasn't looking good, and this morning, right before she left, Danny had told her that Josh had decided to do the climb Thursday.

That was tomorrow.

All she could hope now was that she could keep the

charade going until then, and if he survived, that he wouldn't loathe her forever when she had to disown him, just like his family had done. Maybe when she broke up with him, she would tell him about her dad. Then he would understand why his climbing career wasn't compatible with her sanity.

She could already see Josh's falling expression as she started to explain, the light fading out of his eyes and the cold wall of protection returning.

Cruel. It was horrifically cruel. *How can I do that to him?*

Her breathing bordered on hysterical. She had to get it together before she picked up Michelle. She pulled over onto a dusty turnout and followed her therapist's instructions for preempting a panic attack. She forced her breathing to slow — *in two three, out two three four five six* — and she closed her eyes and focused on the depth of the blackness behind her eyelids.

When it all seemed manageable again, she opened her eyes. She peeked at herself in the rearview mirror. Her sweaty bangs were matted to her temples, and her face was splotched with magenta. She got back on the road, rolling down the windows to blast her face dry and gulping her coffee to make up for all the hours she hadn't slept last night.

Michelle's flight arrived on time, and they were back at the campground parking lot by one.

Immediately, she knew something was wrong. The Walkabout van was already back from the dress rehearsal that should have taken all day, and everyone was standing around the open side doors. Rick was sitting on the floor inside, his leg straight out in a splint. A search-and-rescue guy was kneeling in front of him, adjusting bags of ice on his knee.

Michelle pushed through the group.

"Looks like I tore my MCL," Rick told her. "Thank god it happened in the first mile."

"One of the search-and-rescue trainees is going to drive

him down to the clinic in Mariposa," Danny said to Michelle. "He'll probably need surgery."

Theo was sitting on the van's bumper, frowning at the sequence boards. The team was already spread thin without her. Now, without Rick, they'd be screwed tomorrow.

"Do you think we could get Mario on a plane if we called him right now?" Michelle asked.

"He's in Australia," Danny said.

"What about Remy?"

"He doesn't do heights."

"What about *Vertical View*? They're going to film their interview today, couldn't they send their guy up?"

"It's probably just a writer with a camcorder," Danny said. "Madigan's already called around to the media we know."

"Couldn't Josh wait?" Michelle asked.

"If he's going to climb it tomorrow, it's not our place to stop him," Danny said. "And especially not because we couldn't keep our cameras staffed. We're just going to have to figure out something else."

April was still hanging back, fully aware that the demise of the shoot was her fault, for getting involved with Josh.

She stepped forward. "I can do it."

Silence hung over the group until Theo popped his head around the back of the van. "That would be great. We need you."

"April, you don't need to save us," Danny said. "This is my bad for not hiring more crew. We have the budget for it this time, too. I'm just so used to operating on a shoestring."

"I really think I can do it," she said. "I'll be fine."

Danny was clearly relieved. "Well, if you think you're up to it—"

"No," Madigan said. "You cannot put her in a situation where she's uncomfortable. It's a risk to her and the whole crew."

Danny looked at April.

"I can do it, really," she said. "I need to practice this afternoon, but I know I'll be fine."

"Madigan, do you think you can go with her and—"

"No. I have to haul gear," Madigan said.

"Someone else can do that."

"It was just two days ago she said she couldn't do it," he said. "If I were you, I'd be asking why."

He wouldn't dare bring up her dad in front of all these people.

"*I'll* help you," Theo said. "We'll work over at Celery Slabs until you're feeling good."

"This is not okay," Madigan said.

"She'll be fine," Theo argued. "She'd be fine even if she didn't practice today. And I can work it so she won't have to shift positions. She'll just rap to the highest spot and stay there until Josh tops out. Easy as pie."

"Fantastic," Danny said.

"No," Madigan said. "This is not fantastic."

"You're making a real ass of yourself, Madigan," Danny said. "This is her call, not yours."

Madigan yanked his backpack off the ground. "I refuse to be a part of this." He spun toward April. "If you're going to go ahead with this, you better be bombproof sure you can handle it and not get someone killed."

He heaved the pack around to his back and took off toward the main road.

"Madigan!" Danny yelled.

Madigan kept walking.

"April, I apologize for him," Danny said. "He was way out of line. I've never seen him overreact like that."

"It's fine," she said. "I'm going to go change. I'll be back in a few, Theo."

· · ·

Theo set his pack down at the same section of Celery Slabs that she had climbed before.

"We need to have a chat," he said.

"What about?" she asked, a little concerned.

"I'll just put it this way. I've seen you show up in camp with chalk on your face several times now, and I don't think it's because you've taken up rock climbing."

She stared at him.

"Normally our buddy Madigan would be the one to say this, but in case you haven't noticed, he has quite a thing for you, and I don't think he's aware of what's going on."

Theo, of all people, had noticed her and Josh?

"Now, don't get me wrong," he continued. "I've never been one to follow a rule if I could get away with breaking it, and your secret's safe with me, but filming a climber doing something like this is hard enough. To be—ahem—*seeing* him takes it to a new level. I just want to make sure you're cool with it."

"Don't worry," she said. "I'm totally cool with it."

"Okay, good. I thought so, but I would have felt bad if I didn't check. Congratulations, by the way."

"For what?"

"For bagging one of the best climbers in the world. He's hot, too. Makes me wish I was a woman. Or gay. Score one for Walkabout Media & Productions. *Yee-ahh!*" He high-fived her.

Crisis averted, for now.

"Don't worry about Madigan's tizzy earlier. He just wants to protect you. He's like that. But you'll do great up there. You picked this up quickly, and your skills are solid."

He started pulling gear from his pack. It was a good thing Madigan and Theo had never discussed what they each individually knew about her. If they had, they would have her complete story, and there would be no doubt about whether she should be filming tomorrow.

• • •

True to his word, Madigan stayed away from Celery Slabs, but he appeared in Sorcerer Meadow before dinner for the ground rehearsal of the revised filming choreography.

"I'm sorry about earlier," he said to April. "I was very concerned about you doing this. I still am."

"I did great with Theo today," she said.

"I've never questioned your technical abilities."

"If it makes you feel better, Ernesto's going to rappel with me to my spot, and he'll pick me up on the way back up. All I have to do is sit in my harness and run the camera. Hopefully you're not worried about that part."

"April, this is serious. I know you're just doing it because you don't want to let the team down. But I saw what happened to you up there, and I don't think you're ready. I was hoping you'd come around, but since you haven't, I feel like I have an obligation to say something to Danny."

"No, please don't!"

Danny looked up from the sequence board he was analyzing with Theo. "Everything okay over there?" he yelled.

"Yes, fine!" April said.

She had to stop Madigan from talking to Danny. Josh already knew she was back on for filming. If Danny yanked her off the crew because of her dad and word got back to Josh about it…she didn't even want to think about that.

"Listen," she whispered to Madigan. "I backed out because I was afraid. You're right, the thing with my dad has had a terrible effect on me. I'm afraid of everything. After we had our talk on the Sorcerer, I completely chickened out inside. My confidence in myself was gone. But I was so ashamed when I told Danny I couldn't do it, I wished I could take it back. Today, I had that opportunity. I'm not doing this for the crew—I'm doing this for *me*. It will be hard, but I *know* I can do it. Please don't take that away from me."

The lies were coming so easily now.

Madigan stared across the meadow. "Okay," he finally said. "But just know that it's perfectly fine if you change your mind at the last minute."

Vera, who was sitting in a camp chair on the edge of the meadow with Gabby, waved her hand at April. April jogged over, relieved for the excuse to get away from Madigan.

"I hope I'm not interrupting anything," Vera said.

"No, we haven't started yet."

"I'm taking Josh out to dinner tonight. He'd like you to come along."

"Me?" she asked, plastering a surprised look across her face.

Theo whistled for the crew to gather in. "Uh, I've got to get over there. I won't be able to come tonight. I have dinner duty back at camp."

She jogged over to Theo's huddle. The best scenario with Josh in this situation was that she wouldn't see him again until he passed through her camera lens at the top of the Sorcerer tomorrow. Him not being at the Walkabout site for dinner was great news. With all the stuff happening today, there would be no reason he'd be alarmed by not seeing her, and he could embark on his climb on the high note of their conversation in the meadow last night.

After the ground run was over, they all walked back to the van, past the cluster of media still waiting to interview Josh. Michelle was with a few producers, jotting a note on a clipboard. She waved to them.

Josh himself was standing in front of a cameraman and

a well-dressed female reporter, in a spot where the fearsome Sorcerer loomed above the trees in the background. His shoulders were tense and his eyes as dark as the tower's black rock.

As they passed behind the cameraman, Josh stopped talking and his eyes followed April. Vera gave her a pointed look.

The reporter's voice drifted their way. "What do you think it would feel like if you fell?"

April winced. She should have been there with him. Protecting him from all those reporters, or at least giving him confidence in front of the camera.

"Are you sure you don't want to join us tonight?" Vera asked.

April glanced back at Josh, who looked like he was ready to bolt from the interview. She hated that he was spending what could be the last hours of his life doing the one thing he hated most.

"I'd really like to," she replied to Vera, "but I have to be up at four thirty to hike up the Sorcerer."

Vera stopped at her SUV, where a driver was waiting. She slid into the passenger seat. "I understand." She grabbed April's hands and gave them a quick squeeze. "Good luck tomorrow. I think you're very brave to film up there, and I'm so glad it was you who Danny hired for this film."

• • •

April stared into the campfire. The reds and yellows and blues swayed with the invisible wind of combustion. She was hyperaware of the time, her chest getting tighter with each passing hour.

It was eight o'clock now, which meant there were only twelve hours left until Josh started the climb.

A log cracked and slipped into the center of the fire. Her hand jerked, sloshing beer across her feet. Embers from the cracked log sprayed out of the fire pit, then floated over the crowd like fireflies, going dark one by one.

It was the tallest fire and the biggest crowd the Walkabout site had ever seen. It seemed the whole campground was there, along with every member of search and rescue. With the many conversations tumbling over one another, Madigan, who was standing next to her, hadn't noticed how quiet she was. Although the campfire had turned into an unofficial good-luck-tomorrow party for Josh, Josh himself was absent.

And then he wasn't.

He was across the campfire, sweatshirt on with the hood up. His face glowed yellow and warm in the reflection of the flames. He made eye contact with her.

"I'm going to get more beer," Madigan asked. "Want a refill?"

"I'll come, too," she said.

"I've got it. Stay here to hold our spot."

"It's our campfire!" she said, but he had already disappeared through the crowd.

Across the fire ring, Josh had disappeared, too.

A pair of large, strong hands landed on her shoulders and massaged her a few times.

No! Not right here in public!

Josh leaned in, his hood brushing along her jaw. "I'm going back," he whispered. "Come meet me, okay?"

He squeezed her shoulders once more, and then he was gone.

Shit.

She wouldn't go. She'd tell him later that she couldn't get away. But when would she do that? As he climbed past her on the Sorcerer? Assuming he made it that far.

Madigan returned and handed her a beer. She didn't want

it, but it gave her fidgety hands something to hold on to.

She'd been nervous like this the night before her dad died, but it was because the next day, at the air show after-party, she was going to tell him she had been accepted, starting junior year, to the bachelor of arts in film program. This would reveal the truth that her career plans after college had nothing to do with airplanes.

She looked at her watch. Eleven hours and thirty minutes until the climb. Josh would be back at his campsite by now. Soon, he would be wondering where she was.

Her stomach tightened. No. She couldn't let that happen. She had to get to him before he figured out something was wrong.

"I'm going to go to bed," she announced to Madigan.

She didn't bother faking a trip to the bathroom, instead heading straight through the woods to the search-and-rescue camp.

Chapter Twenty-Five

Josh's campsite was dark and still.

"Over here," he whispered.

He stood up from the hammock. She collapsed into his arms. The protective shell she'd built during the day disintegrated.

If only he wasn't climbing the Sorcerer tomorrow. If only he had been born satisfied with team sports and video games.

But then he wouldn't be Josh.

He held her tightly, resting his chin on the top of her head. "I missed you like crazy today."

She would miss him for the rest of her life.

"You're shaking," he said. "Let's go in my truck. It's warmer."

She wasn't shaking because she was cold. She was shaking because she was petrified.

They took off their shoes and crawled across the tailgate into his truck. He closed the back and cracked the side windows. The crisp night air flowed in, mixing with the scents of chalk, metal climbing gear, ropes, and fabric softener.

With the curtains drawn, it was too dark to see. She heard Josh take off his jacket and crawl under the blankets. She did the same.

His hands felt for her waist, and he pulled her to him, giving her a sense of what it was like to be a climbing hold beneath his powerful grip.

"How are you feeling about tomorrow?" he asked.

"*Me?* How are *you* feeling about it?"

"April, don't underestimate what you're doing. It's really high up there. Most people couldn't do that. Especially considering that you and I—"

"Don't worry about me," she said. "I practiced with Theo today. You just focus on the climb."

"I'm sure you'll be fine," he said. "I just wish I could be right there with you."

You will be, she thought, clenching her muscles to prevent her body from shuddering.

She scooted closer and rested her forehead against his. His eyebrows were tense. "How are *you* feeling about tomorrow?" she asked.

"I'm just looking forward to having you all to myself afterward. You're going to love Tuolumne."

"Stop it, Josh, really."

"To be honest, I'd be a lot happier right now if the climb was already done."

Her veins ticked nervously. "I'm sure that's normal for the night before."

"Not at all."

Her insides locked up with horror. "You don't have to do it. Our film, all the media—we don't matter. No one will be mad if you change your mind."

His fingers twisted her watchband slowly around her wrist. "I know. But I'm still going to do it. I just have to stop thinking about it so much."

He tucked his forehead into her collarbone. His hair smelled faintly of campfire smoke. "It's all about the feeling. The lack of feeling. How everything falls away and it's just me and the rock. It's been harder for me to get there lately."

His words lingered across her neck. When the heat faded, she was chilled to the bone. She could not lose him.

She ran her hands slowly up his arms and across his chest, wanting to memorize every detail. How the skin on the inside of his bicep was baby soft and warm despite the granite hardness beneath it, and how the intricate muscles of his forearm danced against her shoulder every time he touched her face.

She laid her hand over his, tracing his fingers one at a time. He was right there with her, but still, she ached for him. How would she muster enough willpower to go back to the campsite tonight?

He closed his callused hand around hers and lowered the knot of their hands to the tight, safe place between their bodies.

"Will you stay with me tonight?" he asked, his voice tinged with desperation.

Was it possible he was as scared as she was?

"Please," he whispered.

"Okay," she said. "But we need to get to sleep. It's already late."

His shoulders relaxed. "Deal." He kissed her and then sat up. "I'll find you some clothes to wear."

He dug through a bin at the foot of his mattress and handed her a pair of warm-up pants and a T-shirt. Her eyes had adjusted enough to make out the big white Esplanade logo against the fabric of the T-shirt. She squinted. The *red* fabric of the T-shirt from the first interview.

She sat up and pulled her sweater off. "You're making me wear the problem shirt?"

"Consider it payback."

She laughed, but she was also aware that Josh had removed his shirt. The moon had slid out from behind the clouds, and there was enough light now to clearly see the smooth, clean skin of his upper body as he unzipped his pants. She couldn't keep her eyes off him. He looked over at her and suddenly she was too shy for the simple task of unbuttoning her shirt and replacing it with his T-shirt.

She fingered her top button, struggling to pop it free. As she reached for the second, Josh moved closer to her, his fingers slowly sliding the second button through the hole. He exhaled as he felt for the next button, his warm breath flowing down her open shirt and making her heart beat wildly.

His mouth moved onto hers as his fingers felt for the fourth button. The rest of the buttons were a blur, and she was only vaguely aware of him pulling the shirt off her shoulders and freeing her arms. She ran her hands over his bare stomach and up to his chest, where his heart was racing like hers. She spread her fingers across his chest and dragged them back down to his impossibly hard abs, where she followed the thin line of fine hair down to his partially open pants.

He yanked her back to him, and they collapsed onto the mattress. Their mouths collided, hot and deep, as she coaxed his pants off. He unzipped her jeans, and she wiggled out of them without their lips ever losing contact.

She'd thought she'd been consumed by him before, but she had been wrong. *This* was consumed. She was absolutely no longer in control of her own body.

His tongue pushed farther into her mouth as she cut her bare legs between his. Josh's hands were everywhere, pulling her tighter, tighter to him. Still, it wasn't tight enough. She twisted her legs around his body. His hips pressed into her urgently, and she could feel that he was hard.

"Do you have condoms?" she whispered.

His breaths were shallow and fast. "I think so."

He rose up to his knees and felt along the canopy's high shelf. Her body trembled without his touch. She pulled the blankets around her to stay warm.

Josh riffled through a tackle box on the shelf and then looked inside an old coffee can. "Sorry," he said. "Let me check one more place."

He stretched over her, reaching through the back windows and pulling out a shower kit. As long as he was eventually successful, his difficulty finding a condom was strangely reassuring, a confirmation that this sort of thing didn't happen very often.

He unzipped the shower kit and another compartment inside it. Then, she heard the opening of a new cardboard box and the crinkle of a wrapper.

Was she really going to do this? And on the night before the Sorcerer?

He pulled the blankets back, his eyes skimming over her naked body. "You are so beautiful," he whispered. Then he placed his hands at her waist and kissed her in the middle of her stomach. Embers flared deep in her body.

"Are you sure about this?" he asked.

"Yes," she said. No matter what happened tomorrow — or after — she wanted to connect with him in this final, important way.

"I want you to know, this is a big deal for me."

She let herself get lost in his eyes, which were dark with the night. "It is for me, too."

He kissed her with a tenderness that turned her bones to liquid. Then he threaded his fingers with hers and slowly, carefully pushed inside her. The world spun, this time in blacks and grays. She was overcome with the sensations of Josh around her, over her, inside her. Nothing else existed but them, together.

· · ·

Slowly their surroundings came back into focus. April shivered as a chilly breeze grazed her damp skin, and Josh pulled his blankets over them. She rested her head on his arm and watched the bottoms of the curtains flutter in the night air. Outside, the crickets and frogs droned on, muted by the occasional rise and fall of the wind through the trees.

Josh twisted a lock of her hair between his fingers. "April?"

"Hmm?"

"Remember when you asked me why I free solo?"

She nodded.

"Do you remember what I said?"

"You said it was for the peace."

"Well, there's somewhere else I've found it." He swallowed. "You."

Her heart surged, and tears sprang up in her eyes. To be here in his truck, under his blankets, with his lungs expanding and contracting against her—it was all she needed in this world. She wrapped her body around him and clung to him like a buoy at sea.

· · ·

April's eyes popped open. She was filled with the lingering dread of nightmares she couldn't remember.

She looked at her watch. It was two thirty a.m. on Thursday.

This was the day Josh was going to die.

Chapter Twenty-Six

April silenced her alarm at 4:05 a.m., ten minutes before it was supposed to go off. She was already awake because she had never been able to fall back asleep.

She carefully detangled herself from Josh. The plywood creaked as she sat up. Josh murmured and rolled over. She froze, and then relaxed, seeing that he was still fast asleep. He looked so vulnerable, so human, lying there. So unlike the superathlete who was about to attempt the impossible.

She wanted him to wake up so she could tell him that she was scared. She wanted him to assure her everything would be fine, even if it wouldn't be.

Instead, she leaned down and kissed him ever so softly on the temple.

Good-bye, Josh.

He stirred and reached for her.

"April," he said groggily, "don't go."

"I have to. It's time to get on the trail." The effort to make her voice sound casual was gargantuan. "I'll see you at the top, okay?"

He closed his eyes like he'd fallen back asleep, but when she scooted toward the tailgate, his grip on her hand tightened and he pulled her back.

"What I'm doing today is risky. Just in case anything happens—"

"It won't. I know it. You're going to do awesome."

"Listen," he said in a voice still heavy with sleep. "There are two things that I want to tell you. The first is that my real last name is DeVincenzi."

"Josh—"

He cupped her face between his hands and looked directly into her eyes. "The second is that I love you."

April let him kiss her and then lingered in his embrace for the count of fifteen.

"I gotta go," she whispered, and then slipped from his grasp.

. . .

The shock—physical and mental—hit as she slid off the tailgate.

Her hands were like blocks of cement as she struggled to put her shoes on. The panic raging through her body made her feel like she was being pummeled with stones, like there was cellophane plastered against her nose and mouth, making it impossible to breathe.

She rushed through the dark forest back to the Walkabout site. Spiderwebs broke across her face and thorny branches clawed at her hair. She dodged a swooping bat and sideswiped a tree trunk. Her toe hooked on an unyielding root, throwing her to the rocky ground. She staggered to her feet and kept running.

Madigan was right. She was in no way stable enough to film on the Sorcerer, but she was going to do it anyway.

Chapter Twenty-Seven

The Sorcerer hike was ruthless, but she didn't care. She wanted the pain.

"Excuse me, guys," April said as she squeezed past Ernesto and Russell on the trail.

She pushed her legs until she was practically running. The dew-covered ferns and the tree-striped blackness jiggled in the narrow beam of her headlamp. Her skin was hot and swampy beneath her clothes, but her bare arms were goose-bump cold in her self-generated wind.

The gap between her and the guys widened quickly. Now her own breath was the only thing she could hear, heavy and loud as she pushed up the elevation.

She turned onto a switchback, and the trail steepened into rail-tie stairs. Her pack was fully loaded, and there was an extra fifteen pounds of rope on top that she'd volunteered to carry. Her thighs wobbled under the exertion at each stair. She pushed harder, welcoming the misery.

Her radio earpiece crackled.

Danny: "Just checked the weather. We're clear until

tonight."

The closer she got to the top, the more frequently the reports came in.

Theo: "On top."

Danny: "At the base with Madigan."

Michelle: "Josh is awake. Eating breakfast."

At the top, April wasted no time switching into dry clothes and putting on her harness. Below, she could see Ernesto and Russell's headlamps just entering the talus field. They still had a long way to go.

She walked directly to the end of the fin, recklessly forgoing the safety line until she got to the anchors at the end. Theo had already rappelled down to check everything out. She sat and waited for him to come back up.

The sky across the valley was alive with magentas and purples. The main road below was empty, and the meadow where Michelle soon would be with all the media cameras was still and pristine.

It was a glimpse of the valley as it had been centuries ago, before lodges and tour buses and 1.5 million visitors a year. Surely, in this kind of beauty, Josh couldn't fall.

April hugged her knees. When he told her he loved her, she hadn't said it back. With all her lies and misleading, couldn't she have just returned the sentiment? He'd opened his heart to her, and she'd left him with silence.

If only she'd been able to think of him instead of herself in the moment. If he did fall, at least he would die thinking that she loved him. Then, this morning, at the base of this terrifying spire, he'd be embarking on his great feat in the glow of the knowledge that the girl waiting for him at the top loved him, too.

He'd been half asleep when she'd left his truck, but now that he was awake, he would be fully conscious of what she *hadn't* said. Her silence would invade the very psyche he was depending on to be quiet and blank.

Her father would be so ashamed of her. Instead of boldly breaking the rules and embracing the consequences, she'd waded in so slowly that she didn't realize she wasn't testing the waters until she could no longer touch the bottom. Once there, instead of making a decision and sticking to it, she'd betrayed everyone she cared about, sneaking behind their backs, keeping secrets that could hurt them gravely, all in the name of crafting the safest version of life for herself.

She'd taken all of the rewards but none of risk. Her father's definition of a coward.

Michelle: "Heading to the van with Josh."

Go back! she wanted to scream through the radio. *Go back to your truck, Josh. Tell them you've changed your mind.*

Russell: "Four of us up on top now."

April spun around. Russell and Ernesto were taking off their packs. *Pull yourself together. Don't be weird.* She transferred her daisy chain onto the safety line and walked off the fin.

"How was the hike?" she asked them.

Russell ran his hand across his forehead, flicking a huge spray of sweat across the rocks next to him. "Do you even have to ask?"

She forced a laugh. "Danny should give us bonuses every time we have to come up here."

Ernesto snorted. "Or at least free dinner. And somewhere other than the campground."

Danny: "Josh at the base."

April stretched her stiff arms and legs. They had several hours before Josh would be near the top, but they would be getting in place soon, so as not to accidentally push any rocks down on him while he was climbing.

Madigan: "I'm anchored in at position two."

Theo: "Ropes are all looking good, I'm heading back up."

She, Russell, and Ernesto met Theo out on the end of the fin for a briefing. When it was time to go down, the steps of rappelling off the edge that had once required so much focus came automatically to her. Ernesto was keeping an eye on her, as per Theo's instructions, escorting her on the short rappel to her fixed spot on the wall.

"I'll be leapfrogging past you to get set up on top once Josh is done farther below. You'll film from here until he's all the way over the top," Ernesto said. "Then I'll go back down so we can come back up together."

"Okay," she said, and he continued down.

April carefully pulled the camera out of her backpack and clipped its tether to her rope.

Danny: "Josh is ready. Is everyone set?"

She looked through the camera and zoomed in at the ground below. Media vans now lined both shoulders of the road, and a crowd of camera crews and onlookers with telescopes and binoculars were clustered in the meadow. A Park Service SUV idled on the road with its lights on while a pair of rangers directed cars though the bottleneck.

Danny: "Hands on rock. We're a go."

She turned the camera off and rested it on her thighs. She shifted her feet and settled into her heavily padded harness seat. The one benefit of the Sorcerer being so steep was that Russell was the only member of the crew she could see. Everything that was going on in the reports might as well be happening across the country. At least that's what she would pretend.

Madigan: "I've got it on two."

Danny: "Filming done on one."

April's stomach did a flip. Josh was now too high to change his mind and down climb, and until position six, he wouldn't be high enough for his parachute to work if he fell.

"He will be fine," she whispered. *He will be fine. He will be fine. He will be fine.*

The radio reports were flowing in fast now, reflecting Josh's speed on the climb. She wasn't sure if this was good or bad. *He'll be fine. He'll be fine. He'll be fine.*

Across the valley, the sun peeked over the rim next to a waterfall that she could hear whenever there was a lull in the breeze. Hawks circled in the air below her.

Danny: "Filming on five."

Five! She might be able to see Josh now.

Do not look down. He will be fine. He will be—

She looked down.

She *could* see him. The top of his unhelmeted head and the red hump of his parachute backpack were the size of an asterisk—too small and abstract to induce panic just yet. She could just make out Theo, too, moving up to film at his highest point. Over to the side, Ernesto was ascending to a position between Theo and Russell.

She was supposed to start filming once Josh passed Ernesto's second position. She turned her camera on and rehearsed her pan at the speed Josh seemed to be climbing, and then played it back in the viewfinder. Her hands had been shaking so badly that none of the footage would have been usable if it had been the real thing. And that had been with blank rock with no one on it. How would she do when the guy who loved her was in the frame without a rope?

She shifted her legs and repositioned the camera. Zooming in, she could see hands and arms, and the peach color of his face.

Even from this distance, he was not the invincible Josh from multiple covers of *Vertical View* magazine but the Josh she'd been with last night. The Josh who had taken her hand on the slackline and the Josh who'd danced with her so tenderly in fake Yosemite and again in the meadow just below them. The Josh she'd do anything for, in exchange for him surviving this feat.

Except tell him that she loved him.

The height seized her. She gasped and grabbed the rope. Looking down, she made sure her harness was doubled back and checked the rope's path through the Grigri. Her mind drew a sudden blank on how it was supposed to look. She checked her ascenders, too. Without the stoppers hooked right, the slightest movement could undo the ratchets and send her sliding off the ends of the rope.

He'll be fine. He'll be fine. You'll be fine. You'll be fine.

Her right foot slipped off the wall, making her shoulder slam into the rock. She stifled a scream and reached frantically for the camera. Thankfully, it had been pinned safely between her thigh and stomach.

She took a breath of relief, but her eyes still felt wild, like they were rolling in their sockets. Think what could have happened if that scream had escaped and Josh heard it! *Get a grip. Get a grip. Get a grip.*

April closed her eyes and forced herself to exhale every ounce of old air, all the way down to the lowest lobes of her lungs, until her rib cage was a sucking vacuum screaming for more oxygen. She held off for a full count of ten longer, until the pain overrode any other thought or fear. Only then did she let the new air flow in.

Russell: "Rolling on seven."

She opened her eyes. It was time for her to start filming.

This time when she looked down, she could see the silhouette of Josh's windblown hair and the point of his nose. She could also see the color of his shirt. Bright orange. It was the same bright orange shirt he'd worn to dinner at Tall Pines, when he'd stealthily wrapped his ankles around hers beneath the picnic table.

She raised the camera and hit the record button. Nothing happened. She pressed it again. Still nothing. This could not happen, not right now, of all times. She was fully hyperventilating.

She flipped to the control panel, trying to visualize the troubleshooting table in the front of the camera's technical manual.

What are the symptoms? Viewfinder black. Error light on. The lens cap.

She felt the front of the camera. The lens cap was on. Damn it! She refocused on Josh. "Rolling on eight," she said into her earpiece.

Below, Josh released a hand from the rock and dipped it behind him into his chalk bag. As he drew it out, a white cloud billowed like ashes behind him and into the vast air below. A shiver coursed through April's body, making the camera shake.

This was important footage for the film, and she was a professional. There could be no more shaky hands or rookie mistakes. She steadied the camera and zoomed in to the stops. The extra ten degrees gave her Josh's face, his forehead wrinkled as he scanned the rock above him. He slid his hand into the crack like a knife.

She kept the camera in place but looked away as he shifted his weight onto his hand. Her heart beat out of her chest. *He chose to do this. There's nothing you can do to help him now.* All she could do was to wipe the terror off her face before Josh reached her position.

She refocused the camera on Josh. His hair was wet with sweat, and he was definitely peaked. His heels were jackhammering—delicately, barely perceptibly, but jackhammering. Not good. She told herself it didn't matter. He would be fine.

He was so close to the top now. The hardest parts were behind him, and he was high enough that the parachute might be able to catch him if he fell. It was possible he might actually survive this. In a half hour, she could be throwing her arms around him at the top.

He was getting closer and closer to her, so close that she was now getting the footage that would be used in the film. She panned out at the same rate Josh was climbing until she was zeroed out. In minutes, he would be passing by close enough to touch. He was *almost* there.

Now, she had a clear view of his face, which was not marked by the indifferent coolness of every other climbing video of him she'd seen. His placements were solid, but his soft eyes were clouded with exhaustion. His words echoed in her ears: *I love you.*

The balls of his feet were smeared on invisibly small protrusions. His left fingers were clamped against a rounded corner while he reached up to jam his right fingers in a shallow crack. As he did, sand flowed out of it like a waterfall.

Beads of sweat popped up on Josh's forehead. He blew the sand off the rock in front of him that would be his footholds on the next move. He reached up and situated his hand in the crack again.

There was a grinding of rock against rock, and then a sickening crunch.

Josh blinked, and then his hand flew out of the crack along with a plate of granite that sliced though the air before shattering against the side of the cliff.

"Rock!" Josh yelled. He lunged to regrip, but as he did, his feet lost contact with the wall. In terrible slow motion, he was sliding down, clawing at the rock. Then, the friction gave out, and he was plummeting through the air.

Chapter Twenty-Eight

"Noooooooo!" April screamed.

Her mother grabbed her. "Shh! It's a new trick."

Someone in the crowd snickered, but the nose-diving black biplane was falling faster and faster, closing in on the red line, and her dad wasn't pulling out.

A cloud of thick black of smoke flowed out of the Pitts.

Nooooooooo! she screamed, this time silently in her head.

He still wasn't pulling out and he was almost out of altitude. He had to pull out now, *right now*!

The crowd was impressed, holding a collective breath as the plane began to tumble tail over nose. A few people gasped in awe. But this was no bonus maneuver. It was the result of the unbalanced aerodynamics in her dad's desperate attempt to get the engine going.

Slow motion hit. The Pitts was plummeting toward the ground. April was shrieking hysterically.

The crowd caught on as the plane veered toward the grandstand with no sign of slowing. The shrill scream of a woman high in the bleachers joined April first, then a dozen others, their screams uniting into the unrecoverable mark of a banshee.

The whole place erupted in chaos. People stampeded to get out of the stands, running frantically in all directions. Parents flung themselves in front of their children.

She knew the plane would land close but not in the stands, and thus, stood frozen in the milieu, watching the Pitts's whistling descent.

Even as the plane flowed vertically past the control tower, her father was trying to restart the engine.

It was so big up close. She'd never been this near to the Pitts when it was in motion. It was such a beautiful plane.

In an instant, it was a tangle of crumpled metal with flames exploding from it.

April hurdled over the fence and sprinted with the fire trucks across the runway.

Two uniformed men caught her just before she reached the wreckage. They turned inward and redoubled their grip as she strained against them, the force slamming her down to the tar-covered pavement.

She didn't want to see what was in front of her, but she couldn't look away.

The Pitts was a sphere of rolling flames spewing smoke so black and heavy it sank to the runway like octopus ink before rising up in a column. The erratic wind parted the smoke just long enough to get a glimpse of something familiar before the heat blasted the air into a shimmering mirage and the smoke rushed back in.

A disembodied propeller blade, the melted logo, a wing tip curled in on itself.

Her throat was scalding, and she was choking on the vile avgas fumes, but she couldn't stop screaming. A third man clamped down on her and started pulling.

"It's going to explode, ma'am, you've gotta get back," he

yelled.

They were dragging her away. But Dad! She had to wait for her dad! The smoke would open and he'd walk out. He'd be laughing. The joke would be on them. It was all part of the show.

She dug her heels in and threw her body toward the flames where the smoke was even thicker. She was coughing hard. She couldn't breathe. She vomited on her captors and then everything went black.

Chapter Twenty-Nine

She was in a harness, slumped over, with her helmet resting against the rope that was holding her in the air. Down on the ground, SUVs with revolving lights were everywhere, their sirens muted in the terrifying vertical distance between her and them. The pounding of helicopter blades echoed off the black rock from somewhere below.

"April!" Madigan yelled into her earpiece.

Her mind was blank. All sensations were numb. What did he want?

Josh.

He'd fallen.

She was still clutching the camera. It slipped out of her hands. She grabbed the rope. The camera jerked when it reached the end of its tether, then dangled like a pendulum.

"April!" Madigan yelled.

She swallowed hard and felt for the radio. "I'm here."

"Thank god!" Madigan said. "Don't move, Ernesto's almost there."

Josh—he was gone. Josh was gone forever.

And she'd had a direct hand in it all. Her peripheral vision turned fuzzy and started closing in.

Ernesto was suddenly next to her, gripping her shoulder. "Let's get up to the top, okay?"

She pulled the camera back up. It was still rolling. It had recorded everything. She wanted to tear it off the leash and throw it into the depths that had claimed Josh.

She switched her gear and started ascending. Far below, the helicopter lifted off and flew away.

Josh's family wouldn't be at the funeral, but she would be. Even if his hands were crushed and soft like Play-doh, or stiff with death, she would hold them one more time. She would kiss his cold lips and smooth his wild hair. And once he was buried, she would stand vigil six feet above him. He would not spend his first night in the ground alone.

Once they were off the fin, Ernesto put on his pack and waited for her to do the same.

"Go ahead," she said. "I need a minute before I go down."

"I'll wait—"

"Please. Go."

Reluctantly, he left. As soon as he was out of sight, she sat on the ground and tore into her backpack for the things Josh had asked her to bring to the top: his gray hooded sweatshirt, a change of clothes, a water bottle.

She put on his sweatshirt and bunched his clothes into a pile to wrap herself around. She inhaled deeply, trying to breathe him back to life within her by his familiar smell.

This, right now, was so much different than three years ago, mainly because she herself had not been injured as a result of the accident and, therefore, had not awakened in a hospital where she had immediate access to sedatives that made the pain disappear.

But in one way it was exactly the same: it was the long slide down into gaping chasm of hell that was the permanent, irrevocable loss of someone she loved.

Because, yes, she *loved* Josh.

She loved his crinkly hazel eyes, the intense caring that filled his soul, and how just being in his presence made it feel like his arms were around her. That lopsided, sheepish smile of his! The way he twirled his highlighter between his fingers when his textbook passages turned boring. That gray hood, always up in public, hiding his rumpled hair. She loved everything about him.

Tears ran down her face. Sobs broke loose, and then she was falling, just like he had.

Madigan was talking to her in the radio again, but she couldn't move. She didn't want to move; she didn't ever want to move again. Inside her frozen body, her mind raced, replaying every moment together with Josh.

I wanted you to know the answers to the questions you were asking me.

I don't want us to be over.

The only reason I'm even sitting here is because of you.

I didn't care what happened to me. And no one else did, either.

I care about you too much already.

I wish this, right now, could last forever.

Tonight, she would find a way to sleep in his truck, surrounded by his smell. If there were ghosts, and if his spirit were still lingering on earth somewhere, maybe he'd find her there and know the truth of what she hadn't said aloud. She would stand up right now and she would walk down the trail, if for nothing more than to meet him there at his truck.

She pushed herself off the ground, her mind in a numb haze. Her body shook with cold and tension as she started walking. Halfway down, there was Madigan, practically running toward her. Her trance exploded, and she collapsed into his arms. He held her tightly and rocked her gently. The tears flowed with no end. "It's all my fault."

"April, it's not your fault."

"No, it is. You don't understand. It really is." Josh would never know that she loved him. That she would always love him.

"Shh, shh. It's okay. Just stay right here until you're ready." Her tears flowed fresh.

When she was too exhausted to cry anymore, Madigan put his arm around her and helped her walk down the trail.

"Where will they take him?" she whispered when they were just a few switchbacks from the meadow.

"Sacramento."

"I'd like to go there to see him, if that's okay," she said.

"Of course. Everyone else is already on their way."

"Danny and Theo?"

"And all of Josh's friends. Did you see the huge crowd in the meadow? Most of them are headed to the hospital."

"The hospital?"

Madigan stopped walking and looked at her. "You know, he was hurt pretty badly, April. I assumed you knew that."

"Hurt?"

"He's in bad shape, and he's not conscious, but he's breathing on his own."

She jerked away and stared with disbelief. "You mean, he's not dead?"

"You thought he died?"

"I saw him fall. He wasn't pulling his chute."

"But then he did. It slowed him just enough. Didn't you hear us on the radio?"

She didn't bother responding. She was already jogging down the trail.

"Wait, April!" Madigan called. He ran to catch up with her. "Just so you know, the rangers are probably going to want a report since you were closest when it happened."

When they hit the melee at the base, she tore the SD card out of the camera and shoved it at the nearest park ranger. "This is exactly what I saw," she said.

She gripped Madigan by the elbow, and they ran for the Walkabout van and jumped inside.

"Drive fast," she said.

Chapter Thirty

She saw nothing at first except Josh's chest rising and falling. He was alive. He was truly alive.

His leg was in a cast and elevated while his arm rested in a clear, inflatable tube, with metal screws protruding from it like a gauze-covered pincushion. Cuts and dried blood covered his skin, along with orange iodine stains. The IVs and beeping monitors were everywhere. An automatic blood pressure cuff came alive and clamped tight around his poor, bruised bicep.

He was so out of place in the sanitary whiteness of the hospital room and bright lights. She was out of place, too, caught between her public and private relationships with Josh.

Only one visitor at time was allowed in his room, so technically they were alone. But there was an uncurtained window into the hallway, and right around the corner was the waiting room filled with climbers and her crewmates standing vigil.

She wanted to fling herself across Josh and kiss him until he woke up and gave her a smile that assured her everything would be okay. Instead, she pulled a chair next to his bed and slipped her hand beneath his. The warmth of his skin was her final proof that he had indeed survived a three-thousand-foot fall.

"Josh, it's me, April," she said. "I got here as soon as I could."

She checked the window. No one was there except the nurse typing at a computer stand. April rested her head on the mattress near Josh's thigh. She searched his broken face for signs of the familiar, but there wasn't much. His nose was flat and swollen, his skin yellow, and even if he were conscious, his eyes were so puffy he wouldn't have been able to open them.

She sat up and leaned closer to him.

"I love you, Josh," she said. "I'm sorry I didn't tell you last night, but I do. I have since the beginning."

Tears filled her eyes, but she stifled them back. "When you wake up, I'm going to be here for you. As soon as you're well enough, we'll go to Tuolumne. And after that, we'll find a way to make it work. I promise we will."

His mangled body made her sick, but it couldn't touch the euphoria of being in his presence. He *hadn't* died, and furthermore, the one thing keeping them apart was gone. He would not climb again, and he would never know she'd planned to break it off with him after the Sorcerer. She could give her heart to him freely and wholly.

What *would* he do next? He was working on the business degree, but he'd never mentioned what he wanted to do with it. And of all the places he'd temporarily resided, where would he want to live permanently? Maybe he'd come to Seattle after shooting wrapped, and he could work on his degree while she finished the internship.

She was getting ahead of herself. Right now, she needed to focus on the present. He was in a coma. She needed to do what she could to help him wake up and heal.

April leaned over him just to feel his weak but warm exhalation against her cheek. She carefully shifted his hair aside and used the backs of her fingers to stroke his temple.

A nurse came in the room and dimmed the lights. "It's time to say good night," she said as she adjusted the drips on Josh's IVs. "Even though he's in a coma, he could be aware of everything that's going on, and we need to give him time to rest."

April nodded and then leaned over Josh. "I have to go now," she whispered, "but I'll be back as soon as I can tomorrow. I love you so much, Josh."

It was physically painful to walk away from him. The overflowing waiting room made her dizzy after the solitude of Josh's room. There were so many conversations going on, so many pairs of eyes.

Vera appeared at her side and guided her to an alcove near the emergency exit.

"How is he?" Vera asked.

April choked back tears, and Vera rubbed her shoulder. "It's okay," she said. "I know it's scary to see him like that."

She nodded, and Vera handed her a tissue.

"I was so frightened for you up there," Vera said. "Especially when you weren't answering the radio. We could see you in the telescope, all slumped over."

"I thought he was dead," she said. "I didn't know until I got down that he survived."

"Oh, honey. You've already seen too much for a lifetime." Vera hugged her long and hard. "Just so you know, he told me all about you two."

April looked at her, alarmed.

"It was at dinner last night. I'd already suspected, though." Vera gave a reassuring smile. "It's hard to miss with the way you two look at each other."

April couldn't hold the tears back anymore. "I'm so

sorry," she said.

"For what, honey?"

"I shouldn't have let it happen. It was unprofessional. I shouldn't have crossed that line."

"Oh, sweetheart, pooh on *unprofessional*. Look at the footage you two were producing together! And I hope you know you couldn't have stopped it if you tried. It's obvious Josh cares about you more than anything in this world. And that's saying a lot for a man who's been alone for so long."

"You know about his family?"

"Vic told me once, before he died. So I could keep an eye on Josh after he was gone."

"Do you think I should call his family?"

"I already did." There were tears in Vera's eyes now. "His father hung up on me."

April didn't understand how a human being, his father, could be so ruthless.

"I know," Vera said. "It's unfathomable. Just know that Josh always had Vic. And me."

It was, indeed, a huge relief to April.

"Josh had a rough patch after the first time he climbed the Sorcerer," Vera said. "He was out of money and looking for work, but Vic convinced him to stick with climbing. Josh found a job at the gas station in El Portal, which kept him close to Yosemite, and it wasn't long before another sponsorship came along. Then he tackled Thorpe's Wall over in Switzerland, which proved he wasn't just a flash in the pan."

"How did you feel about Vic climbing? Weren't you ever afraid for him?" April asked.

"You would have to know Vic. Before rock climbing, it was mountaineering. Before that, he was a competitive cyclist. He was always pushing himself. He thrived on that kind of thing and, boy, he was good at it. I always thought of it this way: How can I be afraid for someone who is doing what makes them happiest? You have to let it go and let them *live*."

April thought of Josh alone in his hospital bed, and she started crying again. Vera wrapped her arms around her.

"I love him," April whispered.

"He's going to be okay. I know it," Vera said. "Just wait and you'll see. He's going to be just fine."

• • •

At first, April had faith in Vera's assurances, but as the days ran together and turned into a week, she started to doubt. Other than the bruises fading, there hadn't been any change in Josh's condition. Where there was once euphoria, there was now the deep-rooted dread that things would soon be turning south.

She stood vigil at Josh's side, grudgingly rotating with Danny, Madigan, Theo, Lars, Vera, and Josh's closest climbing friends to keep up appearances that she was no different to him than anyone else. Theo returned to Yosemite to bring back a load of clothing for everyone, and Vera rented two hotel rooms for the Walkabout crew, where they took turns sleeping when they weren't at the hospital.

As soon as Theo brought April's laptop back from Yosemite, she looked up Josh's real last name. He had been omitting a lot more than just a name. The DeVincenzis were filthy rich. In that picture of his family on the Strip, the casino they were posing in front of was *their* casino, and they owned a second casino-hotel in Henderson. That designer polo in his pile of shirts probably hadn't been a thrift-store find, and it was no wonder he'd looked so natural in a tux. Obviously, he hadn't really needed help with his bow tie at the gala.

There were other businesses in the DeVincenzis' Las Vegas empire, as well as an alarming number of news stories over the years about investigations into their operations. That would explain his family members' fear of disobedience.

April generally avoided the hospital waiting room, where Josh's climbing friends were gathered. The climbers were friendly to her—the camerawoman who had the close-up view of the fall—but they talked about Josh all the time, and it was too hard for her to listen to. The stories of his death-defying climbs and almost-fatal expeditions were troubling but not nearly as much as the stories that illuminated who he was as a person. Stories of his kindness, of him going out of his way for his fellow climbers. Stories about his patience and spontaneity.

In these stories, he was alive, but a few feet away in his hospital bed he remained as still as ice.

Instead, she had her own sanctuary at the hospital: the Walkabout van in the underground parking lot. There, she was using all the footage she'd hidden from Danny and the guys to make a short film for Josh. She was recreating her own vision of him, and of them together, one that matched what was embedded in her soul. The sound track was an extended cut of their Jackal Legs song.

Today, she was working on the final segment, which would be him jumping into Flying Sheep Lake. The raw footage from that day was over an hour long, and she'd never had reason to watch the whole thing. Now, any new second of footage of him was invaluable.

She started her media player and settled into her chair to watch. As Josh stripped out of his shirt and walked toward the lake, she felt exactly how she had in the moment. Back then, Josh was still an enigma. She had been so attracted to him, but she'd also hated him for being a jerk. If she hadn't been feeling guilty for him catching her asleep that day, their entire story would have been different.

On the screen, Josh made his picture-perfect leap into the lake, and then it was her turn. She watched herself swim into the frame, sputtering and splashing. As she climbed out of the water, she was facing Josh, and also the camera, which she had forgotten was running. Her connection to him and the joy in her smile was obvious, even though she had hardly known him then.

She watched them lie together on that perfect, soft carpet of mossy grass. Her arm was draped across her stomach, and it relaxed and slipped to the side as she fell asleep. Josh slowly rolled to his side and watched her while she slept.

Wait a minute.

They had barely known each other then.

On the screen, Josh studied her face and then scooted closer.

For the whole week after, she'd doubted there was any way he could possibly have feelings for her. What he told her after the gala, he hadn't been exaggerating. It had been mutual all along.

She stopped the clip and replayed it in slow motion. After he scooted closer to her, he touched one of the loops of her wet blond hair. He drew his hand back carefully and made a cushion for his head on the ground, where he presumably also fell asleep.

She thought of him sleeping against her that last night in his truck. She missed him so much. He had to wake up, because she was dying inside without him.

Someone yanked the van's back door open. She jumped. It was Madigan, and she was caught red-handed with slow-motion footage of her in a skimpy jog top and a shirtless Josh lying entirely too close to her.

She scrambled to minimize the clip. Her face was burning hot. He might as well have caught them having sex.

"All I'm going to say is that he's a very lucky guy." He gave her a sly smile that didn't quite mask the hurt in his eyes. "And now that he's awake, there's only one person he's been asking to see."

Chapter Thirty-One

April bolted through the parking garage and danced on the balls of her feet as she waited for the elevator. Inside the hospital, she forced her legs to keep to a walk. She was breathless with exhilaration and shining like a beacon. The closer she got to Josh's room, the brighter her light.

Climbers filled the waiting room, buzzing with the news. April confidently pushed past them to Josh's door, where Vera rotated out as she entered.

Josh's beautiful brown-green eyes locked on her immediately. She lunged to embrace him. He gave a good-natured groan, and she softened her grip on his battered body.

She leaned back to get a good look at him. His expressions were off with the lingering swollenness, but it was still him. His smile was huge. Her Josh was back.

She leaned in to kiss him chastely on the cheek, and he turned his head so their lips met instead. All the panic and worry from the past week melted away. She sat on the bed next to his relatively unharmed leg and picked up his hand. "I am never letting go."

"Is that a promise?" he asked.

"I promise on my life."

He grinned.

"What do you know?" she asked. "What do you remember?"

"Well, I know that it is Saturday. And that you are my girlfriend, April Stephens, future Academy Award–winning filmmaker."

She blushed.

"I also recall that we had a date scheduled in Tuolumne that I rudely stood you up for."

"Josh!"

He smiled, but his eyes were heavy. The exertion of being awake was already catching up. She saw with renewed perspective the extent of his injuries: the lumps of his battered arm and leg beneath the blanket, the black scabs on his scratches, and the bruises that were dark swirls of eggplant rind and crushed raspberries.

She looked into his eyes. "I love you, Josh. I have, always, but I was afraid to tell you."

"Always since when?" he asked.

"Since that first day at the lake, on the grass. Basically, as soon as you decided to be nice to me."

There were voices approaching in the hall. She slid off the bed and into the visitor chair. The climbers from the waiting room filled his room and the hallway behind the window. Josh was exhausted, but he held it together for them, smiling and nodding to his friends. It was clear that for every family member he'd lost, he'd gained two more within the strong and loyal rock-climbing community.

The climbers were quiet at first, but the volume quickly rose as they edged closer to his bed and tried to talk to him all at once. The nurse swooped in and broke up the scene but allowed April to remain in the chair.

Josh's eyes closed as the nurse fluffed the pillows behind him. As soon as the nurse was gone, April sneaked her hand under the blanket and found his. As he slept, she grew afraid he had slipped back into the coma. She held onto this fear for nearly an hour, until his hand twitched and his eyes floated open. Through the haze of painkiller and drowsiness, he smiled at her, squeezed her hand once, and drifted back to sleep.

. . .

Later that day, Josh sat up in bed. The next day, he had his first meal, a chocolate milkshake. April was there with him when the doctor detailed the extent of his injuries and described his long recovery process. It was her shoulder he held during physical therapy three days later, the first time he stood on his good leg.

Even though Theo, Madigan, and Vera knew about her relationship with Josh, the rest of the crew and Danny didn't, so they continued sneaking their kisses, and hand-holding only happened when they were alone. It was an unspoken assumption that when Danny and Madigan joined Theo back in Yosemite this afternoon to start filming with the other climbers, she would stay on to help Josh until he was out of the hospital.

She walked down the hospital corridor with a decaf iced tea and a lime-green Loftycake for Josh. He had a physical therapy session this afternoon when he would practice walking with crutches and his immobile casted leg. The doctors were waiting for his internal bruising to heal, but he was otherwise making great progress, and he expected to be released by the end of the week.

Josh's door was open, and Lars was in there with him. She hung back in the hallway to give them some space before going in.

"…there's that unscoped wall down in Uruguay. I wouldn't mind getting down there and doing some FAs."

She frowned. That was not Lars's voice, it was Josh's. FA meant first ascent. As in, rock climbing. As in, uncharted realms of hazards unknown.

Josh was going to climb again? After all that had happened? She pressed herself flat against the wall so they couldn't see her.

"When do you think you'll get back on the Sorcerer?" Lars asked.

Josh was going to redo the route that had almost killed him? *No!* She set the drinks on the floor and ducked into the stairwell at the end of the hall, doubling over the banister to try and catch a breath.

He had almost died. And still, he was going to keep doing it?

She leaned on the railing and stumbled her way down the stairs.

He said he loved her, but he wasn't going to stop climbing.

The panic was morphing into fury. Before she reached the ground floor, it burned through her veins like acid. She blinked in the bright sunlight outside and made a beeline down the street to the hotel. Her hands shook as she slipped the key card into the lock to the room where her bags were.

Madigan came out of the other room. "Back already?" he asked.

She pushed her door open. "I forgot something." Without turning around, she stepped inside.

She closed the door, but he blocked it with his foot.

"April, what's going on?"

She grabbed her duffel bag and shoved clothes into it. "I need to go home for a while." She swiped everything from the bathroom counter into the bag and zipped it shut before pushing past Madigan into the hallway.

She punched the elevator button impatiently, fully possessed by the acidic anger boiling in her stomach.

"April!" Madigan yelled.

She thought about Josh right before they'd rappelled Flying Sheep Buttress together. She had been nervous. He'd told her he'd never let anything happen to her.

But you would! You will keep doing what will kill you and leave me burning here, alone, in my own personal hell on earth. You would let that happen to me!

The elevator dinged, and the doors slid open. She lunged into the elevator and pounded on the button to close the doors.

Madigan flung his arm across the sensor, and the doors slid back into the wall. Despite the look of hate she was giving him, he stepped into the elevator with her. The fact that he also looked furious made her rage burn even hotter.

The doors opened, and she walked outside toward the taxi stand, but he stepped in front to block the way.

"Something happened with Josh," he said. "And you're just going to run away? I can tell how much you mean to him."

"I don't mean anything to him at all, really."

She reached up to flag one of the waiting taxis. Madigan yanked her arm down.

"Whatever it is, you will work through it," he said. "Do not walk away from him right now. He needs you."

Men and their heroes. Neil Armstrong. Michael Jordan. Josh Knox.

"You should be happy about this," she said as a taxi rolled to a stop in front of them. "I don't know why you are suddenly on his side."

He opened his hand in reaction, and she escaped his grip just as the taxi pulled up to the curb. She threw her bag in the backseat and jumped inside. She tried to shut the door, but

Madigan was holding it open. He was hurt but also angry.

"April, this may surprise you, but I care about you even aside from my own personal gain. And Josh is a friend. I knew him long before I met you. You are not yourself right now. You are not in control. I'm trying to stop you from doing something that you will regret."

"He's going to keep climbing," she snapped. "Did you know that?"

Madigan stared at her. Now there was a trace of pity in his eyes. "He's a professional climber," he said quietly. "I never thought he wouldn't."

He let go of the door, and April pulled it closed.

At the airport, she bought a ticket to Tucson that cost more than she had made during the internship so far. A text arrived from Madigan before she went through security.

Rethink this, April. You don't have to run. After all that has happened, this could destroy him.

She deleted it immediately. Josh might never forgive her for leaving, but at least he wouldn't be able to die on her a second time.

Chapter Thirty-Two

April relaxed as the stoplights spaced out and the city lights gave way to suburbs, then ranches. She cracked the window and breathed deeply of the desert air. She was almost home.

The taxi dropped her off at the gate, and she walked up the long, steep driveway. The night was black and still, but the heat from the day lingered in the air. When she reached the top of the hill, there was still a pink-gray tinge along the horizon left over from the sunset.

Her mom was on an overnight shift at the hospital, and the house was quiet. She didn't bother turning on lights until she got to her bedroom, where she dug through her nightstand for an old prescription of sleeping pills, took them without water, and then collapsed on her bed.

She awoke late to sunshine through the window and the comforting familiarity of her childhood room. Already, she felt better. Her head was clearer, and the physical distance made everything seem less dire.

Her mom had come home and then left again while she was sleeping. She had scribbled a note for April on the refrigerator whiteboard.

Speaking to the Tucson School District this morning. Two counseling sessions at the hospital after. Early dinner at Schmidt's? I'll come back to pick you up. Love, Mom

Schmidt's. It was where she and her mom used to go for lunch while shopping downtown. Now they only went during happy hour for the specials, which were still an extravagance. The thought of going anywhere in public right now exhausted her.

On the coffee table was her mother's latest enthralling read: *Case Studies in Teen Oxycodone Recovery.* She flipped through it absentmindedly as she waited for her phone to power up and then she texted her mom.

Can we do Schmidt's tomorrow instead?

She read through a string of worried texts from Madigan last night and this morning. She replied to the latest, sent just an hour ago.

I'm home safe. Don't send the police! I'm sorry for what I said yesterday.

He texted back immediately.

It's okay, April. Just glad you're okay. I'm here if you need to talk.

Why couldn't she have fallen for Madigan instead? They had everything in common, and they got along so well. He was a great guy, and he was cute, with those big blue eyes of his. Most importantly, he didn't climb three-thousand-foot cliffs without a rope.

There were three voicemails in her in-box, which she found strange, since no one left voicemails anymore. They had to be from Josh, who would have a really hard time texting on that ancient cell phone with his mangled right hand. Her sadness grew heavier.

Her phone rang while she was still holding it. A 702 number. The same area code as one of her roommates who now lived in Las Vegas. She stared at the phone. Josh was in the hospital at this very moment, his cell phone to his ear. With one push of a button, she would be connected to him, their voices flowing to each other across three states.

But then what? He was still a climber, and there was nothing that would change that. The pain from the three hours when she thought he was dead, and all the worry while she waited for him to wake up from the coma, were still too fresh. After a minute of silence, the phone beeped, announcing a new voicemail. She powered off the phone without listening to it.

She tried to revive her anger from yesterday, but her insides were hollow. How long would it take for Josh to understand she was gone for good? The harshness of her thought made her feel unstable.

She went outside and tried to relax on the chaise lounge, but she was too restless. Instead, she changed into workout clothes and went running for ninety minutes on the shoulder of the sizzling highway, the whole time reminding herself that the end of her and Josh had been inevitable from the beginning. With each passing day, it would be easier to be apart from him. That was how these things worked.

By the time she got home, she was feeling better, but as soon as she walked through the door, she was simultaneously hit by the absence of her father and a vision of Josh lying in his hospital bed.

She took a shower and a sleeping pill and passed away the afternoon in bed. Her mother was making a big salad in the kitchen when she got up. April perched on a stool and watched her slice cucumbers. Salad never would have been the main course when her dad was alive. He was a hearty man who wanted hearty meals.

"That salad looks really good, Mom, but I don't know if I'm going to eat tonight."

"It's okay," she replied. "I'll bring the leftovers for lunch tomorrow."

April hadn't talked to her mom much after the gala, and last night on the phone, she had been vague when she called her about flying home. She didn't want to talk about it, but she felt she owed her mom an explanation for her sudden return and, now, lethargy.

"Josh fell," April said. "On that big climb I told you about. We've been at the hospital in Sacramento with him for a week."

Her mom laid down the knife. "Were you there when it happened?"

April nodded.

"Were you filming?"

She nodded again. Her nose tingled with the tears she was trying to hold back. Mom came around the counter and wrapped April in her arms. "You two are dating now?"

"We were," April said. "But he's not going to stop climbing."

Saying it out loud spun her world out of control again. Everything that happened, combined with being back in her home with her dad's presence, was too much. But one thing weighed on her heart more than everything else.

"He's still in the hospital," she whispered. "I left him there alone."

She cried and cried, supplied with a steady stream of tissues from her mom.

When she finally stopped crying, Mom dished herself up a plate of salad and brought it over to the couch, where they binged on three saved episodes of *Pound Rescue*, their favorite reality show. After, Mom went to bed and April wandered outside to the soft island of grass in front of the house.

The dappled grays of the valley and the hills beyond it were visible in the starlight. Crickets were chirping, and the breeze was gentle and warm. It was a totally different environment, but it reminded her of Yosemite. She might not have ever been tent camping before she arrived there, but she had grown up in a beautiful, wild place.

Tonight, the solace of her surroundings wasn't seeping in. All she felt was the absence of Josh. Her mother had been very kind to not bring up her PTSD theories tonight, but April kept thinking about what Madigan had said about his friend and wondering if the crash was coloring this situation. What happened to people like her when they faced a completely different trauma *in addition* to the old one?

She went into her room and turned on her phone. There was just one more voicemail for the whole rest of the day. Not a good sign. She sat on the carpet, leaned against her bed, and hit play.

Josh's first message was playful, telling her how hard it had been to wrestle her phone number from Madigan (*like he doesn't know about us, jeez*) and how strange it was that they'd never called each other on the phone before. The cheerful tone in his voice stabbed her straight in the heart.

The second message, at five yesterday evening, was worried. *Where are you? Did something happen? Is your family okay?*

The third made her tuck into a ball and cry. His voice was raw and dejected, distant and slow.

April, it's almost midnight. I still haven't heard from you. I was sure you'd been kidnapped or something, but Madigan assures me you're fine. He's still here, by the way. He didn't go back with Danny. But he's dodging all my questions, which makes me wonder—I don't know. Are you not coming back at all? I must have done something wrong. I can't think of what it would be, but if I did, I'm sorry. I love you, April. Please call me as soon as you can.

The fourth message, the one he left this morning, was cold and hard, resigned and resolved.

April, I don't know what is going on, but I know how to take a hint. I am going to call one more time and then I'm going to stop calling. You have my number. It won't ever change.

She couldn't stand to listen to the fifth. She hung up and pressed the cell phone to her chest and sobbed. Madigan was right. What she had done was unforgivable.

• • •

April stood in front of her house with her video camera. That's all it was without her dad in it: a house, not a home. But it was also a theater, where memories came to life spontaneously and replayed themselves in the exact location they had happened. Like right here in the driveway, she remembered games of catch with her dad, and the one time when a downpour hit right as they were leaving for April's dance recital and her dad pulled the car all the way up to the porch so she and her mom wouldn't get wet when they got in.

She couldn't hide out at home forever, and by the time she could afford to come back for a visit again, her mom might be living somewhere elsc. She needed to document everything about the house so she could preserve the memories it invoked. She hit the record button and walked toward the front of the house, capturing the details of the adobe-and-wood front porch and the carved front door with the brass knocker her mom bought at an air show up in the Pacific Northwest.

Inside the house, she went naturally to the right, where her dad's office was. In high school, her days were long because of sports, and he'd get home before her. She'd come in the door and go right to his office to say hello.

Now, she stood in his office doorframe with her camera, panning from left to right. Her father's desk was built into a cherrywood bookshelf that spanned an entire wall. The shelves were filled with books, framed pictures, and all sorts of aviation memorabilia. Model airplanes hung from the ceiling, with the largest, a 1930s glider with a six-foot wingspan, soaring over the leather couch under the window, where one of her dad's jackets was still draped across the arm.

April stopped recording. The office seemed untouched, except that the sunlight streaming in the window revealed no dust. Also, the bills in the in-box were new.

She stepped inside and took a closer look. Paycheck stubs, some lawsuit documents, a copy of her latest UCLA bill with its blaring six-figure balance. It was the eviction notices from the bank that scared her the most. There wasn't a for-sale sign in front of the house, but foreclosure proceedings had already begun and the house was on the market.

April couldn't wait any longer to give permission to sell her dad's business. He'd always put his profits right back into it, and everything there was owned outright: the planes, the hangars, the maintenance equipment. When he'd first died, April had scorned him for putting his business finances ahead of his family's financial security, but now that the lawsuit had succeeded and everything in her parents' names was gone, she saw it differently.

Life insurance for a stunt pilot was tricky business; perhaps her father had been planning all along not only for the worst case but the worst case with a lawsuit. In that light, putting everything into the business and then the business into April's name had been the right move. Perhaps her ownership of the company had been more of a financial consideration, rather than her dad setting her up for a career as a stunt pilot.

Even though the money wouldn't save the house, there might be enough for a small condo in Tucson, and without mortgage payments, her mom would have enough money to make ends meet until she was old enough for Social Security.

And maybe, just maybe, there'd be enough left over for April to make the minimum each month on her student loans until she could work her way up to a job that paid rent *and* the loan payments.

She sat on the couch next to her father's jacket. His smell was still present in the office, which confused her senses. She'd only been in there once or twice since he'd died, and it was only to grab something and leave. It surprised her that it didn't feel strange. Furthermore, the metal airplane replicas and the smell of the leather couch triggered only happy emotions: the excitement of heading down to the airstrip with him as a child, his laughter during the slapstick movies he loved so much, and the anticipation of hanging out with him when she came home from college on breaks.

April dropped onto the floor and opened the cabinet next to his desk chair, pulling out the big, turquoise photo album that was inside. She had pored over all their family albums as a child, but this one was her favorite, as it was the one with the earliest pictures of her parents when they started dating.

Her parents were so young in these photos of picnics, air shows, goofing off at parties, barbecues, tubing on a river, dressed up for dinners downtown, and poolside sunbathing. And every single picture showed how much they were in love. They couldn't have hid it if they'd tried.

This was the kind of love she grew up wanting for herself. Even the way her parents had met was absurdly special. Her mother had been standing on top of one of the Rose River bluffs, doing a photo shoot for the petite clothing section of a world imports catalog. Her dad had been practicing for a show in his red Stearman biplane and had flown directly overhead, tipping his wing to get a better look at her.

The photo taken at that exact moment had ended up on the cover of the catalog. There hadn't been any breeze that day, but the airplane caused a gust that blew her mother's white cotton sundress out to the side and made her grab her straw hat. Her father had flown back to the airstrip and raced out to the filming location in his car to introduce himself.

The plane had been cropped out of the cover picture, but the photographer had given her parents a precrop enlargement as a wedding gift. It now hung in a frame above the fireplace where, forevermore, her father's bright red biplane streamed over a goddess in white on a desert hilltop. Even her own name was a tribute to this momentous meeting: it had happened on the second day of April.

She remembered looking though the turquoise album after her freshman year in college and doubting such a love really existed. In the dorms, relationships were all about hookups and drama. That continued at her apartment sophomore year. After the crash, there hadn't been any relationships at all.

She examined one of her parents' candid wedding pictures at the back of the album.

Natural, easy, passionate, best friends, comfortable.

Now she knew what it was like to have this kind of connection. She put the album away before her mind could wander back to Josh.

Her dad's closet door stood a few inches ajar, just like always, and she nudged it the rest of the way open. His smell was even stronger there, with his flight suits still on hangers. She buried her face in the fabric, wanting to unsee the conspicuous empty hanger among them and the bare patch of carpet in his line of boots on the floor.

All of the sudden, she was overcome with a desire to go

down to the airstrip. After pumping up her bike tires in the garage, she coasted down the driveway to the highway. The first left turn put her onto a gravel road that would take her the back way to the Rose Valley airfield, four miles away.

Chapter Thirty-Three

One of the training aircraft was chocked out on the tarmac, ready to fly. Hal—a thin, stoic, mustached man, ten years younger than her dad—was in the small, glass-walled office in the corner of the hangar, working on a flight plan with a teenage boy.

"April! What a surprise!" Hal said, stepping out into the hangar.

She hadn't been to visit since her father died. Actually, since six months before that—when she'd taken Sophie on a flight.

"So what brings you in today?" he asked in a casual tone that made her feel guilty for staying away so long. Until the crash, Hal had been like an uncle to her.

"I'm doing an internship in Yosemite right now with Danny Rappaport. He's the one who directed *Isles of Winter*."

"I've seen it. You made me watch it with the boys, remember? It was really good."

She had always been such a cinema fanatic.

"Your mom keeps us updated," he said. "I can't believe

Mitch's little Ultra Light is graduating college."

She flinched at her father's ancient nickname for her. "Well, I have to finish my internship first."

Hal waved his hand like it was an insignificant detail, which only made her aware of the oppositeness of the truth. The longer she stayed in Arizona, the weirder it would be when she went back. If she stayed too long, the only excuse that would work would be the truth. Later tonight, she would email some sort of explanation to Danny and tell him when she would be returning.

"How are the boys?" she asked.

"Aiden's starting at Embry-Riddle Prescott in the fall. Aviation management major. Joey's working on his private license."

"Joey? Already?" She thought about the towheaded boy whom she'd occasionally babysat.

"He's right there," Hal said, nodding to the office.

"That's Joey? He's huge! Why didn't he say hi?"

Hal laughed. "He's a little shy around the ladies these days."

The teenage Joey joined them in the hangar. "Dad, I'm done."

"Joseph George, don't you remember me?" she asked him.

"Hi, April."

She gave him a hug. He participated, but with limp arms and a wide space between them.

Hal rolled his eyes. April laughed.

It was wonderful to be back here with people who were like family. How long had it been since she'd been so at ease?

Since two days ago, at the hospital with Josh. A lump formed in her throat.

"April, do you mind if we finish catching up later?" Hal asked. "I've got to get Joey up before my other students come in today."

"Sure," she said.

She moved outside and watched Joey do his preflight checks around the blue-and-white trainer plane. She herself had done the same thing many times on that very plane and could probably still do it today with her eyes closed.

Hal grabbed the chocks and climbed in with Joey. They taxied to the end of the runway and took off. The sound of the engine as it flew by made her homesick for her life when her dad was alive.

She went into the office. For as sharp as Hal had kept the planes and hangar, the office—which had been her mother's domain—could use some help. There were stacks of papers on every surface, and it clearly hadn't been cleaned in a long time.

Her father's desk was now being used to store student ground school binders and logbooks. She slid open the middle drawer, curious if her dad's stuff was still inside. Yep. A broken watch, greasy pencils, the butterscotch candies he'd kept there for her and, in later years, for Aidan and Joey.

She looked through the other drawers, subconsciously hoping to find something he'd left for her. A letter he'd written to her in case of his death or an object of significance that would give her the answer to a crucial dilemma in her life.

Like selling the business. Or Josh.

She scooted some of the binders out of the way and looked at the same pictures that had always been there: a wedding picture of her mom, a studio portrait from when April was a baby, a first-grade April sitting on her dad's lap in the Mooney Rocket, and the relatively recent addition of one of April's high school senior photos.

The Mooney Rocket was out in the hangar. She left the office and climbed inside the plane, shutting the door. Here, her father's presence was more alive than ever. It felt like he was right next to her and they were getting ready to fly. The plane was in perfect condition. Perhaps when Hal got back she'd ask to take it up before she went back to Yosemite.

She *wanted* to fly. This was a huge development. She'd spent time in her father's office at home without having a panic attack, and now she'd come to the hangar and it actually felt good. Yes, she was truly improving.

The two wallet-size pictures on the dashboard were the same ones in all of her dad's planes: a miniature of her mom's catalog cover and a picture of April as a toddler, holding a toy biplane.

"I miss you, Dad," she whispered.

She wished that somehow she could tell him about switching her major to film. She wanted to know that he would be happy that she had found her passion, even though it meant she was not following in his footsteps.

Letting his planes go was not going to be easy, but this visit to the hangar made it feel less sacrosanct. Hal kept the flight school side of the business going surprisingly well, especially considering he didn't have any control to make improvements or take it in his own direction now that the Mitch Stephens Aerial Performances side of the business was defunct. Her mom had told her Hal was still interested in buying the flight school and planes and had even researched some business loans to make sure he would qualify if they decided to sell.

Yes, if the business was not to be run by her, then this is what her dad would have wanted, especially now that both of Hal's boys were showing interest in careers in aviation.

She'd talk to her mom later tonight, and perhaps they could get the paperwork started before she returned to Yosemite.

• • •

April biked back to the house in time to shower before Mom picked her up for a happy hour dinner at Schmidt's.

They sat at their usual table and placed their usual food and drink orders. April chewed a long, thin breadstick while her mother responded to a page from the hospital. Being back at this familiar place that had nothing but good memories reinvigorated some of April's confidence that had once been so easy and abundant.

"How did you stand what he did for a living?" she asked when her mom was off the phone.

"Dad? You mean the flying?"

"The tricks. The danger. I mean, you're afraid of heights. You don't even like flying on commercial air."

The waiter delivered their half-price mojitos. She and her mom clinked glasses.

"I suppose it was because I was young," Mom said. "I don't think I understood the risks. My friends and I thought it was fabulous that he was a stunt pilot."

"Did you ever see him in a show before you got married?"

"No, but we went to air shows, and he had me out for practices. He was just getting started then. He didn't have as much work as…"

Her mother's voice trailed into a sip of mojito. *As he did at the end*, April filled in silently.

"When *did* you figure out how dangerous it was?" she asked.

"Your dad had a good friend who lived near here and also flew the circuit. George. He crashed into Coyote Mountain and died. It was during a practice flight. That's when it sank in for me."

"And then there was Sam Stark, and then Bill's break apart in Georgia, and then that kid who trained with Dad—"

"Listen, April, I know what you're getting at. Does this have anything to do with your climber?"

"No."

"You want to know if I would trade what I had with your dad for someone who would still be around when I was ninety."

"No." April bit the top off a breadstick. "Okay, would you?"

"That's the question every reporter used to ask me. How could Mitch take such risks when he had a wife and daughter at home? And I'm not just talking about the tail slide. They were asking that twenty years before Saguaro Butte."

And with good reason. April folded her arms across her chest.

"The answer to your question is no. Even with the wisdom of hindsight, I wouldn't trade the time I had with Mitch for having longer with someone else."

"But you hated it. You used to keep your eyes closed for his whole performance sometimes!"

"Your dad and your climber are not parallel situations, April. I want you to remember that. I grew up with parents who ran a clothing store. I wanted the excitement. You grew up with a father who you were terrified would die."

April was surprised her mother knew that. She had always been so careful not to speak her fears aloud. Acknowledging them would be like a jinx.

"Then why did you let him do it?" she asked. Her voice was sharp with accusation.

Her mom looked out the window, then back to April. "Sometimes, when I feel bad for myself being alone, I think of my patients. The ones who are widows of police officers and soldiers. There's no reason to come see me if everything is going well. They find me after their worst fears have come true."

"Dad made *your* worst fears come true."

"Honey, listen to where I'm going."

April dabbed at the condensation on her half-empty mojito glass.

"There are police officers and firefighters in every city and county," her mom said. "There are millions of soldiers. Construction and manufacturing can be dangerous, too. Men leave behind young kids, wives, parents, best friends. We're not alone in this—always remember that. Fear of losing your loved ones is something everyone faces. And no one is exempt from that fear coming true."

"Dad wasn't protecting anybody or saving lives," she said. "Dad was an entertainer. Like a magician or actor. There's nothing noble about that."

Her voice was too shrill. She was saying things she knew she would regret later. This wasn't the direction she had wanted this conversation to go.

"I know Dad loved what he did, and he was the best at it," April said quietly, "but I'd rather he still be here with us."

Her mom laid her hand across April's. "It's okay that it still hurts, honey. It does for me, too. Every day."

• • •

That night, after Mom was in bed, April returned to her father's office. She sat on the floor in the beam of moonlight pouring through the open curtain and pulled the turquoise album out again. Her parents' happily-ever-after had been short, but it had been powerful.

She thought about Josh, and whether he could see the same half-moon from his hospital bed. It would be so easy to pick up the phone and call him. It was late, but she didn't think he would mind. He'd be furious at her, of course, but she could explain everything about her dad. Wouldn't he be relieved to know that it wasn't something he had done? That this ending had been inevitable from the beginning?

But instead of calling Josh, she texted Madigan.

How's Josh?

He replied five minutes later.

He's healing really well. Might get released the day after next.

April: *Thanks for being there with him. Please don't tell him I asked.*

The news of his release deeply unsettled her. For now, he was captive in the hospital, but as soon as they released him, he would disappear on the road in his truck-house. Surely the doctors wouldn't allow him to drive with his arm and leg in casts, but that wouldn't stop him. If she didn't catch him now, she'd lose him forever.

She decided to listen to Josh's fifth message. She dialed voicemail, but the message wasn't from Josh.

Hi, April. It's Vera. I hope you don't mind me calling your cell phone. Listen, I don't know what happened between you and Josh, but I think you'd want to know that it's really taken a toll on him. He's putting on a brave face, but I can tell he's not doing well.

The guilt stung her hard.

I know you left in a rush and you probably feel like you can't come back, but you can. Take it from this feisty old lady who was married to the love of her life for forty years. It's not too late. It's never too late if you've found someone you can't live without.

April hung up the phone. Vera had nailed it. A person she couldn't live without. Exactly the crux of problem. Josh would eventually die, and she wouldn't want to live without him. Even so, Vera's words kept running through her head. *It's not too late. It's not too late.*

April stared at the planes on the ceiling. "Dad, what should I do?" she whispered.

She went back to her bedroom and turned on her laptop. She opened the picture of her and Josh together at the gala.

Her yearning for him was not getting weaker with time. It was more intense than ever.

Just for the night, she gave in to the yearning, falling asleep with the laptop in her bed, watching some of her clips of him from Yosemite.

• • •

April's mom poured two cups of coffee, which they drank with the English muffins April had just pulled out of the toaster.

"Your dad loved entertaining, but it wasn't why he flew aerobatics," her mom said.

April frowned. "Can we talk about something else, please?"

"You brought it up, dear."

"That was last night."

"Well, I have more to say. Aerobatics was a calling for your dad. It ran deep in his veins. He uniquely could do those tricks, he taught himself all the mechanics to maintain his own planes, and he built a business out of it."

"Dad was different than other people. I know that. He wasn't afraid. As in, literally. He physically didn't feel fear."

"People experience different manifestations of the flight-or-fight response. Some people are disabled by it. Others are freed by the lack of it. And some people are able to control it."

Her mom sipped her coffee. "I was in love with your dad, and flying was part of who he was. Now that some time has passed, I can be grateful for the twenty-five years I had with him. I'm lucky to have found that kind of love at all. How I see it, every day was a gift. A treasure. I didn't think about it like that in everyday life, when I was living it, but it's something I can hold on to now. Mitch and his flying were one and the same. Take the flying away, and he was no longer Mitch."

Without climbing, Josh would no longer be Josh.

April picked at her English muffin. She had come home to help herself move on in a place where there were no constant reminders of how badly she had betrayed Josh and how her love for him had not been unconditional.

"What am I supposed to do?" she asked. "*I* can't live like that."

"I read an article online about Josh's fall," her mom said. "I saw how massive that tower is. If he fell from the top and you saw him fall, then you had to be at the top, too. I wasn't aware *that's* what you were talking about when you said they were going to let you start filming the athletes. And now, knowing what Josh meant to you…April, my god! No wonder you ran away."

"I didn't run away," she said. "I chose to leave."

Mom gave her a look.

"Why do I feel like you're pushing me to go back to him?" April said. "You've never even met him."

"I'm not. I'm just reminding you that you can't underestimate the long-term impact of what happened at Saguaro Butte. Not what happened to Dad, but what happened to *you*. As you pointed out last night, I had my eyes closed for most of it. You didn't, and on top of it, having experience with those stunts, you knew what was happening a full minute before everyone else."

Mom finished her coffee and looked at her. "The situation you had to face on that cliff put you up against everything you fear, and now it's become tangled with someone you care a great deal about. Just know that there are underlying brain-chemical survival reactions that are driving your decisions even now."

"They didn't become tangled," April said. "The two were one and the same all along. I was wrong to have let it happen. I take responsibility for that."

"It's not about taking blame, it's about making a decision."

"Not this again! I made a decision. I left. I would have broken up with him anyway, after the climb."

"Let's be real, April. You didn't make a decision by coming here. You evaded a decision."

Her mom glanced at the microwave clock. "I'm sorry to cut this short, but I have a group session this morning." She slid her dishes into the sink and gave April a hug. "I hope I'm not being too hard on you, honey. I just want you to remember that when you operate through avoidance, you are letting your fears control you."

These were her father's words.

Mom gathered her things at the door then looked back into the kitchen.

"People are more resilient than they think," she said. "*You* are more resilient than you think."

The door clicked closed. April stared at the cabinets on the other side of the kitchen. She hopped off the stool and ran to the front door and peeked out. Her mom was getting into the car.

"How did you know I was so close to Josh?" April asked. "That it was serious?"

"I didn't. But you just confirmed my hunch."

Argh. Psychologist mom. Wait until she heard Josh's family was shunning him like the Amish. She'd have a blast analyzing that.

"You're not a girl who sticks around guys you're only lukewarm about," her mom said. "And you've certainly never fled home to Arizona because of one. Besides, even over the phone it was impossible not to tell how you truly felt about him. It's just one of those things."

· · ·

April went for a run.

This time, she didn't feel like she was trying to outrun something. Her strides were long and smooth. She was pushing hard, and she was moving fast. She felt strong and capable. Powerful.

When she got back, she stretched on the front porch. Something was shifting inside her. She couldn't put her finger on it, but she was warmly content, and it wasn't just the effect of the run.

Later that afternoon, she took a bubble bath in her parents' bathroom. She rested her head on the edge of the tub and closed her eyes. In front of her was Josh, leading her through the moonlit meadow. The same crystal-pure happiness from that moment floated near her like a ghost, lingering just out of her grasp.

It wasn't over, not for her.

And it didn't have to be.

She loved him, and she had a choice.

After she dried off and put pajamas on, she crawled under her sheets, pretending it was Josh's bed in the back of his truck. Her skin tingled as she remembered their bodies naked together.

She loved Josh, and he was a climber. He did it because it was his calling. It wasn't about pushing the limits or putting on a big show, it was about solitude and self-reliance. Reaching a place of complete stillness that could not be found by road or trail. Climbing took him to places so sublime she could have never believed they existed had she not gotten a taste of them herself.

There might not have been a modeling shoot and a stunt

plane involved when they met, but there had been a twinge of magic just the same, and it had ridden all this way on an undercurrent, even through his abrasiveness in the beginning and her denial at the end.

She was a girl who hated haunted houses, jumping off the diving board, and had never gone on her friends' annual white-water rafting trip. She had never rock climbed before Yosemite, and now that her dad wasn't making her, she didn't fly stunt planes.

These were all *physical* fears. The one she was facing now was mental, but it was just as powerful.

Her test was her fear that Josh would die.

Everyone died eventually, as her mom pointed out. Car accidents, old age, cancer, natural disasters, heart attacks, bee stings, airplane crashes. Perhaps she would die this year. Or next month. Tomorrow, even. She could be sideswiped by a car while running on the highway, and Josh would be left to deal with the aftermath. That was, if he forgave her and let her back into his life.

When you operate through avoidance, you let your fears control you.

Could she do this? Could she love Josh freely, even if he was going to die?

What good is life if you're not living it?

She felt Josh's hand tight around hers as they leaped from the log into the lake. Yes. She could do this. She would take this risk. It was worth it, even if it was only one more day with him.

April reached for her phone. She didn't know what she was going to say to him, but if there was any hope of salvaging what she had done, she couldn't wait another second. She picked up her phone and dialed his 702 number. The phone rang, but he didn't pick up. She left a message and prayed he would get it right away and call back immediately.

Chapter Thirty-Four

April awoke with a start. Her phone was still in her hand. It was seven o'clock in the morning and there were no missed calls or texts.

Suddenly, she was in a straitjacket buckled too tight to breathe.

What you've done is unforgivable.

Maybe Josh's phone was charging and he couldn't reach it from his hospital bed. Or maybe his ringer was off.

She didn't believe any of her own excuses.

Unforgivable. Yes, in light of his family's abandonment of him, this was unforgivable.

Her hands shook as she redialed his number. Hearing hostility in his voice would crush her, but she couldn't *not* try again.

The call went straight to voicemail, and she collapsed on her bed. A permanent loss, by choice. It was just as bad as death.

She had hurt him in a terrible way and didn't deserve to feel sorry for herself. She struggled to muster the energy to sit up, then dialed Madigan's number. He didn't pick up, either, so she left a voicemail and also sent a text.

She paced the room, willing her phone to ring. Five minutes passed. She called Theo, who picked up right away. "Theo!"

"What's going on?"

"I called Josh, but he hasn't called me back."

"They released him yesterday."

Her heart panicked. "Where is he?"

"He's here in the park. Madigan drove him back, but I don't think he's sticking around for long."

"How long?" Her voice was desperate, but she didn't care.

"I don't know."

"A day? An hour?"

"They got in late. He's probably asleep right now. He still needs to pack up this morning, and he promised he'd meet with Danny at ten."

She rushed into her father's office, where she'd left her laptop and searched for plane tickets. There wasn't anything out of Tucson until the afternoon.

"How upset is he? About me?" she asked.

"We haven't talked about it directly, but I'd say very."

No! She couldn't lose Josh like this. If only she could explain to him what happened to her father. Perhaps he would never forgive her, but at least before he disappeared, he'd understand and know that there was someone who loved him, unconditionally.

Overhead, the big red model of the Stearman biplane swayed on its fishing line. She stared at it, then snapped the laptop closed.

"I can get there in five hours," she said to Theo. "Can you help stall him?"

"Aren't you in Tucson?"

April ran into her room and threw clothes into her

backpack. "I'm leaving. Right now. Try to stall him. Take his keys if you have to."

"I'm not going to physically restrain the guy."

"I'm not joking, Theo. Please don't let him leave before I get there. I'll take your dishes duty for the rest of the filming."

"Well, in that case, I can't say no."

"Can you find Madigan and tell him what's going on? But whatever you do, don't tell Josh that I'm coming."

She hung up with Theo and called Hal. "I need a huge favor."

Chapter Thirty-Five

"Mind if I drive?" April asked Hal as she threw her bag in the back of the Mooney Rocket.

"When was the last time you got in a plane, girl?"

"My license is still valid." He'd already done the outside walk around. She pulled the chocks and climbed into the left seat.

Hal handed her the flight plan, which she skimmed and then started preflight checks. Even though it had been more than three years, she followed along the preflight checklist, clicking switches and checking instruments like she had just flown yesterday.

She started the engine, and the plane roared to life. She checked her wings and made her calls to ground as she putted past the row of hangars.

The runway stretched long and straight in front of her, tapering to a pinpoint where it met the sandy desert. She'd always loved this view and the anticipation of the acceleration to come. It was like staring down the straightaway in one of her hundred-meter races in high school track, only here she could run so fast that she would lift up into the air and fly.

"You sure you remember what you're doing?" Hal asked.

Yes. She truly did, and she was ready for it.

She checked the magnetos and the propeller and waited for the high-pitched roar to even out. After a quick glance at her gauges, she entered the runway and made the final call to ground. She released the brake, and they were barreling down the runway, faster and faster. The end was nearing and the speed was right. She nosed the plane up and it gave in to the lift, its wheels rising off the pavement like a heavily loaded honeybee.

A morning inversion made them drop as they gained altitude, but the plane recovered quickly. When they reached cruising altitude, April turned the plane to the first course on the flight plan.

It was a great relief to be in the air and on her way to Josh in her dad's fastest plane. She felt bad that Hal had had to cancel lessons, but not terribly so, as flight students were always canceling on their instructors. Besides, her dad used to take impromptu trips like this all the time.

They cruised up to Prescott, then eased the course westerly toward Las Vegas. All that lay between her and Josh was the sparsely populated desert of the Great Nevada Basin. And she was *flying*! It seemed like no time at all until the peaks of the Sierra were rising ahead on the horizon. She smiled to herself and nosed the plane up for the gradual gain to pass over the mountains.

Her landing at the Mariposa airport was rusty but not bad. She parked the plane at the fixed base operator to refuel. She tried to give Hal some money but he refused.

Across the street, there was an elderly couple coming out of the convenience store. They looked like tourists.

"Gotta run," she said to Hal. "Thank you so, so much for helping me get here."

"Any time, April. Come by for longer next time you're home."

She bolted across the street to the couple now getting into their sedan.

"Excuse me," she said. "Are you going to Yosemite?"

"Yes," said the man.

"I hate to ask," April said. "But I've gotten myself into a predicament and don't have a way back to my campsite. Do you think I might be able to catch a ride into the park with you?"

The couple exchanged glances, and the woman nodded. Perhaps they had a granddaughter her age and felt sorry for her.

She hopped in the backseat with her bag, hoping that if Hal was watching, he would assume that she knew these people. She did her best to be a pleasant passenger, asking where they were from and sharing trivia about the park, but the conversation did nothing to distract her from the fact that Grandpa was driving forty-five miles an hour and they hadn't even hit the curvy part. She was losing all the time she had gained flying fast from Tucson.

Her panic grew as the minutes on the clock rose higher. If she didn't get there soon, she would miss Josh. It was a far-fetched idea that Theo could actually stall him in the first place. Josh would want to get out of there as fast as he could. What if he was already gone?

After an eternity, they arrived in the valley, and the couple dropped her off in front of the search-and-rescue camp. She was aware of the familiar smell of pines and chatter of squirrels, but she could take no pleasure in either.

Halfway through the camp, she spotted the grille of Josh's truck in its usual spot. She slowed when she reached the last row of tents and rounded the corner carefully.

There he was, standing at the tailgate. He was markedly

thinner, balancing on one crutch while struggling to maneuver a plastic bin with his good hand. Tears streamed down her face.

She walked toward him. He looked up but turned away as soon as he saw who it was. He riffled though the bin in front of him, refusing to acknowledge her, even when she was at the tailgate next to him, close enough to touch.

"I'm sorry, Josh. I'm so sorry."

Hostility permeated the air around him, making her weak.

"There's something I never told you. My father was a stunt pilot. And I watched him die. Almost three years ago. In a crash at an air show. I lost it when I heard you tell Lars you were going to try the Sorcerer again."

Josh kept his eyes forward, but at least he had stopped digging through the bin. His good hand, which was still covered in scratches and bruises, rested on the edge while he considered her words.

"I've always vowed that I would never get involved with a guy who risked his life for a living, but somehow I fell in love with you anyway."

He shifted, and she paused, afraid he was going to walk away, but he was just easing the weight on his crushed leg. She was all too aware that what she had done to him was much worse than any of the physical injuries to his torn-up body.

"My mom thinks I have PTSD from seeing my dad's crash. I blacked out as soon as you fell. I didn't see your parachute open. I thought you were dead, Josh. I didn't know you were alive until I got down to the meadow."

Still, he refused to look at her. She had lost her dad and now she was losing Josh.

"I know what it feels like to have you die," she told him. "I didn't think I could go through that again."

He shoved the box the rest of the way into the truck. "I didn't know where you'd gone. You just disappeared."

He wobbled, and his crutch fell to the ground, sending up a loop of dust. She reached to steady him, but he swiveled away like her hand was a branding iron. She watched helplessly as he fumbled for the crutch in the dirt below the truck.

"I thought you'd been attacked or something," he said. "But then I found out you'd left on purpose."

He lifted his eyes, slowly, like they were made of lead. His skin sagged against his newly prominent cheekbones. He looked at her in exactly the way he used to look at other people's camera lenses, like he was waiting for her to steal his soul.

"You promised you would never leave," he said.

She looked at the ground in the most terrible kind of shame.

"I told you everything about my family," he said. "How could you just leave out what happened to your dad?"

He looked at her, waiting for a response. She didn't think he could bear the truth, but if there was any hope of regaining his trust, she had to be absolutely and completely honest.

"I didn't tell you about my dad because I thought it would mess with your head on the climb." She forced herself to keep eye contact despite her shame. "Because if I told you, you'd figure out that I never intended to let this go beyond the filming."

He looked away so fast that he almost lost his balance. Even if he could find it in his heart to forgive her, she didn't know if she could forgive herself.

"I resented my dad for flying. I resented him for dying. For choosing his airplanes over seeing me graduate from college. For choosing a new tail slide sequence over walking me down the aisle someday."

She gripped the edge of the canopy. "I watched my dad's plane fall from five thousand feet and explode on the ground. I got so close to the wreckage that they hospitalized me for smoke inhalation. For a long time, I was one bad therapy session away from the insane asylum."

New tears rewetted the ones that had dried on her cheeks. "I had to get some space. I had to figure everything out. Not just with you, but with who my dad was and how what happened to him was affecting me. I truly understand now that you would not be the person I've fallen in love with if you didn't climb. You and climbing, you're a package."

He adjusted his crushed leg. He wouldn't look at her. He might never look at her again.

"You have to believe me, Josh," she pleaded. "I want to be with you even if it means I have to lose you all over again someday."

He traced the IV tape remnants on the back of his hand, his face giving away no emotion.

What more could she do? There had to be some way to show him how much she regretted it. How much she loved him, how much she needed him.

The movie she had made while he was in the coma. She dropped to her knees, digging through her backpack for her flash drive.

"Here," she said, holding it out to him. He made no move to take it.

"I made a film. Of us. When you were in the hospital." She laid the drive on his bed. "If you don't believe me, this will tell you everything. It's the .avi file with your name."

Finally, he looked at her. His eyes were despondent. Her heart split in two.

"I believe you," he said, his voice barely above a whisper. "But it's too late."

Chapter Thirty-Six

She stood frozen as Josh struggled into the cab of the truck with his casted leg, begging with her eyes for him to not start the engine. That he would stop the truck. That he would glance at her in his rearview mirror as he drove away. That he would turn around and come back.

Nothing.

She was panicking on the inside. Ruthless copper wires wrapped tighter and tighter around the muscle of her heart until he turned a corner and was out of sight.

He was gone. For good.

The void of his emptiness sucked harder and harder until it imploded, cracking her ribs wide-open.

She raced through the trees behind the search-and-rescue camp and partway up the boulder-strewn hillside where she and Madigan had once practiced top outs. Her heart ached with a fierceness she would never survive. She would never love anyone as much as Josh.

How could she have done this to him? Josh was out there in the world, totally alone. Josh, who was in such pain that he couldn't even get in his truck without flinching and sucking in his breath. All those internal injuries that needed rest. He was gone…off to god knew where in his truck-house. She'd never find him again. He'd never speak to her again. She'd never know that he was okay.

• • •

"Okay, that's enough now." Theo stood right in front of her. He clapped his hands twice like she was a dog. "You've been back here two hours. Let's go."

She was too startled to speak.

"So I was right about him being pretty upset? I probably would be, too," Theo said. "You left him without an explanation when he was lying in a hospital bed."

And Theo didn't even know the half of it. She started crying again.

"Oh, jeez." Theo sat down next to her. "Okay, Hollywood, let's talk about it."

"I don't want to talk about it. I'm a terrible person. That's all there is to it. And now he's gone…" She swallowed the lump in her throat. "…forever."

"Yep. That happens sometimes."

"I love him. Loved him." Yes, *loved* him. She had to accept that she and Josh were past tense now. She was never going to be able to stop crying.

"Oh, man." He gave her a hug. "I know it's hard. You probably don't believe me, but I do know. You have to find a way to make it through."

"I made a huge mess out of this internship. There's no way I'm ever going to get a job now."

"Is this about the employee conduct thing again? Danny knows that you guys were dating."

"Madigan told him, didn't he?"

"He had to. You kind of went missing, remember?"

"What did Danny say?"

"Something about how he should have made me be Josh's buddy at the gala instead of you."

"Oh."

"You know, I don't think he really cares. It was kind of an exceptional circumstance, don't you think?"

"I guess."

"Well, this should cheer you up. Danny has been giddy ever since Madigan told him you're a pilot. You know, to help explain about your disappearance. Why in the hell didn't you tell us that before? So rad. Anyway, in the series we're doing this winter, we're going to be doing a ton of aerial filming and drone work. Let's just say, I'd bet all the beer in our campground that you'll be getting a job offer quite soon. A pilot-filmmaker? You're going to have the most amazing career."

Finally, it was the words she'd dreamed about but never thought she'd hear. And she'd never considered what an incredible asset her pilot's license would be in film, because she'd never thought she would fly a plane again. She couldn't bring herself to care about any of it. None if it mattered now that she'd lost Josh. She'd rather just go hide out back home with Kids Are Wee.

"So are you okay? Let's walk back. We're having a crew meeting soon with Ernesto and Russell, and you can meet Scotty Knight and a couple of the other climbers who got in yesterday."

It was nice of Theo to come find her. The pep talk was a good distraction. But she was certain the minute he stopped talking, or that she was left alone, she would crumble again.

"Sorry, Theo. I don't know if I can."

"I'll tell you what. Why don't you take another half hour, and if I don't see you in camp by then, I'm coming back and we'll walk down together?"

She nodded.

Theo made his way down the rocks.

He was right. She had to pull herself up and get to that crew meeting. But she didn't know how she was going to manage it. Josh, he was so real and all around her in this place, yet gone. Her whole life was gone.

Her phone buzzed with a text.

Josh: *I'm in the meadow.*

She leaped up. "Theo," she yelled. "Josh texted. I'm going to go meet him."

He gave her a thumbs-up and kept walking.

· · ·

Josh was sitting on a foam backpacking mattress in their interview meadow, facing the Sorcerer. She slowed to a walk, her stomach sick with dread.

His posture was crooked and strained from his back injury and casted leg. It was only a short walk from where he'd parked on the side of the road, but she didn't know how he'd managed it.

She had no idea what to expect: Was he willing to talk now, or was he just giving her the courtesy of an official good-byc? A courtesy she hadn't given him.

She stepped out across the meadow, her heart racing. This was it.

"Josh." She sank onto the grass, facing him. The bruises on his face were deeper, his eyes more tired.

He twisted a long blade of grass in between his fingers as he studied the Sorcerer's sharp profile.

"I think about the night before the gala, when you came to my truck," he finally said, keeping his eyes carefully away from her. "I was so nervous. All I wanted was to be near you. All the time. And I also wanted it to be real, not just the portion of me that I let everyone else see."

His voice was gravelly, like he hadn't talked in months. "I took such a chance on you. Getting to know you. Trusting you. Letting myself fall in love with you. You have no idea how scared I was, every step of the way." He looked at her. "I'm scared right now, telling you these things."

"Josh—"

"Every single time I told you how I was feeling, it was a huge step for me. It was a conscious choice I made. It was bad enough when you disappeared, but now...today...to know that you would have just cut the whole thing off if I hadn't fallen? I *trusted* you."

"Josh, please—"

"You are the only person I've told about my family other than Vic. You're the first person I've dated since I left home. You are the *only* person I've loved, ever. You gave me hope that someone, someday, might not only love me but love me unconditionally."

Tears streamed down her face.

"Don't you know that I would do anything for you?" he asked, letting go of the blade of grass he was still holding. He looked at her, his hazel eyes damp and searching. "I tried to leave, but I couldn't. I turned around at El Portal to come back here and think." He swallowed. "I came back here for you."

Her stomach dropped, and her heart floated free. She didn't know it was possible to love someone this much. She reached for his bandaged hand, holding it carefully, exactly as he had held hers that night before the gala.

He cupped her face with his good hand, wiping a tear away with his thumb. "I watched the movie you made. I see us how you see us. How you see me. I came back because I believe you."

Her face followed the light pull of his hand, guiding her lips to his. It was the falling and the spinning of the very first time all over again. The return to something so familiar, so right. She opened her mouth to his tongue, her heart racing. She leaned into him as he wrapped his arm around his waist.

His shoulders tightened. She stopped kissing him. "This is hurting you."

"I'm okay," he said, gripping her hand so she couldn't pull away. But even as he did so, he winced in pain.

"You're not okay."

"I've been better." He shifted his broken leg. "I didn't take any painkillers this morning."

So he could drive away from here. From her.

"You've only been out of the hospital a day," she said. "You need to rest. And take some medicine."

She walked out to his truck on the shoulder of the road and brought back painkillers and a bottle of water. She helped him ease on to his back, then laid her head on his chest.

"I think I know what you heard at the hospital," he said. "Lars asked me when I was going to get back on the Sorcerer. Didn't you hear what I told him?"

"No." She hadn't waited around to hear his answer.

"I told him I wasn't planning on it. The truth is, I don't even know if I can climb *anything* again."

She gently fingered the pins sticking out of his bandaged hand. With anyone else, she would have agreed. Because he was Josh Knox, he would be healed and back at it in six months.

He rolled cautiously over onto his side to face her. "But if I can, I will promise there will never be another free solo. I decided that the day I woke up from the coma and you were there, waiting for me."

"You don't have to quit climbing for me. Didn't you hear

what I said earlier? I'm okay with—"

"Hey, now, let's not get ahead of ourselves." He laughed. "I did not say I'd quit climbing for you. I said I'd quit free soloing."

She smiled. "Oh, I see. So no free soloing, but what about free BASEing?"

"No more free BASEing, either."

"What about highball deep water bouldering?" she asked.

"That's quite some lingo for a nonclimber."

"I do my research."

"There will always be a rope. How about that?"

"Climbing with a rope, that's child's play. Who wants to do that?"

His eyes sparkled in the sunlight as he laughed. A smile lingered on his face as she laced her fingers through his, and in that moment she knew everything would okay between them.

Josh took off his hoodie and bunched it under his head as a pillow. "So, I've been meaning to ask. How'd you get back here so fast?"

"I flew my dad's plane."

"You flew the plane?"

"Yeah. To the Mariposa airport."

"You fly?"

"It had been a while, but I did fine."

"Terrifying."

"Not really."

"And what after that? How'd you get the rest of the way here?"

"I hitchhiked."

"You've turned into a real Yosemite bum, April Stephens."

"Is that supposed to be a compliment?"

The corner of his mouth quirked up in a smile.

Then she was kissing him, her hand slipping up his shirt, running across the warm granite of his abs. His hand was under her shirt, too, on the skin of her stomach, her waist, her lower back. All of his touches were brand-new again. His mouth moved to her neck, sending tingles down her spine.

She pulled away just enough to see his smoldering eyes. "Theo told me Danny wanted you to stay here with us until we're done shooting."

"He did. You saw me leaving. I had turned him down."

"But you could change your mind." She kept her eyes locked on his. "Will you change your mind?"

Amusement flitted across his face. "On one condition. Scotty's having a fire tonight. And I kind of need a date. Someone to make sure I am sufficiently social in case any millionaire benefactors stop by."

"Me?" She put her hand to her chest. "I would be honored."

"Good. I really want you to meet my friends."

"So then, you're going to stay?"

He reached for a section of her windblown hair, twisting it in his fingers. "Yes, I'll stay."

The most enormous smile broke free across her face. They were going to be *together*.

"But what after that?" she asked, her eyebrows tightening.

"Our trip up to Tuolumne?"

"I know you know that's not what I mean."

"Well, it depends."

"On me?"

"Yeah."

She dropped her head onto her arm and scooted closer until their foreheads were touching. "What if I wanted you to come to Seattle with me for postproduction?"

He pretended to think. "Then I would say yes."

She slid her lips over his and kissed him gently, then harder, deeper.

Josh's touch was firm, but stiff, like he was trying to protect his healing injuries. Lying on his side was uncomfortable for him, even with the painkillers starting to take effect. She nudged him over on his back. He put his arm around her and squeezed her shoulder.

"April, I'm really sorry about your dad and how you had to be right there to see it happen."

She swallowed hard against the sudden lump in her throat.

"I knew about your dad before you told me today," he said. "After you'd been gone a couple of days, Vera gave me some printouts of articles about what happened."

Her throat was still knotted up. She nodded against his chest instead.

"I've always had this sense that there was something more going on with you. That we were alike somehow, that you understood me. But it didn't change the fact that you'd disappeared."

She placed her palm on his chest next to her face, feeling the texture of his T-shirt, the rise and fall of his chest. This was Josh. She could talk to him about this. She closed her eyes.

"I was so resentful about my dad, even sometimes before the crash. I loved him with all my heart, and we were really close, but I didn't understand how he could love flying more than my mom and me. That he would risk *us* for his own ambitions. Now, I'm so close to being able to forgive him and move on from that. But I just can't kick the shadow from being there when it happened. I keep seeing that plane falling. I keep seeing the explosion. I keep expecting to see my father walk out from the smoke. Over and over. Almost every day I see it."

A single tear rolled from the corner of her eye, wetting the fabric beneath her cheek. Josh placed his hand over hers, curling their fingers together.

"It feels like I'm a rabbit in a cage. I can see everything

around me, and I'm safe inside, but all these random things make me panic anyway. I have this feeling that even if the door was wide-open, I wouldn't know how to escape. Maybe I wouldn't even want to. But I do want to, now. Once I get to Seattle, I'm going to start seeing a therapist again."

He squeezed her hand. She watched the clouds beyond the Sorcerer, his breathing steady beneath her head.

"You did the right thing in not telling me about your dad," he said, his voice a touch groggy. "I would not have had the mental capacity for free soloing, but I would have done it anyway. If I fell any lower than I did, the chute wouldn't have been able to catch me in time."

He pulled her tighter against his side.

"I also know that you didn't back out of the Sorcerer because you were afraid of rappelling. I know you did it for me."

She slid her head over to the crook of his shoulder so she could see his face better. He gave a faint smile with eyelids that were drooping from the painkillers. She traced some small swirls on his chest with her fingers.

Natural, easy, passionate, best friends, comfortable.

"I love you, Josh. Unconditionally."

His eyes were drifting lower. He gave a small smile and reached for her hand, threading their fingers tightly together. Moments later, his body relaxed into sleep.

She was exhausted, too, but she had also never felt this alive. This free.

The late-afternoon sun cast warm yellow beams of light across the aspens and into the meadow. She looked up at the sharp tip of the Sorcerer, so high and far away. And, strangely, not as foreboding as it once was.

An aircraft contrail floated through the puffy clouds overhead, much too high to be heard. She thought about her dad. For once, there was no grief. No anger. No panic.

She knew, deeply, that he'd be happy that she'd found a passion and career that she loved as much as he'd loved aerobatics. He'd be even happier that she'd found the kind of love that he had had with her mom.

She felt Josh's strong, familiar hand in hers, holding tightly, even in sleep. Her father hadn't walked away from the smoke that day at Saguaro Butte, but she would.

Acknowledgments

First, and most importantly, thank you to my husband, Eric, for not only humoring this mysterious compulsion of mine to write and write and write, but to enable me to do so through the balancing of our jobs, household duties, and care of our little Wild Things. It was our many trips together to Yosemite Valley and Tuolumne Meadows that inspired me to form a novel set in the surreal beauty of this park, and our countless hours of watching rock-climbing movies that sparked my curiosity about what it would be like to be the person filming these amazing and terrifying feats.

I owe a huge debt of gratitude to new adult author extraordinaire Cora Carmack for selecting my manuscript to mentor during Brenda Drake's Pitch Wars contest. I don't think I'll ever have a bigger publishing squee moment than when teams were posted and I saw the title of my manuscript next to your name. The insight you shared about story, character, and publishing in general was, and continues to be, invaluable. Your cheerleading was the magic superhero cape that turned three thousand feet of "no" into something that was totally climbable. (And thanks to Brenda, too, for the countless hours she spends creating and running her fantastic series of contests that are such an inspiration and bridge for so many aspiring novelists.)

I am grateful to my editor, Karen Grove, for championing this book out of the slush pile, being patient with all my rookie questions, and expertly steering my manuscript and ironing out all the wrinkles. I am thrilled that *Lessons in Gravity* found a home here at the innovative and reader-centric Entangled Publishing, where the new adult genre is supported to the point of it having its own devoted line. Thank you to my agent, Melissa Edwards, for taking a chance on rock climbing and laying the cairns for me in this epic adventure of novel writing.

I was fortunate to be able to consult with several subject matter experts about some of the technical details surrounding this novel, all of whom were incredibly gracious with their time in responding to my questions. For adventure filmmaking guidance, thank you to Alexandra Kahn of As Inspired Media, Kelly Pope of Pope Productions, and attorney/UCLA MFA directing grad Merlin Camozzi. For aviation guidance, thank you to my pilot sister-in-law, Crissy Field (who aptly shares a name with the historic San Francisco airfield).

Finally, to my friends and family members, thanks for being such excellent listeners when I gave a fifteen-minute answer to your simple question, "What's your book about?" and for having more faith in me than I did in myself that you would someday hold a copy of this story in your hands. Thank you to Kelly, especially, for years—and I mean years—of me dominating our phone calls with plot dilemmas and imaginary people. Thank you to Gram-Mer for so many trips to Southern California and taking such good care of the Wild Things while I write.

About the Author

Megan Westfield grew up in Washington State, attended college in Oregon, and lived in Virginia, California, and Rhode Island during her five years as a navy officer. She is now a permanent resident of San Diego, along with her husband and two young children. Aside from writing and her family, her great passions in life are reading, candy, and spending lots of time outside hiking, skiing, camping, running, and biking. In their early years of dating, Megan and her husband took lots of weekend climbing trips to Yosemite, where she was first inspired to write a story set completely in the incredible, sublime beauty of the park.

Connect with Megan Westfield and learn more about her upcoming books at www.meganwestfield.com.

Discover more New Adult titles from Entangled Embrace...

BELIEVE
a *Brightside* novel by Katie Delahanty

Never in my wildest dreams did I expect to fall for the adorable bass player of my favorite band. I'm a doctor beginning a five-year residency, and there's no room in my life for fairy tales — only patients and perfection. But I can't stop thinking about him. Could he be the One? Am I ready to risk everything I've worked for? All for a chance at a happily ever after I never believed possible.

WILDER
a *Renegades* novel by Rebecca Yarros

He's Paxton Wilder, five-time X Games medalist and smoking-hot leader of the Renegades. The world is his playground, and for the next nine months Leah Baxter is stuck as his tutor on the Study at Sea program. If she can't get him to take his academics seriously, she'll lose her scholarship...if she doesn't lose her heart first.

BRANDED
a novel by Candace Havens

The last thing I need is a Texas princess like Cassie messing with my head. But there's something more to this spoilt little rich girl than the perfect image she works so hard to keep. There's only one rule to keeping my job and a roof over my sister's head: stay away from the boss's granddaughter. But I'm not always great at following the rules.

CPSIA information can be obtained
at www.ICGtesting.com
Printed in the USA
FSOW01n0733281116
27891FS